# A STEAK IN MURDER

## CLAUDIA BISHOP

BERKLEY PRIME CRIME, NEW YORK

A STEAK IN MURDER

A Berkley Prime Crime Book / published by arrangement with the author

PRINTING HISTORY
Berkley Prime Crime edition / July 1999

The Penguin Putnam Inc. World Wide Web site address is http://www.penguinputnam.com

ISBN: 0-425-16966-9

Berkley Prime Crime Books are published by The Berkley Publishing Group, a division of Penguin Putnam Inc., 375 Hudson Street, New York, New York 10014.
The name BERKLEY PRIME CRIME and the BERKLEY PRIME CRIME design are trademarks belonging to Penguin Putnam Inc.

PRINTED IN THE UNITED STATES OF AMERICA

10  9  8  7  6  5  4  3  2  1

*For Les Stanton
from his loving daughter*

**ACKNOWLEDGMENTS:**

*No Hemlock Falls novel ever gets completed without the patience of my editor Natalee Rosenstein, the calm of my agent Merrillee Heifetz, and the support of the people I love: Helen, Les, David, Sarah, Julie, Jason, John, Lyn, Harry, Jenn, and as always, Nick.*

*And special thanks to Jason Schwartz for the Naming of the Wines*

# CAST OF CHARACTERS

## THE PALATE GOURMET RESTAURANT

Sarah "Quill" Quilliam . . . owner, manager
Margaret "Meg" Quilliam . . . owner, chef de maison
Doreen Muxworthy-Stoker . . . owner, facilities manager
Bjarne Bjornson . . . master chef
Various waiters and waitresses, including Kathleen Kiddermeister, Dina Muir, and Peter

## THE INN AT HEMLOCK FALLS

Marge Schmidt . . . owner
Betty Hall . . . the cook
Royal Rossiter . . . a guest, owner Royal Land and Cattle Company
Colonel Calhoun . . . a guest, owner Calhoun Cattle Company
Jack Brady . . . cattle manager
Leonid Menshivik . . . a Russian emigré, member of R.I.C.E.
Vasily Simkhovitch . . . a Russian emigré, member of R.I.C.E.
Alexi Kowlakowski . . . a Russian emigré, member of R.I.C.E.

## CITIZENS OF HEMLOCK FALLS

Myles McHale . . . a private investigator
Andrew Bishop . . . the town internist
Harland Peterson . . . president, Agway Farmers Co-op
Elmer Henry . . . the mayor
Adela Henry . . . his wife
Dookie Shuttleworth . . . minister, Hemlock Falls Church of the Word of God

Howie Murchison . . . town attorney
Davy Kiddermeister . . . town sheriff
Harvey Bozzel . . . president, Bozel Advertising
CarolAnn Spinoza . . . tax assessor
Miriam Doncaster . . . librarian
Esther West . . . owner, West's Best Dress
    Shoppe

## MEMBERS OF Q.U.A.C.K.

Sky . . . a vegetarian
Normal Norman Smith . . . another vegetarian

# A STEAK
## IN
# MURDER

# PROLOGUE

❧

It was early summer in Hemlock Falls. The fresh, green gold light of a rising spring sun washed slowly over Hemlock Gorge. The silver spray of the waterfall hung mist in the air like a gauzy blanket. Sunshine crept across the rocks, touched the newly mown lawn in front of the Inn, struck light off the metal pen surrounding the rose garden.

The dog sniffed at the three-bar gate. He was an ugly dog. His coat was a muddy mixture of grays, browns, and tan. His ears were floppy, and his head was too big for his clumsy body. But the disgracefully colored fur was clean and shiny. His eyes were a deep, alert brown. The expression on his doggy face was a happy one. He sported a leather collar with a large tag that clanked when he trotted briskly through the village on his morning constitutional. The tag read: *My name is Max. When you find me, please call Sarah Quilliam at the Palate Restaurant* and listed a phone number. Underneath in very small type was the message: *Please don't call the dogcatcher.*

Max was a gypsy and an escape artist. Where he'd come from before he'd wriggled into Sarah Quilliam's life, the god of dogs only knew. And where he went on his early morning rambles was the despair of his owner. Nothing seemed to keep Max inside when Max wanted to be outside. And he wanted to be outside on this astonishingly lovely morning.

He sniffed thoroughly around the metal pen. None of his mark was on it. His mark was all over the little stone pond with the statue of Niobe, the brambly thicket of the Queen Elizabeth roses, the tidy length of brick pathway. If Max had been able to deduce, he'd have known that the pen was new. But he was just a dog, so he sprayed two of the metal posts, lifting his leg with an intent, faraway expression. That finished, he trotted briskly down the path to Peterson Park. Breakfast was in order, and soon.

There was a lot to distract him in the park. The trail leading to a woodchuck den. The statue of General C. C. Hemlock. A Hershey's chocolate bar wrapper, with no chocolate in it. A man lying folded in a shallow grave behind a stand of huge oak trees. Max, a friendly soul, spent some time sniffing the man. The clothes smelled of laundry soap and fabric softener. And cows. Max was fond of cows. The blood pooling on the man's chest was drying but not dry. The man himself was breathing in a way Max thought of as *not there* in the same way that other human beings in Max's uncomplicated life were *not there* when they breathed at night on the beds where Max was not allowed to jump, or even bark, since humans wanted to be *not there* until the sun came up.

The breathing slowed. Stopped. The murmur of the beating heart jumped and bounced. Max barked twice.

The man's heart went thumpty-thumpty. He began to breathe, slowly, deeply.

*Not there, then.*

Well. A lot of important jobs awaited him at home in the village. They were planting tomatoes today (Max knew this because the flats had been set out the night before), so there was a lot of digging to do. And he was hungry. He sniffed at the body one more time. Wagged his tail. The man sighed in his different sleep.

So Max went home to breakfast.

# CHAPTER 1

It was Saturday afternoon, and hot for July.

"Cows." Doreen Muxworthy-Stoker leaned over the picket fence and regarded her employer and the scruffy dog at her heels with disapproval. "That Marge Schmidt's settin' up a corral fulla cows right where the old rose garden used to be."

Sarah Quilliam slammed the spade into the tomato bed. Max the dog snapped lazily at the clump of dirt that flew past his nose, then curled up and went to sleep. "Why are you yelling at me, Doreen? I didn't book the cow people at the Inn. And who cares, anyway?"

"Whole town's gone cow crazy. You oughta see what Nicholson's Hardware Store has on the sidewalk. Fake cow. Big as life and twice as natural. You oughta care about cows. There's a big deal going on about cows."

Quill gave up. "Why cows?"

"Texas longhorns," Doreen said. "Them are cows with horns. Big ones."

"And?"

"And some association's having their annual meeting right here in Hemlock Falls in two days, and you don't even care."

"I don't have to care, do I?" Quill said mildly. "I mean, after all, it doesn't matter who eats at the Palate, does it? Although," she added doubtfully, "I suppose I could talk Meg into scheduling some sort of beef thing on the menu."

"Marge'll have beef on the menu up to our Inn. You can bet on that."

This got to Quill, as Doreen knew it would. "If I have to remind you one more time that we don't own the Inn anymore and Marge's business is none of our business, I am going to scream." Quill punctuated the verb with a vigorous jerk of her arms and brought up a shovel full of earthworms. One of them was cut right in half. Max woke up, looked at the worm, and rolled his eyes at Quill. Conscience-stricken, she let the dirt slide back in the hole. Maybe it was true that you could split an earthworm in half and it would go on its way. Maybe she'd just cloned something.

"It's gonna look like bloody Jehoshaphat," Doreen said. "Buncha cows running all over that backyard. And the mess. I'm here to tell you cow manure's the sloppiest manure this side of a chicken with the runs. Not to mention the stink. We get a north wind off'n the Gorge and that stink's gonna blow right through the dining room after it stinks up the kitchen, of course, and after stinkin' up the dining room it's gonna stink up the foyer and after it stinks up the fo—"

"Stop," Quill said.

"I know about cows," Doreen said. Her frizzy gray hair haloed her face in the June heat, making her look like an obstinate cockatoo. Quill glanced at her with exasperated affection, then wiped her forehead. The garden at the back of their new restaurant was hotter than it should be, despite the breeze. At home—at Marge's Inn, she corrected herself—the breeze from Hemlock Gorge was cooled by the waterfall. Their new restaurant was in the village, at the foot of the hill where the Inn at Hemlock Falls had sat for over three hundred years, and the breezes from the Gorge blew right over Main Street and the old stone house that contained the Palate Restaurant. (Sarah Quilliam, manager. *Maître* Margaret Quilliam, *chef de maison.*) Quill wiped the sweat from her neck. She, Meg, and Doreen had exchanged the Inn, with its load of debt, for Marge's Diner two months ago. There'd been enough cash on hand to make some necessary renovations to the kitchen and the small dining area, but there hadn't been a reason to keep on Mike the groundskeeper. There weren't any grounds to speak of at the Palate. The backyard was sixty feet wide and eighty feet long. Not nearly enough room for an outdoor patio and a vegetable/herb garden, too. And they needed a garden. There were some essentials Meg couldn't do without. Fresh dill. Chives. Oregano. Tomatoes. Quill looked at the flat of unplanted tomatoes and sighed. It was late to plant.

"You want I should put a coupla those in for you?" Doreen shoved open the gate with one sneakered foot and stamped into the yard. "Not near enough room for all of those, you know. Not and the Swiss chard and the broccoli."

Quill's feet were hot in her Wellingtons. She squelched over to the little wooden bench tucked against the fence, sat down, and pulled her boots and socks off. She wiggled her toes in the rich dirt. Max, who had followed her to the bench, gnawed thoughtfully at one sock. She ran muddy fingers through her hair. "There's not enough room for anything," she said glumly. Doreen sat down beside her. She smelled of starch and lavender. "There's not enough room for people to eat, the kitchen's too small . . ." she bent her head back and squinted up at the second story, ". . . and my bedroom's stuffy."

"We made a mistake," Doreen said. "We shouldn't have sold out."

"Meg doesn't think so. Meg's having a wonderful time."

"Meg ain't here half the time."

This was true. Word that the Quilliam sisters had sold the Inn at Hemlock Falls had swept through the small world of professional gourmets. In less time than it took to evacuate a beach from an imminent hurricane, Meg had received three offers to cook at prestigious restaurants in New York City. She'd decided to work at Levade, a restaurant so historic signed photos of Diamond Jim Brady were still hanging by the bar, and so prestigious that New York's fringe society had to book tables a year in advance. Meg usually cooked midweek, leaving Hemlock Falls for New York by train Tuesday morning, and returning Friday afternoons. She left Bjarne, promoted from *sous*-chef to head chef, in charge of the kitchen. In New York, her career took off like a space shuttle. Within weeks, rumblings that *L'Aperitif* was going to award Meg an unprecedented fourth star rocked the kitchen at Levade. Lally Preston, the current arbiter of middle-class taste, sent a columnist from her magazine to interview Meg for a cover story, and ended up giving her a column. HGTV was talking a cable show for Meg.

Selling the Inn was the best thing that had ever happened to Meg's career. She'd said that just last night, in Quill's bedroom, just before she went off to her own room. "And yours, too. Look at the money we're raking in."

This was true. Even with the expenses of refitting the Palate's kitchen, they were turning a profit. Quill wished she could shake the notion that in the current economic upswing, a gourmet restaurant run by Muammar Khadafy would make money. She shook her head, then ran her fingers through her hair. "You aren't serious about the cows, Doreen. In the rose garden?"

"Yes, ma'am." Doreen's use of the term "ma'am" was for emphasis only. If the Pope himself came to Hemlock Falls, Doreen's notion of her own place in the universe versus everyone else might permit an honorific such as "Hey, Pope." If her arthritis weren't bothering her. "You know them little metal fences?"

Quill didn't.

"They're portable. Harland Peterson got 'em for Marge down to the Agway. For free on account of the publicity about the cows. They're temporary, like. Got his hired man settin' 'em up. Fact. Saw it myself. Ast him, too. Les, the hired man, that is. 'Them is for cows, Mz. Stoker.' That's what he said."

The back door banged. Max raised his head and barked happily. Meg came out onto the porch. When the old house had been Marge's Hemlock Home Diner (Fine Food! And Fast!) Quill had thought it was full of charm. Built of limestone blocks, with a slate roof and a covered porch that wrapped three sides of the building, the place dated back to the 1830's, when Hemlock Falls had been the center of a thriving farm economy. The back porch was freshly painted (white) and miniature climbing roses twisted gracefully up the trellised sides. Quill regarded the contrast between Meg's dark hair, the white fence, and the tangerine roses. It made an attractive, if somewhat sentimental composition. As pretty as it was, the back porch was squashed between the house and the dinky little garden. Any place that made Meg look big was too damn small. Like this place.

"Don't get up too fast, or you'll trip over your lower lip." Meg bounced down the three short steps to the garden. She was wearing denim cutoffs, sneakers with no socks, and a baggy T-shirt with a cow on it. "Are you all right?"

Quill smiled at her. "Just a little hot, that's all."

"Don't you guys want some lunch?"

Quill nodded. "In a minute."

"I'm trying a cold cantaloupe soup. And a sort of a fig and cheese croissant. Figs are big right now in New York. And croissants are back."

Doreen said, "T'uh!"

Meg pushed her lower lip out. "What's the matter, guys? You both cranky? Shall I finish putting in the tomatoes?"

"Where'd that come from?" Quill pointed the trowel at the T-shirt. It wasn't really a cow, she saw now, but a cut of tenderloin steak with two longhorns on either side of it. TEXAS BEEF! it read. LONG ON TASTE! SHORT ON FAT!

Meg tugged vaguely at the neck. "Picked it up at Esther's shop. She was running a special, three for ten dollars, and I can't find the box with my summer clothes in it, Quill. I thought we unpacked everything, but a lot of my T-shirts are missing."

Doreen eased herself to her feet with a grunt. "Coupla boxes still in the basement at home. You want I should go take a look?"

Meg frowned a little. "This is home, Doreen."

Quill drew her sock from between Max's paws, exchanged her Wellingtons for sandals, and got up. "I'll come with you. We should have picked up the last of that stuff weeks ago. We'll take the Olds."

"Nobody around here likes change," Meg said suddenly. "That's it, isn't it? I mean, we've been here for months . . ."

"Two months and three days, exactly," Quill said.

". . . and things couldn't be going any better, and you're still calling the Inn home, Doreen. Which is kind of not logical, because you've got a home anyhow with Stoke. . . ."

"Anything else you're missing?" Quill asked. "I've got a master list of all the boxes and furniture somewhere, and I think I crossed off everything but about six packing cases."

"Don't you like it here?" Meg asked. "Quill? Doreen?"

"It's fantastic," Quill said. "No debt for the first time in nine years, no grouchy guests. No corpses! It's wonderful. Isn't it, Doreen?"

There was a long silence.

"What I'd like is some lunch," Doreen said. "My stomach thinks my throat is cut."

Meg nodded. "Come on, then. The last of the lunch trade is just leaving, so we can sit in front." She bounced to her feet. When Meg was in this kind of mood, those in her orbit frequently found themselves being pulled along in her wake, like flotsam in the wake of a speedboat. Doreen and Quill followed her into the interior of the Palate, Max at their heels.

According to the cornerstone on the north wall, the original building dated from 1832. At some point during the turn of the century, the entire back wall of both stories had been opened up, and the space was doubled. As

far as Quill knew, the Palate had been a single family
home until the fifties, when one of the multifamilied Pe-
tersons slapped black-and-white linoleum all over the
ground floor, paneled the wainscoted walls with fiber-
board, and turned it into a Laundromat. Marge Schmidt
took the space over in the early eighties and changed the
color of the linoleum to hospital green. She added a utilitarian restaurant kitchen and the skilled services of her
junior partner as short-order cook. The Hemlock Home
Diner thrived on local business until two months ago,
when Meg and Quill exchanged the Inn, with its load of
debt, for the Palate.

After a month of intensive remodeling, the ground
floor, at least, had regained much of its early charm. They
hadn't been able to salvage the butternut flooring, but
they'd substituted maple, which lightened the entire dining area. Almost all of the original plaster and beam walls
had been saved, and a dozen of Quill's acrylic paintings
hung against the creamy surfaces. It was a beautiful
room, as beautiful as the Tavern Lounge at the Inn had
been.

But it was small. Where the Inn had seated one hundred and twenty people in the main dining room, and
twice that in the Lounge, the Palate had eight square tables seating four people each. The tables were pushed
together for larger parties, but it didn't change the total.

Doreen went to the table in front of the large windows
overlooking Main Street and sat down with a grunt of
relief. Quill settled next to her, and they sat without
speaking while Meg went into the kitchen. She reemer-
ged a few moments later with a tray and set it down in
front of them. Cold pears, a creamy blush color, and
croissants layered with a rich fig walnut dressing.

"I think I'll pass," Quill said. She lifted the mass of

hair off the nape of her neck. "It's too hot to eat."

"The soup's all gone. So I took out chilled pears baked in red wine," Meg said. "With that cream cheese filling." She sat down with a happy sigh. "Bjarne is just terrific, isn't he? He's adding some menu items I never even thought about. Especially with the fruit. Who would have thought Finns would be as good with fruits? Try the pears, Quill."

Quill shook her head. "I need to stretch my legs. I think I'll take a walk. I'll go up and get your shirts, Meg. Doreen's right. I think we left a couple of boxes in the basement."

"You want I should go with you?" Doreen asked. "I can show you what I mean about them cows into the garden."

"No," Quill said crossly. "I don't give a rat's behind about the cows, and I need the walk. So does Max."

Max went, "Woof," in approval.

Meg and Doreen exchanged a look that wasn't lost on Quill. It'd been a busy day already, with a full turn at breakfast and a turn and a half at lunch. Of course, full days at the Palate were nothing like full days at the Inn. Despite the line of customers waiting for tables, Quill had found herself with enough time on her hands to count the week's receipts—which had been satisfyingly healthy, more than enough to justify the two new waiters they had hired, and the under chef to help Bjarne in the kitchen. Every day was like that. She'd even found time to serve on the town Zoning Board, which, given her often-expressed desire to accomplish more in the way of civic duties, should have made her feel virtuous, but didn't. The Zoning Board dealt with even more volatile political issues than the Chamber of Commerce, where she served as secretary, and that was saying something.

"A walk is a good idea," Meg said. "Your afternoon's free, and if you go up the back way, you can sneak in without running into Marge. And the cows."

"I do not need to sneak into my own—I mean Marge's Inn." Quill pushed her food around with her fork. "I wonder what the Zoning Board will have to say about those cows?"

"Why should they care?" Meg demanded.

" 'Course they should care," Doreen grunted. "It's their job to care. It's their job to poke their pointy noses and pointy little heads in where they don't belong and drive normal folks crazy with screwed-up rules and regulations. It's their job to—"

"Doreen," Quill said mildly. The Zoning Board had gotten a little sticky over the request they'd made for a liquor license, which was one of the reasons Quill had decided to volunteer to serve when the seat had opened up unexpectedly. Better to join them when you can't beat them. "For goodness sakes, don't bring those darn cows up at the Zoning Board meeting. I spend enough time looking at leach fields and right-of-ways as it is. Before you know it, the mayor will call an ex-whatis meeting and I'll be spending the next couple of weeks listening to Marge Schmidt try and pull the mayor's ears around his socks." She shoved herself away from the table and got up. She was feeling cross.

Meg rolled her eyes, shook her head, and blew out with a "phut!" "You sure you're okay?"

"I'm fine. Just need a breath of fresh air. I'll be back in a bit."

"We booked solid for dinner?" Doreen asked. "If you need me, I can work tonight. So you take your time." She stretched the back of her neck with an air of nonchalance, a sure sign that her shoulders were aching with arthritis. "Whyn't you go see Sher'f McHale? Drive on down to Syracuse and get some dinner with him. I can take care of the cash register here."

"He's on that job for GE, isn't he?" Meg asked. "The industrial espionage thing?"

"And he wouldn't appreciate my company on surveillance," Quill said. "Things will be fine, Doreen. Running this place is duck soup compared to . . . I mean, I've got it all under control. You go on home to Stoke. Kathleen will be in to give Peter a hand with the tables from five to ten. And I gave Dina a call. She's going to wait tables from eight on, when we're the busiest."

"You sure?"

"I'm sure." She snapped her fingers for Max. "And I'm gone. You two enjoy the pears."

She did need to walk. The past two months had sped by in a blur of floor joists, PVC pipe, cranky electricians, and Zoning Board meetings. They'd begun a limited lunch and dinner service almost immediately, and the customers had been almost genial about the construction debris and waiting for the liquor license. Between minimizing the disturbance to diners and coping with the contractors, spring had zoomed straight into summer without notice. But the work was done, except for the garden, and the Palate was profitable.

She took a deep breath. Time. She had some time. She would stroll up to the Inn, retrieve the last boxes of clothes, and stroll on back. She didn't care what Marge may have done to her carefully tended bushes of Scented Cloud, Apricot Nectar, and Kordes Perfecta. Not a bit.

The air was fresh, rainwashed from the night before, and Main Street was cheerful with geraniums. Max was sitting on her feet. She bent down and patted him.

"Walk?" she said, which brought him to his feet with a joyful leap.

They walked briskly past Esther's dress shop (the window theme was heavy on denim, sagebrush, and fake turquoise jewelry), the bank (with a banner reading WELCOME CATTLEMEN) and turned onto the path to the Gorge by Nicholson's Hardware (pitchforks, Western saddles, and a life-size acrylic cow on the sidewalk). Doreen was right. The village of Hemlock Falls was mad for cows. Why, she couldn't begin to imagine. Everyone she knew was backing off beef, conscious of the spate of mad cow disease terrifying Europe, which, she remembered suddenly, was the whole point. Who was it who had been telling her that native American cattle were totally free of that disease? Howie Murchison, that was who. When he and Miriam Doncaster had been in for dinner two nights ago.

She realized she was standing still, gazing thoughtfully at a clump of early wild iris. Her hand went to her skirt pocket, where she kept a small sketch pad. She'd been letting her painting go, as well. And with Myles off on a fairly long job for General Electric, with the Palate running as smoothly as it could under the circumstances . . . why not? This is why they'd sold the Inn, wasn't it? To give herself a chance to work, to get more time for Myles, to free both herself and Meg from the endless, frustrating details of running a twenty-seven-room Inn buckling under the weight of too much debt and too little custom.

"It was the right thing to do," she said aloud.

Max jerked to attention.

"Oh, Max," she said. "It was the wrong thing to do."

Max stiffened, nose pointed toward the brush. Maybe she ought to sketch Max instead of the iris. She cocked her head at him. Could she do a dog without being sentimental? Or without the kind of sarcasm that made William Wegman's work so repellent? She hadn't been sure about having a dog. They demanded a lot of attention. They were smelly. They had to be taken to the vet. They loved you without question.

Nope. She was too fond of Max to do him well.

Max barked.

Quill bent forward and rumpled his ears affectionately. Max barked again, furiously. "Good old Max. You don't have to listen to every word I say, but you do, don't you?" The iris rustled. Max dashed forward, knocking her flat into the mossy base of the tree. He leaped over her and flung himself at the iris, forepaws extended, ears up, growling. Quill looked up at the canopy of oak leaves overhead and sighed. She could feel damp moss seeping into the back of her neck and mud seeping into her sandals.

"You don't think you're a person Max, you think I'm a dog. That's the whole trouble. I've just figured it out." She rolled over and propped herself on her elbows. Max dashed toward her, teeth snapping, then dashed back to the iris. Two black eyes rimmed with white stared at her from the brush. The eyes advanced. The brush parted. A furry white face with a black muzzle stared at her. Quill stared back. It was a cow. A very large cow. With horns that must have extended two feet on either side. Foam dribbled from the muzzle. A stray gleam of sun caught at the ring in the cow's nose and made it twinkle. Quill closed her eyes tight, then opened them again. She didn't know a whole lot about cows, but she did know that they didn't put rings in female cows' noses. They put them in bulls' noses.

"Don't move." The voice was low, curt, masculine. And very Texas. "Ma'am."

"Not for the world," Quill whispered fervently. "You tell that bull I'm not moving an inch. I'm not even going to breathe."

"He ain't gonna do anything. We're just out for a walk."

"You're walking your bull?"

"And you're gonna get a nice mess of dead raccoon on that pretty skirt. Hang on. You stay right there. And you," this apparently addressed to Max, "you shut up and sit."

Max shut up and sat. Quill, philosophically, remained where she was, frozen into position, right hip elevated, left elbow digging into the ground. The brush parted and a tall, middle-aged, bowlegged man in jeans stepped onto the path. He held a red leash in one hand. Behind him walked the bull. The leash was attached to the ring in his nose. "Name's Royal," he said. "This here's my bull, Impressive."

"It certainly is." Quill bit her lip, swallowed hard, and extended her hand. "My name's Sarah Quilliam. People call me Quill. How do you do?"

Royal, who had bright blue eyes, heavily tanned skin, and a nice brown mustache in approved cowboy style, grasped her hand and pulled her gently to her feet. She and Impressive looked at one another. Up close, she could see that his eye was mild and that the foam on his nose was more like drool.

" 'S the heat," Royal said laconically. "He drools when it's warm." Impressive lowered his head and swung his horns from side to side. Max chuffed in a warning way.

"Just wants you to scratch his nose," Royal said. "See

here? Like this." He scratched hard behind Impressive's ears. The bull half closed his eyes in pleasure. "The missus called him Impy. But that," Royal said severely, "ain't no name for a prizewinning bull. If you get my drift."

"I do," Quill said. "Are you from, ah . . ."

"The Dew Drop?"

"The what?"

"The Dew Drop Inn. Marge Schmidt's place up yonder?" He waved his arm in the direction of the Inn at Hemlock Falls. "Got some of my prize stock up there. Ms. Schmidt fixed up a terrific corral. Tore out a bunch of brambly ol' roses to do it, too."

"She did what? She's calling it what!?"

Impressive opened his eyes and began to swing his horns, this time in a decidedly less friendly way than he had before. He snorted. Max pulled his lips back from his teeth and growled.

"Now, ma'am," Royal said nervously. "Now, ma'am, begging your pardon, but you don't want to go a-shriekin' round this bull."

"I was NOT—" Quill made a determined effort to lower her voice. "I was not," she continued in a calm and dispassionate tone, "a-shriekin'."

"There, now, see that?" Royal grinned at her, his teeth tobacco-stained. "He goes nice and easy when he hears that pretty voice of yours. You headed up thisaway?"

Quill smiled, hoping she didn't look as outraged as she felt. The Dew Drop Inn? The Dew Drop INN!! That did it. That just did it. She was going to march up there, confront Marge, and demand to buy her home back. Royal? You bet your cute little cowboy butt I'm headed that way. Aloud she said, "Yes. Are you going back yourself?"

"We'll walk right along with you."

The progress up the hill to the Inn was no odder than
the Women's Auxiliary Float at the Hemlock Home Days
Parade—a version of the musical *Showboat* with baby
pigs dressed as the main characters known as *Shoatboat*—
perhaps even less odd. If Quill hadn't been plotting ways
and means to get her old home back she would have
enjoyed it. Impressive ambled along amiably enough, and
Max, notoriously phlegmatic about everything except
mailmen, trotted at the bull's heels with a pleased expression. Royal didn't say much, except to cluck en-
couragingly when Impressive stopped for a bite of a
willow shoot or timothy grass. And the weather was
splendid.

"There's the rest of the herd," Royal said as they
topped the hill.

Quill came to a halt, dismayed. In one form or another
the Inn at Hemlock Falls had sat over the lip of Hemlock
Falls for close to three hundred years. First a log cabin
run as a makeshift bar for trappers, then as a mansion
during the Revolutionary War period, then as a home for
General C. C. Hemlock after the Civil War. Built of
stone, with a copper roof, the Inn sprawled elegantly in
front of the waterfall, surrounded by stone terraces,
shaved lawn, Quill's carefully landscaped gardens . . .

. . . and six Texas longhorn cattle. Eight, Quill corrected herself, if you counted the two little red calves.
Marge (or somebody) had created a pen of six ten-foot-
long metal gates, of a type she'd seen in dairy farms all
over Tompkins County. Unlike the dairy cows Quill was
familiar with, these cattle were all different colors. One
was black and white, like an Indian pony. Two more
were white with big red splotches, one was dun, and two
were speckled like a rampant case of measles. All the

adults had horns ranging from four to six feet, end to end.

Quill realized why Marge (or somebody) had selected the rose garden; the stone Niobe in the middle of the fishpond recirculated the water, which meant it could be used as a watering tank. All sorts of cow-y equipment was scattered around: bright blue plastic buckets, bags of feed, bales of straw and hay, and pitchforks.

"Do cows eat fish?" she asked after a long moment.

"No, ma'am. They do not," Royal said.

"I mean, we have a dozen koi in there. Had, I mean."

"I eat fish," Royal said with a helpful air.

"They weren't fish to eat, they were fish to look at," Quill said crossly. "Where is Marge, anyway?"

"Said she was bringing the spreader up to the pens. Had to go down to Harland Peterson's to get it, and she left before I took Impressive for his constitutional. So she oughta be back by—yep, there she is."

"Spreader?"

"Manure spreader." Royal unlatched one of the metal gates, led the bull inside, then took off the leash. Or lead. Or whatever it was. Then he leaned over the fence and watched Marge drive up on a huge green tractor with a spiky metal trailer attached to the rear.

"Yo, Quill."

Quill nodded but didn't say anything. Marge rotated the tractor wheel with careless ease, then began to back the trailer up to the pen. She was a short, stocky woman in her late forties with a determined chin and sharp gray eyes. Her gingery hair was newly cut in a more or less fashionable style that owed a lot to hair spray. Quill saw with surprise that she was wearing lipstick.

"Yo, Royal," Marge said. She blushed and smiled. "You want I should help you pitch?"

"Help yourself," Royal said with a generous air.

Marge shifted the tractor into neutral, hopped off, and let herself into the pen. She and Royal each took a pitch-fork and began to toss cow manure over the gate and into the trailer. Quill noticed that Royal puffed in the heat. His face was red with effort. He obviously didn't want Marge to notice.

"Just where are you going to—um—spread it?" Quill asked. She ought to help. Whenever she saw anyone working, especially an older person like Royal, she felt as if she ought to help, but she absolutely did not want to. Even though the cows looked rather nice. Even if there was cow manure all over her rosebushes that would probably burn the heck out of them. "I feel as if I . . . Marge?"

One of the cows with a calf at her side, the largest and the blackest, began to swing her horns and moo. She nudged her calf behind her and advanced slowly on Marge, nose lowered to the ground. Then she tossed her head in a semicircular motion.

"Marge, maybe you should let Royal finish . . ." Quill took a deep breath and shrieked, "RUN!"

The cow sprang forward with an astonishing burst of speed. Marge was just fast enough. She swung herself up and over the fence and sat down hard on the other side. Royal stuck his pitchfork in the ground, leaned against it, and chuckled in a tolerant way. "That Faithfully. I warned you about that Faithfully. Don't want anyone near that calf except me and Impressive."

Marge got to her feet and dusted the seat of her plus-size khakis. "She'll get used to me, Royal. I like cows. And they like me."

"Maybe Royal could finish up here, and we could go

into the Inn and talk for a minute," Quill said. "There's just a couple of things . . ."

"You okay with that, Royal?"

Royal nodded slowly. "Sure am. Nice day to be cleaning the pens."

"See you for an early supper, then. Got some of that Kielbasa lying around, made it with that sauerkraut you like."

"Sounds good to me."

They smiled at each other. Quill cleared her throat. Twice.

"All right, already," Marge said. "Let's go into the Skipper's Schooner."

"The what?"

"The Skipper's Schooner." Marge glowered impatiently. "The Tavern Lounge, you used to call it."

"But this isn't a ship, Marge, it's an Inn. The nearest ocean is three hundred miles due east."

"So?" Marge stumped across the grass to the flagstone terrace that led to the bar. An arrangement of garden gnomes, windmills, and small plastic mushrooms flanked the right side of the French doors. Inside, it took Quill a moment to adjust to the dark interior. Fishnet hung in great swathes from the tin ceiling. The votive lights on the bar tables were encrusted with seashells. A painting of a bare-breasted mermaid smiled invitingly from behind the bar.

"Hey, Quill!" Nate the bartender raised a hand in greeting. When Quill and Meg had laid him off, in the dark debt-ridden days before they'd sold the Inn, he'd gone down to work at the Croh Bar on Main Street, swearing he would never work for the notoriously stingy Marge. Her management style, he claimed, was a direct descendant of how the Wermarcht ruled over Poland, and she, Quill, and her sister, Meg, had been the best bosses he'd ever had. All other women were terrible bosses. Terrible. Most of 'em thought that employees should dress up in silly uniforms that all matched each other and wear stupid hats.

Nate shoved his sea captain's hat to the back of his head and smiled ingratiatingly at Quill. The brow band read "Cap'n Nate." "Can I get you a glass of wine?"

"Yes," Quill said firmly. She made a point of ignoring the hat. She settled herself at the bar next to Marge. "So. Marge. First about those cows in my rose garden."

"It's my rose garden, and it's good business," said Marge. Her brow lowered. "You tell that Davy Kiddermeister there's no law against the temporary pennin' of show animals on the grounds of a commercial establishment like the Dew Drop Inn. I checked it with Howie Murchison, on account of that Doreen of yours called the state and complained. You should keep a better eye on that Doreen."

Nate set a glass of red wine in front of Quill. She took a sip. Gallo, and zinfandel to boot. She coughed and glared at Nate. Nate blinked innocently. "Best we've got, Quill. Not like the old days."

Quill sent him a fierce mental message—Will you take off that damn hat!—which he ignored, and another—I can't drink Gallo!—which he didn't, because he blushed, and took the glass away. Quill said, "She is not 'my Doreen,' Marge. And if she's complaining to the state about cows in the garden, there is nothing I can do about it. Doreen never listens to me. Or anybody else, for that matter."

Marge grunted in acquiescence. Doreen's stubbornness was well-known in Hemlock Falls, and had been, town opinion had it, the death of her second husband. Or maybe her third. "So what is it you wanted to see me about? If it's the boxes in storage, I told you, they're not a problem. Least not until I clear up the downstairs room to put in the games arcade."

"Games arcade," Quill said. "Good. Fine. Marge, I'm reconsidering this sale. I'm thinking that perhaps I might talk to you about buying the Inn back."

"Oh?" Marge folded her arms under her considerable bosom and tipped her stool backwards. This posture made Quill extremely nervous. "You and what mortgage bank?" She laughed: Ha, as if this were a particularly funny joke.

"Well. I was thinking." Quill took a deep breath. She hadn't thought about it at all, actually. At least not the financing part. But she had thought that Bjarne was doing a terrific job as the master chef, and that Meg could continue with her trips to New York and that perhaps she and Doreen and Dina and Kathleen could run the Inn themselves. "I was thinking that maybe we could just kind of do the exchange again. You know, we've put quite a bit of work into the restaurant, I mean, your diner, and honestly, Marge, we have people coming in all the time wanting to know if we're going to serve the same delicious food that you and Betty did, and of course it's terrible to disappoint them . . ."

"You send 'em right up here."

"And of course I send them right up here, but I know that you couldn't have paid down that debt load we were carrying, and we could just swap. Back."

"Of course I did," Marge said.

"Of course you did what?"

"Paid off that three hundred grand you owed Mark Anthony Jefferson down to the bank. You were carrying that sucker at nine percent." Marge lowered her chin to her chest and looked upwards, shaking her head. "Damn dumb."

"You made enough money in two months to pay off that three hundred thousand dollar mortgage?"

"Not all of it," Marge admitted. "But I wasn't about to carry that kind of interest, so I dipped into some other funds." (Marge, one of the wealthiest residents of Tompkins County, had a number of other funds.) "And of course, I got a good price in advance for the bookings for the summer."

"Bookings for the summer?"

"We're full up through the summer."

"There were a lot of years when we were full up through the summer, too," Quill said defensively.

"Yessir. But you were full up renting the rooms at one hundred and eighty per. Can't get anywhere doing that. Way too expensive."

"But you and John Raintree and everyone else told me that we couldn't run the Inn at that price because it was too cheap!" Quill said. "And don't you sit there and tell me you're making more money by lowering the room rates, Marge Schmidt, because it makes no sense at all."

"Sure it does. Rent the rooms for seventy—"

"Seventy dollars!"

"And charge a booking fee of ten grand."

"A what?!"

"Sure. Take these Texas fellas." Marge's round cheeks flushed a shade deeper. "Like this here Royal. Rossiter. You know who Royal Rossiter is, don't you?"

"I haven't the foggiest."

"Only the richest Texan in Texas."

"One the richest married men in Texas," Quill said. She immediately regretted her ill temper and muttered,

"Sorry," but Marge either hadn't heard or chose to ignore her.

"And that's saying something. And the friends he's got here for this Longhorn Association meeting? Well, they're the second, third, and fourth richest guys in Texas. You give 'em the room for seventy a night, and the rest of the inn for five thousand a day, and it don't make no never mind to them."

"Don't make no never mind?" Quill said faintly.

Marge wriggled a little. "Well, you know, you hang around those guys and you start to pick up the language, like. And," she added somewhat irrelevantly, "Royal's gettin' a divorce. Anyways. You just kind of fiddle with what people think things should cost. Get it? Take these Russkies—"

"Russkies? You mean Russians?"

"That's right. Got a whole mess of 'em coming in for a big sales meeting tomorrow. Figure they ought to get along with the Texans just fine."

"Texans and Russians?"

"Of course Texans and Russians. Since that whole Commie thing collapsed you can't find a more motivated bunch of guys to find out about the capitalist way of life. Figure those Texans'll teach them a thing or two. And, of course, we get another booking fee for the Inn from the Russkies. So. That's how I sort of got the cash to pay off that mortgage, and like I said, I shook out a few old overcoats to pick up the rest. You were payin' far too much, Quill, in interest."

"I should have listened to John."

"You should have listened to John. Good business manager, that boy. Too bad he had to take it into his head and leave for that job in Long Island." Marge's beady little eyes narrowed shrewdly. "If that was the reason he left," she added carelessly.

Quill didn't want to think about the reasons why John Raintree had taken the job in Long Island. She'd called him once, after he had gone, after the Inn had been sold, after she'd realized how much she'd hurt him. The call had gone well, considering. She fiddled with a glass of ginger ale Nate had left on the bar for her. "I don't know what to say, Marge. You've done a great job here."

"It's what I do."

"But. Now that you've done it, don't you want to rescue something else? Take on a new challenge?"

"Got enough of a challenge right here."

Quill drew a circle on the mahogany bar with her thumb, then another. She lifted her head and looked up at the tin ceiling. She knew if she went outside, crossed the green grass to the Falls and looked at the water, she'd cry. "It's a great place, isn't it?" she said after a long moment.

"It'll do."

"Would you at least think about it? About trading back, I mean? I was just thinking—"

"Yeah, I know what you were thinking. You were thinking now that I got this place up and running and profitable, given it a little pizzazz, you could waltz right in and grab it back." Marge shook her head. "No way, cookie. NO way."

"If you were to consider it," Quill said, picking her words with care. She should know better than to plunge right in with a bald-faced offer. You didn't get a darn thing accomplished in Hemlock Falls that way. You had to negotiate, step sideways, walk away and stroll back again. It'd be days before she could even get a dollar amount out of Marge. "Let's just say we're—ah—blue-skying it, here. What would a ballpark figure be?''

"Half a million," Marge said bluntly. "Bottom line. All cash."

Quill's mouth dropped open. Nate sucked his teeth in sympathy. The phone rang. In the days to come, Quill was to consider that phone call the start of the whole sorry mess. Nate picked it up. "Dew Drop Inn," he said. Then, "Ahuh. Ahuh. Yep. Got it. Yes, ma'am. Yes, ma'am. I'll tell her that." He held the phone away from his ear with a grimace.

"Sounds like that Adela," Marge said, loud enough to be heard. The indignant chatter from the receiver stopped abruptly, then resumed. Nate put the phone back to his ear. "She's right here."

Marge put her hand out to accept the phone with a resigned air. Nate handed the phone to Quill. "It's for you."

# CHAPTER 2

It was inevitable, given the nature of small towns, the arrival of strange horned cattle, and the interest that the Inn held for most Hemlockians, that the call would be from Adela Henry, convening an emergency Zoning Board meeting. There had been, Adela said, numerous complaints about the odor, the hazard to voters' health, the welfare of the cows themselves. The mayor felt that a quick review of the ordinances applying to the keeping of farm animals was in order. ASAP.

Quill decided not to tell Marge about the meeting. If there was going to be trouble, Marge would hear soon enough. And she didn't want Marge to think that she, Quill, would even consider contributing to the fuss in her capacity as a (temporary, until the elections) Zoning Board member. After all, Quill had an Inn to buy back.

She made her excuses and drove back to Main Street. Zoning Board meetings were held in the municipal courthouse only, Quill suspected, because it increased the sense of authority fundamental to the well-being of

CarolAnn Spinoza, tax assessor. Quill hadn't encountered
CarolAnn Spinoza before she was nominated to fill the
board seat left vacant by Anton Havecek's sudden demise. Quill liked the Zoning Board, which consisted of
herself, Freddie Bellini, the funeral director; and Harland
Peterson, a taciturn, heavyset farmer who wielded almost
as much power in Hemlock Falls as Marge Schmidt.
What she didn't like was the fact that the Zoning Board
meetings were public, and that a whole lot of political
issues tended to end up there. And where there was politics and public meetings in Hemlock Falls, there was
CarolAnn, even though technically she wasn't supposed
to be there in her capacity as assessor unless asked. So
far, she was only in attendance at those meetings when
the general public was invited. But Quill had a feeling
that this emergency meeting was courtesy of CarolAnn
herself, and that she'd be there no matter what.

When Quill and Meg bought the Inn nine years ago,
the tax assessor before CarolAnn had been second cousin
to the publisher of the *Hemlock Falls Gazette,* and an
old-line Hemlockian. Permits, tax grievances, and re-
quests for zoning variances had been few; the settling of
the issues acrimony-free.

The old assessor retired to Florida to the same condo
complex as his second cousin, where he became a prolific
contributor to the Notes from Florida column in the current *Hemlock Falls Gazette.* He left the tax assessor job
open. An election was held. CarolAnn Spinoza produced
an associates degree in bookkeeping and a perky charm
to sink the only other candidate for the position, a notoriously bad-tempered pig farmer. CarolAnn was an outsider, a flatland foreigner from a suburb of Syracuse
who'd moved her hapless husband and three quarrelsome
children to Hemlock Falls for "country quiet."

She was tall, CarolAnn was, with an out thrust bosom like the prow of a bellicose frigate. The toothy smile and bouncy blond hair concealed the soul of a Pol Pot and the heart of a cannibal. She was possibly the single most horrible human being Quill had ever met in her life. She was certainly the most inquisitive. CarolAnn's pert proboscis (Meg's term), snout (Doreen's), long, ugly nose (Quill's) was into every possible corner of the village, all of them officially unrelated to tax values.

Quill was terrified of her.

So was all of Hemlock Falls. Even Marge. The power of the assessor to affect the lifestyles of Hemlockians for generations to come was awesome. It was widely believed (but not substantiated) that CarolAnn had a lover highly paced in the state General Accounting Bureau, so even your personal income wasn't safe from a thwarted (and thus vindictive) CarolAnn.

It was tacitly—not overtly as CarolAnn's spy network was efficient, omnipresent, and practically invisible—understood that come next election, CarolAnn's impressively sculptured behind was to be booted out of office. Until that time, she held the village in an iron grip.

Mindful of CarolAnn's power, Quill was careful to park in a metered spot, and stick in several quarters. She entered the courtroom just as Harland Peterson and Freddie Bellini took their seats at the long oak table in front of the judge's stand. She barely glanced at the high ceilings, the carved paneling, and the old-fashioned oak pews of the cavernous room. She'd been in this courtroom before, defending a traffic ticket, and the memory wasn't a happy one.

'' 'Lo, Quill,'' Freddie said. Quill always felt guilty that she was a little wary of Freddie Bellini. He was a very nice man and came from a long line of morticians.

"Hi, Freddie." Quill sat next to Harland. He smelled of cows, in a nicely homey way, and she patted his arm. "How are you, Harland?"

"Good." Which meant he was. Harland was a man of few words, unless roused to a pitch of emotion.

"Isn't that a new tie? And a new shirt?" Harland's wife had died three years ago of what Quill darkly suspected was overwork. Farmers' wives in Tompkins County had a hard life of it, almost as hard as their husbands. In the time since then, Harland had stuck to his John Deere coveralls, laundered twice a week by his youngest daughter, Susan. The shirt and tie were quite a departure.

"Yeh."

"Going somewhere after the meeting?"

"Yeh."

"That's nice."

"The Ladies' Auxiliary's meeting at the Croh Bar about eight o'clock," Freddie offered. "The bowling banquet." He winked.

"Oh," Marge was president of the Ladies' Auxiliary. Quill hoped Marge didn't really have her eye on Royal Rossiter. She'd make Harland an excellent wife. "That's even nicer." Quill looked around the courtroom and dropped her voice. "Does CarolAnn know we're having an emergency meeting?"

"She demanded it," Freddie said glumly. "Called up the mayor and got on his case about those cows in your garden, Quill. He called me. Or rather, Adela did. Same thing."

"Nothin' wrong with a few cows," Harland said.

"I agree," Quill said, who, much as she wanted to whack Marge over the head with Doreen's broom on occasion, was not about to betray her to the terrible

CarolAnn. "Did anyone get hold of Howie? He ought to have the ordinances on this sort of thing."

"Adela called," Howie said, appearing from the hall, which led to the judge's chambers, to sit with them. "And here I am." He looked annoyed, which was unusual for Howie. He was a nice silvery sort of fifty, with a comfortable stomach and lines in his pleasant face, exactly the sort of lawyer old-line Hemlockians trusted with probating their estates. He sat down next to Quill, pulled a stack of Xerox copies out of his briefcase and distributed them. The top paper was titled "Zoning Ordinance 7.1: The Keeping of Farm Animals on Commercial Property."

"What is it that's so urgent?" Quill asked. "I mean I hadn't really thought that emergency sessions of the Zoning Board would be a part of this job."

No one answered this. It didn't need an answer. When CarolAnn called an emergency meeting of any kind, property owners snapped to.

Howie looked at his watch and sighed. "We'll wait fifteen minutes," he said, "and if no one shows up, I think we can discuss the violation of ordinance 7.1—the keeping of farm animals in an area zoned commercial—and pass a temporary variance. The damn cows aren't going to be in your rose garden for more than a week, Quill. I checked with Marge. Ordinance 7.21 deals with fairs, exhibits, and festivals, and allows for the temporary pasturing of—"

"I'm *so* sorry I'm a little late," CarolAnn said, jogging down the aisle to the front of the courtroom. She was wearing her usual attire: jogging suit, two-hundred-dollar Michael Jordan athletic shoes, and a sweatband holding back her aggressively dyed blond hair. The sweatband was blue. As usual, she was scrubbed squeaky-clean.

CarolAnn had an entourage of two. One was a round little woman in a bright caftan with dangling wood earrings and unbound gray hair to her waist. The second was a tall thin man with a wispy brown beard and a pained expression. Something about him reminded Quill of Hudson Zabriskie, former manager of the Paramount Paint Factory. CarolAnn tossed her hair. Quill caught a whiff of shampoo. "Is the mayor here yet? This concerns him, as well."

"I'm here." Elmer Henry clumped resignedly down the aisle and sat down at the far end of the front row, a seat that would allow him the fastest exit from the building. "Don't have much time, though, CarolAnn. Got a lot of village business to attend to this evening."

"If by that you mean the party at the Croh Bar for the Ladies' Auxiliary, that can wait," CarolAnn said. "Besides, I think Marge is entertaining another man tonight, Harland. Too bad about your nice new shirt and tie." She twinkled. Harland blushed a painful red. Quill bit her lip to keep from being rude. You never got anywhere being rude to CarolAnn. "Gentlemen, and Quill, of course, I want to reassure you that I am not here in my capacity as a public servant."

"You mean this isn't a tax issue," Harland said.

"Not directly, no. But indirectly it could be. It could well be. As I told you all when I was elevated to this office, the financial well-being of the village *is* my responsibility. The assessment arena covers far more than establishing the value of our homes and businesses . . ."

This would be easier to listen to if CarolAnn's voice weren't so sweet. Icky syrupy-sweet with little upward inflections at the end of her sentences. She blabbered on for a bit about her fiscal integrity. Quill scribbled on the margins of the Xerox copy Howie'd left in front of her: CarolAnn in the jaws of a Godzillalike reptile; CarolAnn squashed under the wheels of a huge semi-tractor trailer; CarolAnn upended in a tar barrel.

"Let's get to the point, CarolAnn," Howie said calmly.

"The point is this. The property owner at One Hemlock Drive . . ."

"Marge Schmidt, yes," Howie said.

"Is currently in custody of a herd of Texas longhorn cattle, which is, in and of itself, a clear violation of ordinance 7.1 the keeping of—"

"I'm familiar with it," Howie said shortly. "But it's my opinion as town attorney, CarolAnn, that the herd constitutes an exhibit. Under ordinance 7.21, it's legal."

"Of *course* it is," CarolAnn said. "I'm perfectly aware of that ordinance." Quill would have bet her best camel hair artist's brush that CarolAnn didn't know beans about the ordinance 7.21 covering fairs, festivals, and exhibits. She was stupid as well as mean as a snake. "But that's not the problem, Mr. Murchison." Trust CarolAnn to have a back pocket strategy when the first one wouldn't work.

"What *is* the problem?"

"The welfare of those poor, penned-up beasts," the little round woman blurted. "The ultimate fate of God's blessed creatures." The tall thin man with the wispy beard set his jaw.

Harland bristled. "Who are these folks, CarolAnn?"

CarolAnn inspected her spotlessly clean fingernails. She smirked. "This is Sky and her collegue Normal Norman Smith."

Quill thought she heard Howie mutter "Oh, shit," but

she couldn't be sure. Harland Peterson said, "Oh, for God's sake."

"I'm sorry," she said politely to Normal Norman and Sky. "Should I know you?"

Quill had the general impression CarolAnn had no eyelids, like a snake. So she was surprised when she blinked. "Sky and Norman are the moving spirit behind Q.U.A.C.K. That's Quell Unfair Animal Cruelty and Killing. A very influential animal rights movement based in Syracuse. They support the right of all beings to a free existence, unen . . . unen . . ."

"Unencumbered by the imprisoning hand of man." Normal Norman Smith had a very resonant voice. "Do you realize how many of our animal brethren live under the threat of execution day by day, week by week? Do you have any feeling for the fear, the terror, the despair of a chicken facing the ax? A cow facing the slaughter of its fellows?"

Quill sketched a duck in a caftan carrying a saucepan labeled "QUACK POT."

"How large is the Q.U.A.C.K. membership?" Howie asked.

"Hundreds," CarolAnn said complacently. "They have a couple of buses."

"And your point?"

"The property values of our town could be severely affected by the adverse publicity resulting from a demonstration." CarolAnn's eyes took on a dreamy expression, making her look less like the cyborg in *Terminator 2*, but not much. "I'm afraid it'd be my civic duty as a private citizen—not in my official capacity, of course—to comment to any TV or newspaper people that would come to cover the protest. Do you know," her eyes got a little larger, "the protest Q.U.A.C.K. staged at the turkey processing plant off the Thruway made the front page of *U.S.A. Today*?''

"That was because they let all the turkeys out of their pens," Freddie said. "And the turkeys ran onto the Thruway and that bus full of kids from the soccer game came to a sideways stop and the Thruway was closed for nine hours while they recaptured all the turkeys. And the eighth graders," he added after a moment's thought. "Remember, most of them hopped over the median and went over the culvert to the pinball arcade right there at exit 38. There was a bigger protest over that than the turkeys."

"What's the *point*, CarolAnn?" Howie said. "Those cows in Quill's rose garden—"

"Sarah Quilliam is NOT the mortgage holder at One Hemlock Drive," CarolAnn said menacingly.

"The cows are legal. If there's nothing else, this plenary session of the Zoning Board is over."

CarolAnn's eyes flashed. "You mean all that mess is legal?"

"All what mess?"

"The—" Her voice dropped. "You know. The poo."

"The poo?" Harland boomed. "You mean the cow manure? Nuthin' wrong with a little old cow manure."

"It's *disgusting*." There was true loathing in her voice. "The smell is *revolting*. I can smell it all the time." She shuddered.

Quill recalled suddenly that CarolAnn's neat little three-bedroom house was about a mile downwind from the Inn.

CarolAnn tipped her chin back, so that her icy blue eyes glittered like chips of mica in stone. "The E.P.A. certainly thinks there's a lot wrong with cow manure."

This struck a sensitive spot with Harland, who'd been

involved in a series of skirmishes over the slurry for his dairy herd with the E.P.A. for more than three years. He bristled like a porcupine. To Quill's dismay, he lost his temper and shouted, "There's nuthin' I can do if you got some weird psycho thing about cow dung!"

"Weird psycho thing?" CarolAnn hissed. She drew herself up. She'd ironed her sweatshirt and there were perfect creases pressed down the front of her jogging pants. She was the cleanest person Quill had ever seen. "We'll see about that, mister. We'll just see about that." She placed a firm hand on Normal Norman's shoulder. "Mr. Smith, did you hear that? Those poor animals are going to remain penned up there until they're sent off to the slaughterhouse." Norman turned pale. Tears filled Sky's eyes.

"You're going to do nothing to avert the fate of those poor animals?" Sky appealed to Howie "You will not move?"

"I'm afraid, madam," Howie said stiffly, "that the fate of the cows is not within the purview of the village government. If you have a protest, I suggest you take it with Ms. Schmidt. Or the owners of the cattle." He stood up. "This meeting's adjourned."

"Oh, yeah?" CarolAnn said softly. "We'll goddamn see about that."

# CHAPTER 3

👥

"And that," Quill said to Meg the next morning, when Meg had time to talk, "was that. What do you suppose CarolAnn's going to do now? I'm telling you, Meg, the woman went psychotic over the cow manure. It's utterly ridiculous."

"Jeez. What about Marge?"

"I've been waiting since yesterday to tell you about Marge." She listed the depredations to the gardens, the kitchen, and the Tavern Bar. Not to mention what the village grapevine had told her about Meg's kitchen.

"Marge renamed the Inn?" Meg's eyebrows rose. "And she pulled out the Aga and installed a microwave?" Meg had the Welsh coloring of their father, gray eyes and dark hair. In summer, her fair skin turned dark gold. As a result, her summer temper tantrums were more visually interesting than at other times of the year. Quill, hopeful of a spectacular display, pressed the advantage. "The Dew Drop Inn. And I told you about the cattle in the rose garden."

"What happened to the koi?"

Quill shrugged. "For all I know, Betty Hall turned them into frozen fish sticks and served them to conventioneers."

Meg shook her head decisively. "No. Betty's a better cook than that. I'm curious about the microwave, though. I can't believe Betty's going to precook entrees. She had the best diner food in the United States as far as I know. Going frozen's not like her at all." Meg remained maddeningly calm. "So the old place has changed a lot, huh?"

Quill looked around the Palate's kitchen. It was at least a third the size of Meg's old kitchen at the Inn, if not even smaller. They'd opted for utilitarian stainless steel, and to Quill's eyes, it seemed like every undistinguished professional kitchen she'd ever been in, and Meg had dragged her into quite a few. Stainless steel worktables stood parallel to one another between the double-size refrigerator and the eight-burner gas stove. The wash sinks and dishwasher were banked against the north wall. Pots and pans hung from chains suspended from the ceiling. Meg's knives were stored in a pullout tray under a workmanlike butcher block. Rubber mats cushioned the old oak flooring. Meg's kitchen could never smell like hamburgers and French fries—as a matter of fact, the air was filled with mint and the scent of fresh strawberries—but to Quill, it looked no different than a Burger King or a McDonald's. "I can't believe you don't miss those birch cabinets."

Meg shook her head.

"Or the open shelving and the cobblestone fireplace?"

"Nope."

Quill took a deep breath. "Well. I do, dammit. And I asked Marge to sell the Inn back to us."

Meg's mouth opened. Then shut. She waited a long moment and said, "You did not!"

Quill walked from the steel storage shelves to the sinks and back again, her sandals noiseless on the rubber matting. "I can't stand it. I miss it all. Everything. The gardens. My room. The dining room. The Tavern Lounge. Did I tell you that Marge has Nate working behind the bar? And that she's got him in a sea captain's hat?"

"A what?"

"She's renamed the bar the Schooner, or something. There's fishing nets all over."

"But there isn't a shipyard within three hundred miles of here, much less a fishing boat."

"I told her that. Meg, the minute I signed that sale contract, I knew we'd made a mistake, and then when I left the place just before we turned the keys over to Marge I knew it for certain. I never told you, did I? I sat right down and called John that day."

"John our former business manager? John *Raintree*?"

"Yes. I told him I was sorry he was gone. That I missed him more than I thought I would. I asked him to ditch that job in Long Island and come back. I told him we could be friends for life, that we could work out all that"—Quill waved her hands in the air—"all that other stuff."

"By all that other stuff, I assume you meant the fact that he said he was in love with you?"

"I apologized for being insensitive—"

"Good. Very good. 'All that other stuff,' *very* sensitive."

Quill ignored the sarcasm. ". . . and irresponsible and muddleheaded and for taking him for granted. Meg, I groveled!"

"Hm. What did he say?"

"He said that he . . . never mind. Just that I'd made the right decision, that I should marry Myles and get on with my painting, that I should leave enough time for myself and not get trapped by that sinkhole."

"He meant the Inn."

"*Our* Inn."

"But, Quill . . ." Meg trailed off, scratched her head with both hands, and sighed. She closed her eyes for a long moment, then said, "We were going broke."

"We don't have to go broke, Meg. Marge's figured out this way to not go broke. She told me a little bit about it, but I'll bet you we can figure out the rest of it somehow."

"You were going crazy with that place. You never had time to paint. You never had time for Myles. Every guest that walked through that door you took on as your personal responsibility. The Inn was taking the place of your life, Quill. You were using it to hide." Her eyes searched Quill's for a long moment. She flushed at the outrage there, and murmured, "And thus my refrain, 'thrust home.' Sorry."

Quill was so angry her jaw hurt. She smiled coolly. "I do feel a little like that poor guardsman Cyrano skewered in Act One. Spare me the cheap psychoanalytic crap, Meg."

"I said I was sorry."

"Fine. Just fine. I take it this means you aren't interested in moving back to the Inn."

"I can cook anywhere, Quill. I'm happy cooking anywhere, as long as I'm not cooking for people who eat lard sandwiches and deep fried pickles. As a matter of fact, I'm going to be late for the train to the city where I am going to cook in a perfectly cramped and horrible kitchen in one of the nicer parts of town for people who think corn dogs are an esoteric breed of hound.''

Quill held up one hand. Some part of her was surprised to see it trembling. ''So, go. Leave a couple days early, what do *I* care? Did I ever tell you you were a terrible snob, Meg?''

''Me?! Go chase yourself.''

''So, *fine*,'' Quill repeated. ''This is just fine.''

''Of course it's not 'fine.' Don't say 'fine' to me in that nasty clipped sort of way. If you want to buy back the damn place and have me cook there, I'll cook there. But you'd be making a big mistake.''

''It wasn't that damn place when I took you there after Daniel was killed in that car crash. It saved your sanity, you said, if not your life.''

Meg turned so pale that the light dusting of freckles on her nose stood out. ''So it's *my* fault,'' she said between her teeth. ''Well, *fine!*'' She turned on her heel, wheeled out of the back door, and slammed it so hard the eight-inch sauté pan fell to the floor with a clang. A second later, she came back in and hauled her duffel bag out of the closet where she'd stored it preparatory to this trip. When she left this time, she closed the door with studied care.

Moving carefully, Quill walked over, picked up the sauté pan, and replaced it on its hook over the counter.

''What in the heck was that rumpus all about?'' Doreen came in from the front dining room, a load of tablecloths folded over her arm.

''Nothing.'' Quill grabbed a broom from the corner rack and began to sweep the spotless floor.

''Pretty loud kind of nothin'. I could hear you two all the way down in the basement. And that's a sixteen-inch-thick stone wall.''

Quill didn't answer. Doreen set the tablecloths on the

prep table and counted the stack. "This here primrose color stinks," she offered after a moment. "Shows all the stains and you can't bleach it worth beans. Told ya when you picked it out. Shoulda gone with the white. Meg thought the primrose stunk, too."

"White's boring. People respond better to color."

"People respond real good to a nice clean lookin' tablecloth."

"So?"

"So maybe you want to think about listening to certain people. When they know what's what. Like, I know laundry, if you see what I mean. So you shoulda listened to me about the white. And Meg knows you."

"Stop right there," Quill said. She set the broom into the rack. "Do you have the list of reservations for this evening?"

"It's on the maître d' stand out front."

"You call all those numbers and tell the customers we're closed for today."

"You're kidding."

"Oh, no. I'm not kidding." Quill smiled sweetly. "Are you listening to me, Doreen? Have I ever told you you should listen more? Well, you should. It'll do you good. Lock the door, put the CLOSED sign up, and then GO HOME!"

The sauté pan fell back on the floor. Quill, shaking with rage, walked slowly out the back door, sat down on the back steps, and put her head in her hands. She felt the door open behind her, and then Doreen's rough palm on her head. She leaned against Doreen's hip and caught the scent of starch, freshly ironed cotton and pine disinfectant. "I'm sorry."

"Never mind." Doreen stroked her hair for a moment.

"Whyn't you go tidy up a bit before the chamber meetin'."

Quill sat up straight and looked at her watch. "Oh, Lord, is it that late already? It is. Damn it. Oh, *damn* it. Marge will be there, too, Doreen. Suppose she tells everyone at the meeting I asked to buy the Inn back."

"Suppose she does?"

"I'll just tell her to go soak her head, that's what I'll tell her."

"Don't you go gettin' into a scrape with Marge Schmidt, Quill. People think a lot of her in this town. 'Course, that's partly because she's one of the richest people in Tompkins County, and partly because she holds a pile of loans for half the village, but *why* they respect her don't matter half so much as the fact that they do. So don't go borrowin' trouble."

Quill was in the mood not only to borrow trouble, but to take out a high interest mortgage. She washed her face, threw on a few strokes of blusher and some lip gloss, and decided to take the Oldsmobile to the Chamber of Commerce meeting. If she floored it and made the light on Main Street, she might even be a bit early. Not as early as Miriam Doncaster, the town librarian, who arrived twenty minutes before every appointment she made, but early enough to forestall a snide remark or two from Betty Hall, Marge's head cook and junior partner, about how some people were always a day late and a dollar short.

Except in the final months of last year's economic recession, the Chamber of Commerce meetings had always been held at the Inn. Marge's acquisition hadn't affected a thing. Quill liked living in a small town—Hemlock Falls was less claustrophobic and inbred than the New York City art world, where she'd moved before she'd

come to the village to stay—but there were times when
the reluctance of its citizens to change direction (or, in
fact, change anything at all) was very frustrating. No,
frustrating was the wrong word. Bummed. That was the
right word. She'd been bummed when the Chamber
members had failed to rise in common loyalty and refused to darken the Inn's doors with That Person as the
owner. When she'd broken the news of the sale in May
there'd been a few clucks of sympathy, one or two
brusque pats on the arm, and a couple of sorrowful head
shakes. She had been prepared (even mentally rehearsed)
a noble speech of demurral when the Chamber members
demanded to have the monthly meetings at the Palate. It
was almost as if the village had expected her to lose the
Inn. And although people could fear Marge or resent her
success, no one actually disliked her. She was a blunt,
decent, shrewd, hardworking businesswoman. And a
heck of a cook in her own right. Just the sort of Hemlockian who would be commemorated with a bust in Peterson Park after her demise.

Quill slammed on the brakes at the foot of the long
driveway leading to the Inn, jerked from her reverie. She
ignored the screech of tires from the car behind her, and
peered out the windshield. A giant black and white cow
stood smack on top of the curved brick wall that used to
bear a discreet bronze sign: *The Inn At Hemlock Falls.*
There was a banner draped over its flanks that read:
WELCOME, COWBOYS! Someone had wound Christmas tree lights around the cow's horns and they blinked
on and off.

"The poor *thing*," Quill burst out.

The cow nodded its head and emitted a "moo" that
sounded as if its entire diet consisted of beans.

And then, Quill said, "It's fake!"

"Of course it's fake," said a voice into her right ear. "You city kids don't know a dang thing about a thing, do you?"

Quill drew back and inadvertently released her foot from the brake. The Olds bucked and stalled. "Hello, Harland."

Harland, president of the local Agway co-op and the biggest dairy farmer in Tompkins County, tugged his Butter Is Better cap more firmly over his forehead. "You gotta watch them sudden stops, Quill."

"Sorry, Harland."

"You can't drive out here in the country the way you do in the city, now, can you?"

"Nope," Quill said.

"Every time I see a cop chase on *World's Scariest Police Accidents,* I'm reminded of you, Quill. Seein' you drive that taxi in New York City when you was a youngster musta been something."

"It was, Harland," Quill said humbly. "Is your truck okay?" She craned her neck over her shoulder. Harland's teal and white dually was the pride of his life, now that Mrs. Harland was gone.

"Just had her washed. You goin' to the Chamber meeting?"

Since Quill was (a.) secretary of the Chamber and (b.) had never missed a meeting since she'd joined eight years ago and (c.) was widely known to avoid showing up at the scene of her business failure except when absolutely necessary, she didn't feel she had to reply to this. "Are we late?"

"I ain't. You might be if you gotta go back to the diner to get the minutes. You didn't forget this time, did you?"

"It's the Palate now, Harland," Quill said patiently. "And I left the minutes book with Miriam Doncaster to transcribe. She's inputting them into permanent storage in the database."

"Waste of a couple of megabytes, far as I can see." Harland straightened up and stepped away from the Olds. "And if you could learn to use that little dingus I showed you all last month, you wouldn't have to input twice. Just write on the pad and whammo, translates your handwriting into regular print and everything. Carry mine with me all the time. Use it for the dairy herd. If Mrs. Peterson could of seen what computers can do for dairy farming, she would have been amazed. S'pose them Texans know a thing or two about computers?" He nodded toward the mechanical cow, who blatted obligingly, as if in response to what Quill considered to be a totally trivial question.

"Well, *I* wouldn't know, would I?"

"Sort of thing you should know, if you're going to invest in the program."

"What program?" Quill asked suspiciously.

"You wait and see. Gonna tell you all about it at the meeting. I'm on the agenda after the Hemlock Falls Street Daze committee report." He pulled his cap all the way off and repositioned it. "Tell you what, though. Marge is buying more than a few shares. More than a few. And she's no dummy, Marge isn't. You could do worse than follow her around, Quill. Might learn a thing or two."

Quill released the brake and accelerated up the drive. Learn a thing or two from a person who put a ten-foot plaster cow smack in the way of one of the most elegant old Inns in Upstate New York? Follow around a human version of a Sherman tank who renamed one of the most elegant old Inns in Upstate New York The Dew Drop Inn? "I don't *think* so," Quill said. She parked right next

to the sign that read Don't Even Think About Parking
Here (she'd always parked in that spot, before) and
marched into the foyer. She'd especially loved this part
of the Inn, the place where guests were first introduced
to the hundreds of years of charm that lay sprawled on
the lip of the Falls. The polished oak floors shone as
mellow as ever. The cobblestone fireplace held a neatly
stacked pile of white birch logs. The cream and celadon
Oriental rug had been replaced by a square of blue in-
door/outdoor carpeting, but it was an inoffensive blue,
and it didn't clash with the two blue-and-white-striped
love seats that flanked the reception desk.

"Hey, Quill."

"Dina?" Quill squinted, as if to bring her former re-
ceptionist into better focus. "Is that you?"

"It's me." Dina closed her textbook (*The Life Cycle
of the Cephalopods in a Florida Freshwater Pond*) and
smiled. "How have you been?"

"Since you saw me last night, just fine. What are—"
Quill stopped. What are you doing here? sounded rude.
Gone over to the other side? was snide. "Fine," she said.
She was beginning to hate that particular adjective.

Dina twisted a forefinger into her long brown hair and
tugged thoughtfully at it. "It's not that I don't love waitressing at the Palate," she said. "I do. It's just that reception work lets me study for my orals and waitressing
doesn't. So I . . . I kind of asked Marge for my old job
back."

"Oh," Quill said.

"And it's only part-time." Dina said anxiously. "I'm
still putting that two days in at the Palate."

"You said you didn't want to work more than two
days," Quill said. "We would have given you as much
time as you wanted, Dina."

"But I've got grad school," Dina said in a tone approaching a wail. "And besides, I'm learning a lot about the business side of things. It's going to be kind of hard to find a job in freshwater pond ecology, Marge says, and she thinks I have a real head for numbers. And," Dina added proudly, "Marge says I'm exceptionally effective on the phone. Of course, Marge doesn't really talk like that, you know. What she said was, 'You give good phone, kid. Lot better'n me.'" Dina blinked her big brown eyes. "And then she said I have a real way with the guests. Isn't that sweet?"

Since Quill found Marge about as sweet as month-old grapefruit, she didn't bother to answer this. "Meeting's in the conference room?"

"It's always in the conference room, Quill. You now that. Oh, hello, Mr. Peterson."

" 'Lo, Dina. See you got your old job back. Better pay, too, I here." He winked at Quill. "Mayor here yet?"

Dina nodded. "Everyone's here, now that you and Quill have come. Except for Harvey."

"Advertisin' guys are always late. Something to do with how much they think of themselves, I expect. C'mon, Quill. We got a lot to cover this afternoon."

Quill stamped down the hall to the conference room with a little more force than necessary, Harland rolling along ahead. The Chamber hadn't met since she'd sold the Inn, and she wanted to see the conference room again. She bet Marge had covered the plank flooring with linoleum. Paneled the walls in fake oak. Or nailed oil paintings on the wall from the Starving Artists show at the Marriott the week before.

She walked into the conference room to a chorus of hellos, and immediately felt ashamed of herself. The conference room was exactly the same as it had always been, and the faces just as welcoming. There were two unfamiliar ones: Royal Rossiter, who had walked his bull up the hill, and a stout pale man in a black Stetson. Marge sat between them, her leathery cheeks tinged with either an artificial blush, or a natural one, Quill wasn't sure. Marge had abandoned her manure-pen-cleaning khakis and sloppy pink T-shirt for a denim skirt and a cheerful, Western-style shirt with silver conchos on the cuffs. A red bandanna was twisted around her neck. This demonstration of feminine vulnerability made Quill feel like a spiteful wretch.

Suddenly she felt awful. She sat down at her accustomed place next to Miriam Doncaster, drew her sketch pad from her purse, and made remorseful doodles in the margins: Quill the Bad Sister, with a booted foot on poor Meg's neck; Quill the Resentful Meanie, biting Marge Schmidt's hand with long sharp teeth; Quill the Arrogant Bitch, back turned to a baffled-looking Myles.

"My goodness!" Miriam Doncaster said, looking over her shoulder. "You *have* had a bad time since you bought that restaurant. And I thought things were going so well."

"They are." Quill flipped to a fresh sheet. "It's just me. I'm behaving like an ungrateful wretch. Everything feels so different, Miriam. I feel as if my entire world has turned upside down. Nothing's the same."

Miriam patted her hand sympathetically. "There's a marvelous new self-help book in, *Managing Change: Ten Tips to Avoid Self-immolation.* There's a tip per chapter. It's the case history approach, you know, like "Can This Marriage Be Saved?" in *Ladies Home Journal.* I'll set it aside for you, if you like."

"Does it have a case history on a painter turned inn-keep turned totally confused?"

Elmer Henry, who, in addition to being mayor of Hemlock Falls, was president of the Chamber of Commerce, rapped his gavel authoritatively on the mahogany table. Miriam gave a disgusted "tcha" and said, "Use the *rest,* Mayor. You'll dent that table yet."

Marge Schmidt said, "Get on with it, Mayor. I got things to do." Just like every Chamber meeting she'd been to in the last nine years. Harvey Bozzel, president of Hemlock Falls' best (and only) advertising agency, rushed in late, his briefcase bouncing off his pin-striped trousers, and breathlessly sat down, patting his blond hair with a manicured hand and muttering greetings. Dookie Shuttleworth, minister of the Church of the Word of God, raised his hands for silence and everyone bent their heads in prayer. Quill glanced up from her folded hands and looked around the table. Most of the core Chamber members were there—Howie Murchison, town attorney, Davy Kiddermeister, county sheriff, Freddie Bellini, the mortician—and they all waited obediently for Dookie's invocation. . . . *Plus ça change, plus c'est la ça même chose.*

Dookie stared sweetly at the ceiling. Quill hoped he'd abandoned his current enthusiasm for Christian Mentalism (C-Ment), which involved telepathic messages to the Almighty rather than verbal sermons, but with Dookie you were never sure if he was transmitting, or simply being absentminded. "Amen," Dookie said aloud, which didn't answer Quill's question at all. Dookie might be under the impression he had already said the opening prayer aloud.

Elmer cleared his throat. "Well, thank you, Padre. It's been a while since we've had a meeting—not since that bad business with the fire here some months back, and it's good to see everyone again. Norm? How's 'bout that football team of yours? Them two seniors you got on the defensive line been recruited for PAC-10 yet?''

Since Elmer saw most of the village every day at the Croh Bar for coffee (now serving inexpensive breakfasts, with the closing of Marge's Diner), and since the topic of Norm Pasquale's coaching abilities were thoroughly discussed each day, this was met with less interest than might have been expected. Harland Peterson smacked his knee with one callused palm and enjoined Elmer to get on with it, for God's sakes. ''And let's skip the old news, anyhow.''

''It's not 'old news,' Harland,'' Esther West said patiently, ''it's old business. It's part of the agenda, every time we meet. You'd think you'd know that by now. Old news. My goodness.'' She patted the spit curl over her left ear.

''Yeh, well. I want to talk about investing in this cattle business before the day gets much older, Esther. And I want the rest of you folks here to get in on the ground floor.''

''What cattle business?'' Quill asked. ''I haven't heard anything about a new cattle business.'' What she meant was that Doreen—who knew everything that went on in Hemlock Falls, and who had an entrepreneurial spirit of the highest order—hadn't mentioned anything about the cattle business to her.

''Y'all been pretty busy setting up the restaurant,'' Elmer said kindly. ''So it's not surprisin' that you haven't heard a thing.'' What he meant was that no one had yet told Doreen about it, since everyone thought the Quill was wholly uninterested in investments of any kind.

''Hm,'' Quill said. ''What about it?''

''We'll get to it,'' Elmer said tolerantly. ''But first,

like Esther said, we got the old business to go over. Any old business, Quill?''

Quill accepted the minutes book from Miriam and flipped back to the notes she'd taken at the last Chamber meeting several months ago. It had occurred just before the resolution of what she mentally called "the crafty ladies case," and since her mind had been on the investigation of a series of particularly brutal murders, her meeting notes were sketchy, at best. "Aug dog," she read aloud doubtfully. "FWD. America." She blinked. "Forwarding something? Did I promise to forward something? A dog to America?"

"Hemlock Falls Celebrates America Days," Harvey said briskly. "My idea of how to make some tourist money in the dog days of August. I mean, why stop with the Fourth of July? America is America three hundred and sixty-five days of the year."

"Amen," said Colonel Calhoun, startling Dookie out of his reverie.

"And with the addition of Mr. Rossiter's fine herd of that true American breed, Texas longhorn cattle, to our little town, my ideas for America Days are going to knock your socks off."

"Calhoun cattle," said the pudgy man in the black Stetson. "Royal's foundation stock is from my herd. So you'd want to say the Rossiter-Calhoun herd. Or words to that effect." He shifted in his seat with the confidence of a man deserving of attention. His voice was both high-pitched and resonant. There was a slight twang to his speech that Quill couldn't place. It wasn't a Texas drawl, nor the slur of the deep South, but something altogether different. Quill's notion of geography was a little fuzzy (she'd spent most of the eighth grade discovering that she could draw, to the detriment of both geography and algebra), but she placed the accent south of Washington State and north of California. Calhoun turned to Elmer with a pleasantly expectant air. "May I introduce myself and Mr. Rossiter to these good folks? Give them a little background on the fine opportunity that may be waiting here for us all?"

Elmer rose halfway, nodded vigorously, and sat down again. "Please Colonel Calhoun. Y'all take all the time you need."

Quill looked at her watch. Twenty after four, and if, as she suspected, Doreen had taken her orders to close the Palate with her usual indifference, the kitchen staff would be gearing up for dinner. She should be there. Besides, the track record for the Chamber of Commerce in municipal investment had been problematic, at best. There'd been the mini-mall fiasco, rescued from bankruptcy by a retired Japanese tycoon, not to mention the endless harebrained civic celebrations cooked up by Harvey Bozzel that ended up costing the town its tax money, rather than bringing it in. The infamous Jell-O Architecture Contest. Hemlock History Days and the witch squashing. Quill was pretty sure she didn't want to listen to any more of the same stuff.

She slid the notepad with the minutes in Miriam's direction and tucked her head near Miriam's ear.

"No," Miriam said firmly, before Quill could speak. "N. O. No. I'm not taking minutes for you."

"I take awful minutes."

"Don't you know?" Miriam smiled. She had huge blue eyes and attractively styled gray hair which somehow combined to give her a perennially youthful expression. "That's why we keep voting you in as secretary. If you kept really great minutes, we'd all realize how incompetent we are."

Quill made a face.

"It's true."

"Ladies?" Elmer knocked his gavel lightly on the table, then tucked it hastily into his breast pocket at Miriam's minatory look. "If we could have your attention, please."

Quill stood up with what she hoped was a firm air of authority. "I'm really sorry, Mayor, but I've got to get back to my restaurant. We're fully booked for dinner, and Meg's in New York."

"Meg's in New York, all right," Marge said. "I seen her get on the train myself. But that restaurant of yours has a great big whacking sign on the front door. CLOSED FOR REMODELING, it said. What are you remodeling now, Quill? You about gutted that place already. Totally unnecessary, I might add, in case you folks think I left her with a crumbo kitchen."

"It was a very nice kitchen," Quill said. "We didn't need all that freezer space, and Meg had to have an oven that hit six thousand degrees."

"Only need an oven that hot if you're doin' pizza," Betty Hall said. "Thought Miss Gore-may Chef Meg wouldn't touch pizza with a ten-foot pole. You put anchovies on it?"

"No," Quill said.

"Smart move. People that don't like anchovies would surprise you. There's a positive prejudice against anchovies."

"I like a good anchovy pizza myself," Colonel Calhoun said. "You own that pretty little restaurant on Main Street? I didn't know you had pizza. Would have stopped in, maybe."

"We don't sell pizza at all," Quill said desperately.

"We sell gourmet food. My sister is Margaret Quilliam. She's a master chef."

Betty Hall went "Huh!"

Colonel Calhoun nodded with a serious expression. "Y'all ever think about selling Texas longhorn beef?"

"We only have a few beef entrées, actually. A lot of our customers are too conscious of fat and calories to invest in it very much. There's always a few die-hard beef eaters, though." And they tended to die hard and early. Quill slung her bag over her shoulder. "Well, everyone, Miriam's going to take minutes and I really—"

"No, I won't." Miriam tugged firmly at her sleeve. "Sit, Quill. Sit. You might learn something of advantage to the Palate."

Quill, knocked slightly off balance by the tugs on her sleeve, sat down with an ungraceful thump. "Do you know," Miriam whispered urgently in her ear, "how rich this guy is? And he's a widower."

"I don't care," Quill whispered back.

"Well, *I* do!" Miriam batted her eyelashes at the colonel. "It's your civic duty to listen to the colonel, Quill. I feel it's *my* civic duty to learn all I can about this great opportunity for Hemlock Falls."

Quill sat. And she learned more about Texas longhorn beef than she had ever wanted to know. That the beef was lower in fat and calories than turkey. That the taste rivaled Black Angus for juiciness and flavor. That Dr. Michael Debakey, famous heart surgeon, believed so strongly in the health benefits of this beef that he had a whole herd at his Texas ranch and very probably refused to eat any other kind of beef, although he, Colonel Calhoun, couldn't tell for certain.

"And now, if you'll bear with me," the colonel said

in his high-pitched voice, "I just want you to see a few
of the wonderful cattle we have at home on our
Oklahoma spread." He flipped open his briefcase,
plugged in the little PC he carried there, and asked the
mayor to dim the lights.

"Slides," Miriam said in a voice of doom. "A slide
show. Oh, my. How . . . interesting. What is it about, exactly?"

"Just a few of the purtiest heifers and bulls you've
ever seen, Mrs. Doncaster."

Miriam hesitated.

"It's our civic duty," Quill said in as pious a tone as
she could manage, "to see these cows as well as hear
about them. Don't you think so, Colonel?" She smiled
brightly at Miriam. Unlike the librarian, she didn't mind
slide shows a bit. If she had paper and pencil, which she
did, she always sketched right through them. Or if sketch-
ing failed, she napped. She liked naps. She'd perfected
the art of napping unobtrusively through a lot of Chamber of Commerce presentations, mostly Harvey Bozzel's.

"Yes, ma'am. Nothing like seeing a copy of the real
thing."

Quill considered this statement from several angles and
decided not to comment. "I would love to see the cows.
We'd all love to see the cows."

"I can see all the damn cows I want right in your front
yard, Quill." Miriam's whisper was low but vehement.

"It's not my front yard anymore."

"This first show," the colonel said, his voice pitched
slightly higher than before, "is going to show you all
how you can make a three hundred percent return on your
investment in the Calhoun Cattle Company."

"Three hundred percent?" This from Harvey Bozzel.

"Yessir. The cattle you are about to invest in go for

maybe twenty–twenty-five dollars a pound for fillet on the open market. And I'm going to show you why."

There was a buzz of excited comment. Quill drew dollar signs on her notepad, then a quick sketch of a sad-eyed brown cow she'd seen in her—rather Marge's—front yard.

"First, I'd like to tell you all about my senior herd sire."

"Beg your pardon, Colonel." Royal Rossiter's voice was low but respectful. "But it's my senior herd sire. Impressive."

The colonel chuckled ominously. "I bred 'im, Royal."

"And I bought 'im, sir."

The tension in the room thickened.

The colonel breathed through his mouth. "Be that as it may, be that as it may. This is Impressive, and ladies and gentlemen, you can see that he is impressive, if you don't mind my little joke."

The bull that had frightened Quill on the path to the Inn flashed on the screen. A Western stock saddle was strapped to his back, and a familiar figure straddled the bull.

"Impressive was broke to saddle at eighteen months," the colonel said. "And on his back you can see—this picture was taken a couple of years ago—the famous star of stage, screen, and television, Miss Lally Preston."

Lally's blond good looks stared cheerfully from the screen. The bull looked puzzled. "This was right before we were featured on her TV show, *The Rusticated Lady*." The slide changed to a photo of Lally in her TV kitchen, a large bite of dripping beef on the way to her mouth.

"Ms. Preston featured new ways to cook our beef on her show, and the call-in response was tremendous. Just tremendous. People wanted to know where to get our beef.'' The slide switched again. This time a young female cow stared out at the audience with sweetly inquiring brown eyes. ''This here young lady was turned into the finest burger this side of Texas.'' The slide switched again, to a plate of rare hamburgers garnished with a pair of long horns made out of pickles.

Quill coughed and looked at her lap. Harland Peterson said in an interested tone, ''What kinda feed-to-kill ratio you get with these heifers, Colonel?'' This time the slide was of another female cow with an adorable calf bouncing at her side. The camera had caught the mother affectionately nuzzling the baby's ear. Quill thought she'd never seen such mild-looking animals.

''Take 'em to market at about eighteen months. Little longer than with an Angus or your similar fatty type restaurant beef.''

Click: and a beef carcass hanging in a meat locker.

''Back fat on these babies is less'n one percent. You can see from this here pitcher that the marbling is fine, diffused, all the way through. Texas A&M done some studies which show what fat there is, is *good* for you.''

Click: back to a third benign-eyed cow with twin calves at her side.

Quill sketched a horrified vegetarian in a long robe that bore more than a passing resemblance to herself, then looked sideways at Miriam. She was gazing at the screen with a thoughtful expression. The lights came up. Quill glanced around the table. Esther West raised her hand. ''Colonel?''

''Yes, ma'am?''

''You said three hundred percent?''

''That's right, ma'am. The demand for these here cattle far exceeds the supply. I'm here to talk to you folks about

setting up a feedlot operation here in Hemlock Falls
that's going to supply the tables of every gourmet in the
country. And then some.''

''Feedlot,'' said Quill. ''Isn't that a place where the
cattle are, um, crammed in and stuffed?''

The colonel narrowed his eyes at her. ''You eat foie
gras, ma'am?''

Quill admitted that she did.

''There is one thing I have to say to those of you. . . . ''
the colonel hesitated, seemed to change his mind about
the word he wanted, and continued, ''who are concerned
about the welfare of these cattle. Texas longhorns do best
when they're running wild and free on the range. They
have a ninety-nine percent unassisted live birth rate.''

There was a low whistle, presumably of appreciation,
from several of the men at the table. As well as Miriam
Doncaster. She caught Quill's astonished look and raised
an eyebrow. ''You knew I was brought up on a dairy
farm. In Wisconsin.''

''And these mamma cows are fierce in the defense of
their young. This here's the only breed of domestic stock
around that can coexist with the federally protected coy-
ote.''

Rumbles of laughter. Quill, thinking of the mother
cows defending their babies, of the beef carcass hanging
in the slaughterhouse, of beef that was good for you, and
above all, foie gras, which was one of her favorite foods,
wished she didn't have to think about this sort of thing
at all.

Elmer, beaming at the waves of interest and appreciation flowing around the room like so many buckyballs,
rapped genially on the table with his knuckles. With the
attention of the room, he said, ''Well, now, Colonel Calhoun, you can see that you might have struck a spark

here with our citizens. Can you tell us what the next steps
will be?''

"I can indeed, son. I've been working with the finest
advertising agency—''

"The only advertising agency," Miriam said tartly.

"—in your fair city, and he's got some perfectly
splendid ideas about ways to celebrate Hemlock Falls for
America Day. Harvey? You want to take the room?''

Harvey stood up with an athletic bounce (he worked
out at a gym in Syracuse three times a week) and shook
the creases carefully into his trousers. He opened the
large portfolio he had placed by his chair and flipped it
upright with a practiced hand, then adjusted a small cassette player carefully in front of it. He smiled. "Ladies
and gentlemen of the Chamber, Colonel Calhoun, Mr.
Rositer, I give you . . . America!''

Harvey punched the cassette and flipped the A-frame
display at the same time. Harvey's voice (a not unpleas-
ant baritone) floated into the air, accompanied by a rather
tinny piano playing "America the Beautiful."

> *O beautiful, that breed of cow*
> *That gives your heart a boost*
> *Their mighty horns stretch far across*
> *Much larger than a moose*
> *The longhorn cow*
> *You ask me how . . .*

"Marge?" Dina Muir timidly poked her head into the
room. "Is Harvey in here? I thought I heard him singing.
Harvey. There you are. Your Russians are here.''

# CHAPTER 4

"My God, Russkies!" said the mayor.

"There's no mistaking them for American," Colonel Calhoun said darkly.

This was true. The three men crowding into the conference room behind Dina were undeniably non-Americans. They wore cheap double-breasted suits and melancholy expressions. Their complexions reflected a diet heavy on carbohydrates and fats. They had a definable, unmistakable otherness in the way they moved, stolidly, as if they each wore heavy boots.

"This your doin', Harve?" Harland Peterson asked.

"Um," Harvey said. "Ah. Yes. Marge?"

Marge heaved herself to her feet and advanced on the Russians like a fat Napoleon on Moscow. The tallest Russian backed up and bumped into the bald one. "Hey," Marge said. "One a you Leonid Mensh-a-something?"

"Menshivik," said the tall one. He ducked his head ingratiatingly and smiled.

"Menshvik," Marge said. "Welcome to the Dew Drop Inn, gentlemen."

"Men*shi*vik," he said. "How do you do. We are very glad to be in this country." Quill blinked. Her ear was better than Meg's (who was tone-deaf), but Mr. Menshivik's accent was so thick she heard, "Tch-how do yew due. Ve are wry glat to bee in theis khun-tree."

The thickness of the accent didn't seem to bother Marge, who nodded and said matter-of-factly, "Glad ta see ya. Betty? We got their rooms ready?"

"Who *are* these people, Marge?" Miriam asked nervously.

"From rice," said Mr. Menshivik. "Call me Leonid, pliz, but don't call me late for dinner."

"Ha-ha," chorused the Russians behind him.

Quill slid down in her chair and looked intently at the ceiling. If she concentrated hard enough, she wouldn't laugh.

"You see," Leonid said, "we haf picked up many gut things while we are in the country, American jokes are very funny."

"Rice?" said the mayor. "You all eat rice? I thought just Japs ate rice."

Quill forgot about giggling and glared at the mayor.

"Sorry. I mean the Japanese. Anyways," the mayor said, "anyways. You all on a tour or whatever?"

"R.I.C.E.," Marge said with more than her usual truculence, "stands for Russians in Capitalist Enterprise. Harvey got 'em here. You tell everyone what this is all about, Harve."

"Yes, well." Harvey smoothed his hair. "If maybe we all could sit down . . . are there enough chairs for everyone?" There was a short silence, then a general shifting of bodies. When everyone in the Chamber settled

back in their seats, the three chairs next to Quill were
empty. Leonid smiled, waved, and ushered his confreres
to the seats.

Leonid sat next to Quill and dipped his head forward
in acknowledgment of her presence. "And how do you
do?"

"Very well, thank you." Quill extended her hand. Leonid enveloped it and shook it hard. "I'm Sarah Quilliam. Please call me Quill. Welcome to the Inn."

"Quill," he said, testing it. He gestured at the bald
Russian on his left. "This is Simkhovitch. Vasily Simkhovitch. And behind him is Alexi, Alexi Kowlakowski."

"Kavlakavsky," Quill said. "And Mr. Simkhovitch."

"Pliz. Call them Alexi, who you will remember because he has this hair in his nose, like our Russian bear,
and Vasily, who has no hair at all on his head. Like our
skinned Russian bear."

"Ha-ha," said Vasily.

"Hair or no hair," the mayor said, "what are you all
doin' in Hemlock Falls?"

"Yes. I tall you all right now." Leonid rose to his
feet. "Thank you all. Thank you. I want to tall you this,
that I have seen much we can do to improve our poor
country since we have the bad luck to lose our way in
the government. By this I mean that we are now no
longer communis." An ominous movement, like a swell
on a heretofore placid lake, rippled through the assembly.
Leonid repeated loudly, "We are no longer communis.
Communis is not good for us now. What we like is capit-
alism. And this, we have our name. Russians in Capitalist
Enterprise. This good capitalist here..." Harvey
smoothed his hair again. Quill began to hope he'd smooth
it right off and be as bald as Vasily. "... has been work-

ing with your capitalist government in Albany to find us
*host* city for our enterprise.''

"And what kinda enterprise are you in?'' Harland
asked.

"We are in capitalist enterprises,'' Leonid said confi-
dently.

"No, no,'' Harvey said. "I mean, yes, you are. But
they're farmers, Harland. Leonid here was the head of a
wheat commune.''

"*Com*mune,'' Colonel Calhoun muttered. "What the
hell?''

"And Vasily and Alexi raised dairy cattle. Just like
you, Harland.''

"Yeah?'' Harland rubbed his hand reflectively across
his chin. His hands were thick, red, and heavily muscled.
"What kind of cows?''

"It is Holshteiners we are trying for,'' Leonid said.
"Vasily and Alexi have not much luck with Angus.''

Harland's thick gray eyebrows rose in astonishment.
"Angus, now. Black Angus?''

"No. No. Red, of course. But we are to buy some
Holshteiners to take with us when we go from this country.''

"You don't want Angus for dairy,'' Harland said.
"What are you, nuts? Russians,'' he said to the ceiling.
"You got cash? None of them, what'd you call 'em, ru-
bles?''

"Cash? You mean,'' Leonid rubbed his forefingers
briskly against his thumb, "like in dinero? Moo-la? We
haf some, yes.''

Harland grunted. Then he grinned to himself. "You
want to see some good dairy cows, then, I might be able
to take you out to see a couple of mine. Holsteins, now.

None of this Hol-shteiners horseshit. A good Holstein cow is a good Holstein cow.''

"Excuse me." Colonel Calhoun hunched forward in his chair. "Y'all said cash, right? Then you may want to look at some real American capitalist beef, like the Texas longhorn cow.''

"And that," Quill said to Meg several hours later on the phone, "was that. By the time I left they were all chatting each other up, and Marge was making Betty run around and serve vodka, and for all I know, they're still up there, singing, 'Moscow Nights,' and getting along like a house afire.''

"There isn't much good about Russian cuisine," Meg said. "Borscht, maybe. They can do some great stuff with cabbage. And they have a reasonable way with a potato blini. But you take beets, cabbage, and black bread away from a Russian and you've got bupkis.''

"Meg!''

"It's true. So what's this International Night Harvey's cooked up?''

"It's not a bad idea, actually.''

Meg gave a two-hundred-mile-away snort. "When has Harvey ever had an idea that worked out?''

"Hemlock History Days wasn't bad.''

"Except we ended up with two corpses—no, three. And as a matter of fact, he was the dolt who first brought that damn gourmet week for Verger Taylor to us and insisted we do it for the prestige of Hemlock Falls, and that was how many bodies? Two, there, even if it was in southern Florida where the homicide rate rivals that of Beirut and murders aren't front-page news. The more I think about it, Quill, the more I think Harvey's a menace. Forget International Night.''

"Just listen, okay?" Quill was unusually patient. But she'd picked up the phone to call Meg with a lot of trepidation. They had always squabbled, from the time Meg could talk. They almost never quarreled. She hadn't known if she had crossed the line into the territory of the unforgiven or not until she heard Meg's hello. "Harvey says that with the economy so healthy, a lot of businesses are looking at partnership with Russia. Setting up the relationship is supposed to be simple, uncomplicated by a lot of government interference."

"Right." Meg's voice was skeptical. "What about the Russian Mafia?"

"What Russian Mafia?"

"Any Russian Mafia. I've read a lot of bad things about them. They're supposed to be more homicidal than the yakuza."

"Than the who? I mean whom?"

"The Japanese Mafia. You really need to keep up more on current events, Quill, I've always told you that."

So. The peace between them did have a price after all. Quill gritted her teeth and said mildly, "Leonid, Vasily, and Alexi are not crooks."

"Phuut! What about those suits you described?"

"That just proves it, doesn't it? Genuine successful crooks can afford to dress better. Just give it a try, Meg. Marge is going to host International Night at the Inn."

"At our Inn?"

"At her Inn. It'll be the Chamber of Commerce people and, um . . . a few others." Quill wasn't sure she wanted to tell Meg about the Longhorn Cattlemen just yet. "And everyone wants you to cook."

"Everyone always wants me to cook." This was said without complaint or vanity. It was true. "But do I have to cook Russian? I told you . . ."

". . . beets, potatoes, and cabbage. We want you to come up with a sort of cross-cultural meal." Quill took a deep breath. "Texas Longhorn beef with a Russian twist."

"No."

"But, Meg. The Russians are talking about investing in this cattle program the Chamber's backing, and—"

"I don't care about that. I told you when I first saw those cows in our rose garden . . ." Quill grinned, glad that Meg couldn't see her. Our rose garden? ". . . I haven't the least idea how to cook that beef."

"It's supposed to be just like regular beef, except healthier for you."

"Well, it isn't," Meg said bluntly. "I mean yes, it is healthier for you, but the fat's all weird. It's diffused evenly through the meat, and it's not as fatty as Angus. You have to cook it for a shorter period of time with higher heat." Meg's voice rose, with that particular note of incipient hysteria it always got when she was under pressure to cook well. "And I'm NOT going to manage a dinner for a million guests . . ."

"Forty-six," Quill said.

"Forty-SIX! Oh, *sure*. Anyhow. Forget it."

"Royal said he'd make all the beef available to you that you need. As a donation. You can practice. And if you don't, Meg, think of this. Harvey's talked the Wine-growers Association into sponsoring the banquet if we don't prepare it. They want to create some private label wine just for the occasion. You want to hear what Harvey's come up with?"

"Probably not."

" 'Cow'-bernet. 'Moo'-lot. 'Moo'-jalais."

"Stop."

"I'll stop. It gets worse. You don't want to hear what

he wants to call the Liebfraumilch. With a little practice on this beef, it'll be a spectacular meal, Meg.''

"Practice. When do I have time to practice? I had forty-two entrées this evening at Levade and I'm pooped. And that stupid column's due in couple of weeks . . ."

"Write about the beef."

". . . and I've got to come up with some idea for Lally Preston's TV show. . . ."

Quill refused to state the obvious. She waited.

"It *might* be interesting."

"I think it'd be fascinating."

"Hm. I'll think about it. How much beef can I get?"

"Whatever you need. I'll talk to Royal in the morning. He can have it airshipped here in twenty-four hours, he said, which is a lot better,"—Quill shuddered—"than his first idea, which was to take one of those very nice mamma cows from the rose garden and—"

"I don't want to hear it."

"I don't want to say it. So. Fax me the list of cuts you want, I'll give it to Royal, and I'll see you day after tomorrow, beef in hand. Or in box, as the case might be."

"Okay." Meg yawned. "I guess I can get my *sous* chef to cover me here. See you, Sis."

It was late, after one in the morning, and fatigue hit Quill like a hammer, but she said, "Meg?"

"What. Never mind. Don't say it. Just think a little, Quillie. I'm here whenever you need me."

"Hey, who's the oldest, anyhow?"

"Who's the cutest? Who's the smartest? Who's the best cook? Me!" Meg put the receiver down with a cheerful bang. Moments later she called back. "Quill? Where's Max?"

Quill looked at the dog curled at her feet. "Right here."

"He's got a rabies shot in the morning."

"Oh, no," Quill said. "Not me. Uh-uh. I'm not taking that dog to the V-E-T. He can't even hear the word without going berserk. If you think I'm going to drag the poor thing into my Olds and drive out to her place with that howling in my ears, you are wrong. We'll wait till Myles gets back."

"Nonsense," Meg said briskly. "He's your dog. He'll be fine." A pause, then she added ominously, "And you owe me."

"That's true."

"Doreen made the appointment with that woman vet."

"Laura Crest?"

"Yeah. It's at ten, I think. You'll do it?"

"I'll do it. Just don't blame me if Davy Kiddermeister arrests me for animal abuse along the way. From the way the animal carries on, you'd think I made a habit of whacking him around." She nudged Max with her toe and said in a foolish way, "*Good* boy."

"I was just wondering. When you take Max in to see her, ask her about the longhorn beef, okay? Anything I can find out about the difference in chemistry would be a help."

"For heaven's sake, Meg." Quill bit her lip. "No problem. She's going to think I'm crazy, but no problem."

"Hey! Who's the craziest? Who's the—"

Quill hung up, ran her fingers through her hair, called Myles to tell him she loved him, and went to bed.

"Now, Max," Quill said. "We're going for a little ride." She knelt under the prep table in the Palate's kitchen and took firm hold of his collar.

"That's a mistake," Doreen said. She dropped the breakfast dishes into the sink with a clatter. Last night's closing had slightly affected the breakfast trade, but Doreen had offered discounted dinners to those customers whose reservations she had canceled, and tonight's dinner hour was fully booked. It was nine-thirty and the sun streamed in the window like a pennant at a parade.

"What's a mistake?" Max, usually the most tractable of dogs, wriggled away from her clutch on his collar and bounded to the back door.

"Talkin' to him in that special cooey voice."

"I was not using a special cooey voice."

"You were usin' the 'this is goin' to hurt me more than it hurts you' voice, and the durn dog knows he's goin' to the vet."

Max flung himself against the back door and barked.

"*Now* he knows he's going because he heard you! Max. Max! Hush. Whisper, Max, whisper."

Max rolled one eye appealingly in her direction. Then he flattened himself on the floor, rolled over to expose his belly, and whined. Quill knelt next to him to scratch his tummy.

"Don't do that," Doreen said. She banged a pot into place on its rack. As soon as Quill reached to pet him, Max rolled to his feet and dashed out the door into the dining room up front.

"That's why. That dog ain't dumb."

Quill scrambled up and went after him. She found him at the front table crouched at the feet of Royal Rossiter and a tall muscular man in a cowboy hat Quill hadn't seen before. "Max," she called, carefully keeping any cooey notes out of her voice. "Here, Max. C'mon, Max. Let's go for a walk, boy. Walk."

Max whined, thumped his tail, and barked. Two

middle-aged ladies at table three frowned disapprovingly. The tall man in the Stetson bent over and snapped his fingers. "On your feet, son." Max got up. The man in the hat ran a knuckle over Max's nose. "You lookin' at a bath this morning? Got a problem?" Max panted happily, a foolish grin on his face. He wriggled blissfully under the strong fingers. Quill crossed the dining room with an apologetic smile in the direction of the ladies. They were both eating Meg's Summer Breakfast Sorbet, a raspberry-filled blini that should have put them into a much better mood. The blonde in the pink pantsuit sneezed hard twice. Quill stopped at their table. "You're allergic," she said remorsefully. "I'm so sorry. He hates the vet, although there isn't any reason to, she's very . . ."

Max reacted to the word the way bulls were reputed to react to cattle prods. He dove between Royal Rossiter's legs and out the front door. Quill let fly a four-letter word, regretted it immediately, and ran after him. Royal and the cowboy followed. Quill refused to acknowledge the grins on their faces.

Outside, Main Street lay peaceful under the morning sun. The red geraniums in the black flower boxes (courtesy of the Women's Firemen's Auxiliary) glowed bright against the warm cobblestone storefronts. And Max was three blocks away, running toward Peterson Park, droopy ears flapping in the breeze.

The cowboy let out a piercing whistle.

Max stopped, turned, and cocked his head inquiringly.

Quill held her breath. The cowboy whistled again, and Max trotted a few steps in their direction, stopped, hung his head, and walked slowly back. The cowboy bent and fondled his ears. "Good old son, aren't you."

Quill grabbed the dog's collar. "Thank you so much,

Mr. . . . ah, um. I don't know why he hates the . . .'' She stopped just in time.

Royal said, ''This is Jack Brady, Quill. He's my cattle handler. And a Texan, too.''

''Ma'am.'' Jack Brady took off his hat and held out his hand. Quill hated sappy romance movies and had absolutely refused to see either *The Bridges of Madison County* or *The Horse Whisperer*. But she was a sucker for broad-shouldered outdoorsmen with a lot of sable hair. His hand was more muscular than Leonid's and had the leathery texture of a saddle. His eyes were blue. Quill was beginning to wonder about blue-eyed Texans. Something in the state must affect the gene pool.

''Thank you very much for getting Max, Mr. Brady. You have a real gift with animals.''

''Cattle, dogs, horses, and women,'' Royal added with satisfaction. ''Brady here's the real thing, Quill. Now, the fella Calhoun has working for him? Dex Fairweather? Guy's straight out of Long-uh Island. Puts on the walk and puts on the talk.''

''You certainly showed that with Max. Could I offer both of you a little more breakfast, as a thank-you? Or perhaps you'd like to come in for a lunch.''

''No, ma'am,'' Royal said, ''we had a bang-up breakfast in there. Little light on the potatoes, but real good. What you could do for us, if you don't mind, is maybe introduce us to his vet.''

Max barked. Brady gave him a look. Max sat at Quill's feet and panted apologetically.

''Dr. Crest? I'd be happy to.''

''Thing is, we got a couple of calves running out on their nine months vaccines. And Class Clown's got a cough I don't like, no, I don't like it at all. And Brady needs somewhere to keep his horse.''

"His horse?"

"Scooter. Best roping mare this side of . . ."

The Pecos, Quill thought.

"The Mississippi. Got her up in what used to be that asparagus bed for now."

Quill hoped she didn't look as if she were baring her teeth.

"Thing is, the local vets usually have an extra stall or two," Brady offered. His voice was easy and direct. "I don't like keepin' her in the open if I don't have to."

"Sunburns her coat," Royal said. "She's a buckskin, nice creamy color lessen the sun gets to it. Turns it into straw."

"We certainly wouldn't want that," Quill said. Was fresh horse manure good for asparagus? She doubted it. "I'm going up there right now, if you'd like to ride along."

"Be glad to take you in the dually." Royal jerked a thumb at his pickup, which was large, chrome-trimmed, and royal blue. The door read *ROSSITER RANCH The Finest in Longhorn Cattle*. "Just hop right in. Got one of them extended cabs, so there's plenty of room."

Quill nodded, a bit reluctantly. On the other hand, the faster they got Brady's horse out of the asparagus bed, the better off next year's asparagus would be. And she was going to get the Inn back, dammit, so she had a right to be concerned about the asparagus.

Max loved the dually. Quill had no idea where Max had been before he'd rocketed into her life two months before, but it was clear he'd had good experiences with trucks. He curled up happily in the back, his head on her lap, and Quill directed Brady down Main Street and onto Route 15, where Laura Crest ran the Paradise Veterinary Practice.

"You think much of this doc?" Brady called over his shoulder as they rolled past the swelling green of Tompkins County. Quill, her attention drawn to the play of colors in the summer light, said nervously, "I've never met her, actually. I hope she's nice to Max."

"Never met the vet?" Royal was as bemused as if she'd admitted not knowing where the post office was in her own hometown. Max whined. Quill patted his head soothingly. "I just got the dog. Two months ago. Meg and Doreen took him to get rid of his fleas and to give him vaccines. But he's due for this second rabies shot. I think."

"First one they give in two parts," Royal said. "Got much problem with rabies around here?"

"I don't know."

"Don't know about rabies?"

"Gentlemen," Quill said firmly, "I don't know anything about cattle, about dogs, about horses or ranching. Dr. Crest handles most of the dairymen's work around here as far as I know, and I'm sure she's qualified to give the cattle whatever."

The dually purred along for a moment. Brady reached down and turned on a country music station. Over lyrics having to do with trains, prisoners, mothers, and bars, Royal said, "Any other vets around here?"

"Syracuse has quite a few, I think. It's the next left turn, Brady. At the Sunoco station. And, of course, Cornell University is about twenty minutes away, and they have one of the best vet schools in the United States."

The Paradise Veterinary Practice consisted of three workmanlike buildings set close to one another, an office, a large barn, and a big lean-to shed with perhaps a dozen fenced runs attached. Quill could see one horse, two cows, and a large wolfish dog in separate runs.

The gravel drive was clean and neatly raked. Three cars were parked in front of the building marked OF-FICE: a van with three kids quarreling in the backseat, a Toyota, and a dirty Range Rover with metal boxes strapped to the hood and the tailgate.

"Rig looks okay," Royal said. Brady nodded. Quill, who wasn't sure whether they were referring to the Range Rover or the facilities, took a firmer grasp on Max's collar and dragged him out of the truck. Max sat in the gravel, splayed his legs out, and refused to move. Brady reached into the truck and took out a leash which didn't look like a leash. There was a clip attached to one end, but it looked more utilitarian than the length of lime-green acrylic Quill had bought for Max. Brady fixed the leash to Max's collar and walked him into the office.

"You've got to show me how to do that," Quill said as they sat down.

"It's in the handling," Royal said importantly.

"I'm sure it is," said Quill. Then, a little nervous of what lay ahead of poor Max, she said chattily, "Why do you suppose every vet's office in the known universe smells like pine tar and has little plastic bucket seats?"

"Easier to keep clean," said Royal.

"I know that. It was more of a . . ."

"Rhetorical question?" Brady smiled. "You know, you bein' nervous makes the dog nervous. See that?" He nudged Max with his toe. Max, who had been gazing pitifully into Quill's face, snapped his head around and grinned at Brady. "It's not bein' here that bothers him. It's you bein' bothered by him bein' bothered by bein' here. Got it?"

"Got it." Quill patted her dog. "So how do I stop—um—'bein' bothered'?"

"Just relax," said a cheerful matter-of-fact voice. "Miss Quilliam? Laura Crest."

The vet emerged from an examining room in back of the reception desk. She was short, thin, with sandy-colored hair pulled into a knot at the back of her head. She had a fresh, athletic bounce to her step and was carrying a syringe. A medium-sized black and tan dog walked at her side. Max jerked to attention and made a rush for the black and tan.

"Down, Tye," Dr. Crest said in a quiet voice.

The dog dropped to the floor in a perfect sit. "Now, that's a dog," Brady said in a voice of approval. "Australian kelpie?" Laura Crest smiled and nodded. Brady shook his head in admiration. "Breed's a challenge to manage. I can see why you keep so fit."

Quill immediately felt under-exercised and that Max was overindulged. She gave Max a guilty pat and said, "My dog's a bit excitable, I'm afraid. Should I take him somewhere?"

"Right here is fine." The vet bent over to pat Max, pinched a fold at the nape of his neck, and the shot was done. This made Quill feel even less of a dog person and more of a wimp. She'd worried a lot about Max crying when he got his shot. She made introductions to Royal and Brady, then drifted away from the conversation, which turned to vaccines, calving procedures, and a cow that hadn't cleansed. She was drawn back when the veterinarian said, "I like your sister, Quill. And Doreen. And I've heard great things about the Palate. I've been meaning to get up to try some of the food, but it's pretty hard to find the time with a solo practice. It seems every time I get a chance to put my feet up and eat, my beeper goes off." She patted her pocket.

"Tell you what," Royal said. "Whyn't we take you

on up to the Palate for a bite of lunch after you take a look at my herd.''

"Well, I don't have a lot on for this afternoon. And, of course, there's always my beeper. And I'd surely like to take a look at these cattle. I've heard a lot about them.''

"I'd almost forgotten," Quill said. "My sister said there's something different about the fat. She wanted to know if you had any information about the chemistry.''

"I can find out for you. One of my old professors at Cornell has a buddy at A&M and they've been doing a lot of research there. I do know that they have a very low percentage of back fat, and the quality of the fat is quite different at the microbiological level. I'll make a few phone calls and meet you up at that pretty inn on the hill where you've got your cattle. What's it called? Something really dumb like the Dun Rovin'?''

"The Dew Drop Inn," Quill said. Suddenly, she liked the vet. A lot. And she hadn't hurt Max in the least.

"Ugh. But it's gorgeous, I hear. Didn't they have some famous painter who owned it with her sister and went bankrupt?''

Quill blushed. "We didn't go bankrupt. We just—sold it. Temporarily. I mean, I thought I would be glad to have all the hassle off my hands, but I really miss it.'' Brady and Royal turned to look at her. Quill tugged her hair in exasperation.

"That was you?" Laura said. "Oh, heck. I'm sorry. You know what they say about horse and cattle people, we save our charm for the animals. Look. Lunch sounds terrific. I'll meet you at the corral,—''

"The rose garden, actually.''

"Right. And if Brady wants to bring his mare over for a few days, we can do that after lunch.''

• • •

Quill rode in the back of the dually with Max; head on her knee and her thoughts scattered in six different directions. "Okay. Mental plan. Priority one. Go to the bank and talk to Mark Anthony Jefferson about a loan to buy the Inn back. For half a million bucks. Number two. Make another plan, since Mark Anthony Jefferson will laugh in your face."

"Who's gonna laugh in your face?" Royal asked. His eyes met hers in the rearview mirror. "You want we should take care of him, Texas style?"

"No. No. Sorry. I guess I was thinking aloud."

"I didn't know you were a painter."

"Sure she is," Brady said. He swung the steering wheel easily to the left and back again, avoiding a garbage bag left in the road. "She's Quilliam. You know the painting of the magnolia you liked in Dallas?"

"That big huge thing?" Royal twisted all the way around in his seat so that he could look at her directly. "A little redheaded gal like you" (Quill was five foot seven) "painted that big huge thing?" He thought a moment. "You know, that painting had balls."

"Well said, boss." Brady's tone was wry but his eyes weren't.

Quill said, "Thank you," conscious of being demure.

"And you and your sister ran that Inn."

"Yes. For eight years."

"And you're sorry you sold it?"

"I am."

"Meanin' your sister ain't."

"Practically everyone ain't sorry, Royal. The guy I'm planning to marry isn't. Meg isn't. Doreen isn't. John Raintree, our business manager, wasn't. Just me. They all loved it, but they all wanted to leave it. And I'm finding out it was because of me.''

"You think you can run that little old Inn by yourself?"

"No."

Royal turned away. "Well," he said to the windshield. "Looks like you got a few options, not many. One is, forget it. Two is, you find some other partners. What about finding some other partners?"

"I don't want other partners. I just want things the way they used to be."

"Huh. So, what's stoppin' you?" He tugged at his hat. Quill wondered if he ever took off his hat. "I'm askin' for real now."

"Basically, everyone thinks I work too hard, neglect too much, and," she added honestly, "that I don't do it very well even though I love it."

"That true?"

"Maybe."

"So can you fix it?"

Irritation hit her like a punch in the stomach. What was she doing talking to a guy she hardly knew about things she refused to discuss even with Myles? And what business was it of his, anyway?

"Thing is," Royal said conversationally, turning around to look at her again, "you got a horse learns he can throw you off if you ride him rough, you stop ridin' rough. That's all."

"Thanks," said Quill. "I'm sorry I blabbered on like that. I don't know why I burdened you with it. Not only is it not your problem, but . . ." She took a deep breath and clamped her lips together.

"But ol' Marge hears about this and she'll take advantage. Tell you what. Ol' Marge is a pretty damn good businesswoman, but I don't tell her a lot. Not by a long shot. So don't you worry . . ."

. . . your pretty little head about it, Quill thought.

". . . your pretty little head about it. What you should do is decide what went wrong with you in charge before and what you could change if you ran it now. Think about that."

"I will," Quill lied. "And thank you. If you could just drop me off at the Palate."

"You don't wanta see Brady's mare?"

"Well, I—"

"She don't want to see the mare, boss."

"Of course I want to see the mare," Quill said. "It's just that I've got quite a bit to do and I really . . ."

Brady pulled to a stop in front of the Palate.

"It'll take just a minute," Royal assured her. "Women like horses."

"Maybe some other time, Royal. But thank you, though." She reached for Max, preparing to get out.

"Thing is." Royal stopped, then started again. "Thing is, I didn't know you were the same person that did that magnolia."

"The one with balls," Quill said.

"Right. You ever paint bulls?"

"You mean your bull?"

"Sure. I'm talking a commission, here."

"Gosh, Royal. Paint a bull? I've done people, of course, but I don't know a thing about a bull's anatomy. I wouldn't really know where to start. I mean I would, but I don't know if I want to."

"Now, you look. You think about painting that bull. And I'll think about helping you get back the Inn. What do you say?"

Quill just stared at him. Oddly, she thought of Marge,

stout in her denim skirt and brave bandanna. Suddenly, she didn't know if she liked men, or people with deals, or even if she wanted the Inn back. She felt trapped in a totally different world, with bewildering rules.

Brady idled the motor.

"Okay," Quill said. "I'll think about it. But I'm not going to make a decision until I talk to Marge about it. All right? She should know if I'm planning something."

Royal nodded. As if she'd passed some test.

"A test for what?" she asked John Raintree that evening. She twirled the phone cord between her fingers and released it. "Could you . . . You must have a little time coming. I really need to see you, John. Please."

# CHAPTER 5

"Darling," said Lally Preston, "we simply cannot cut from that sweet-looking cow to a plate of beef. I refuse to do it."

"It will make a very impressive opening to the show," Colonel Calhoun said.

"It will make a very impressive light show on my phone boards at the studio when my little old ladies call in to protest."

"This meeting of the Special Committee for International Night should come to order." Harvey Bozzel cleared his throat in a tentative way. "Please?"

They were crowded into Harvey's office: Meg, Quill, Colonel Calhoun, Leonid the Russian, Harvey, and Lally Preston. Lally moved in a cloud of perfume so expensive Quill couldn't name it. She was dressed in a skinny slip dress that showed off the anorexic build common to (as Lally's publicist billed her) stars of screen and television, and for all Quill knew, the stage. Except the stage actresses she knew had a healthier respect for their bodies than to starve themselves fifteen pounds thinner than nature dictated. Lally was loud, as well as too thin. And her gold bracelets clanked. Meg seemed to get along with her just fine.

"Miss Preston, I understand the sensitivity of a woman of your artistic—ah—sensitivities," Colonel Calhoun said in his high-pitched voice. "But we're talking cattle, here. You aren't one of the vegetarian groups, are you?"

Lally gave him the Look. Lally was good at the Look. Quill had tried practicing it herself in her bathroom mirror. She gave it up, because she couldn't get the icy-slitted-eye thing right. Her tight-lipped pout, she thought, was not half bad, although it made her lips ache.

"I," Lally said, "am the Rusticated Lady. You are familiar with the show? Perhaps not, since we do NOT feature barnyard animals. Only the best produce off a country gentleman's estate."

"You own a country gentleman's estate?" Colonel Calhoun seemed to be genuinely interested.

"Of course not. I live in Manhattan. Central Park West, if that means anything to you. Which I'm certain it does not."

"Then, you married to a country gentleman?" the colonel pressed on.

"I am divorced. From a stockbroker."

"So what in the name of goodness do you know about what comes off a country estate?"

Quill studied her toes. She was wearing sandals for the first time that year, and she'd painted her toenails pink. It was an odd thing about Colonel Calhoun, she'd decided. He never swore. She had an idea that rough tough cattlemen always swore. So much for stereotypes. She sneaked a look at her sister. Meg was lost in thought, doodling on the pad she used to create menus. Her short

dark hair was sticking up in cowlicks. She was wearing
a T-shirt with a cranky-faced duckling carrying a sign
that read: *I'm Bad*. She was smiling and humming an
(off-key) version of "Strangers in the Night."

"Perhaps we could get back to the point here?" Harvey said. The desperation in his voice made Quill feel a
little sorry for him. This was a tough crowd.

"In Russia, we do not often get to the point," Leonid
said. "I am glad to be in this country."

Harvey had a white board on an easel in his office and
he went to it now. There was a bulleted list on it in Magic
Marker.

### INTERNATIONAL NIGHT
**Sponsors: The American Association of Texas
Longhorn Cattle Breeders (A.A.T.L.C.) and
Russians in Capitalist Enterprise (R.I.C.E.)**
- **The Place: The Dew Drop Inn**
- **The Time: Saturday 8:00 p.m.**
- **Honored Guest: Lally Preston of *The Rusticated
  Lady* show**
- **The Agenda:**
  **8:00 Introductory Remarks, Harvey Bozzel,
  pres. B.A.**
  **8:15 Welcome by His Honor Mayor Elmer
  Henry**
  **8:30 Dinner prepared by Maître Margaret
  Quilliam
  (menu to follow)**
  **9:30 Speech "Why I Love This Country" by
  Leonid Menshivik of R.I.C.E.**
  **10:00 Speech "The Genetics of the Longhorn
  Cow" by Col. Randall Calhoun (ret)**
  **10:30 Brandy and desserts**

•   •   •

"How's the menu coming, Meg?" Harvey asked. "Meg?"

Meg glanced up. She looked at the white board. She frowned. "The mayor's not going to like you giving introductory remarks, Harvey."

"It's appropriate," Harvey said nervously. "None of this would be happening if it weren't for me."

"What does the mayor care? You'd better take yourself off the agenda. And besides, ten-thirty's too late for brandy and desserts in Hemlock Falls. Half the Chamber will be asleep. So if you boot yourself off the agenda, it'll give us an earlier evening." She went back to her menu with a frown.

Harvey raised the eraser, then lowered it with a defiant air. "We're getting a written message from the governor, and I'm going to read it."

"Oh, God," Lally Preston said.

"Your TV show will surely want to feature the governor's message, Miss Preston."

"We surely will not. I'm national. Who gives a shit about the governor of New York?"

Now, Lally, Quill thought, Lally swears like a trooper. Or like I thought a rancher would swear.

"Quill?" From the sound of it, in a little while, Harvey would turn petulant.

She looked up from her toes. Harvey tossed the eraser into the air with nonchalance. It bounced off the easel and onto the table. "Could you show us what you've designed for a menu cover? And the program?"

The afternoon before, Quill had gone up the hill to see if she wanted to draw Royal's bull. She decided she didn't. There was absolutely nothing there. That was the trouble with drawing animals. They were sentient, but there was no *there* there. At least not with the bull. What she had noticed was that all the cows together generated a sort of bovine mega-personality. Cows in a herd were much more "there" than individual cows. They had their assigned duties—nurse the calf, eat, move from one portion of the rose garden to another—and they performed these duties in concert without much obvious communication among themselves. For Quill, this interfered with cows as a subject. Painting, above all, was about capturing the "there," the true part of what you looked at. The true part of a magnolia was in the viewer. The true part of the cow was in the cow. And it wasn't very interesting.

What she had decided, after a lengthy phone call with John about ways and means to buy back the Inn, was that although she had no interest in painting Impressive, she did want to donate a program cover for International Night, especially since John felt there could be some long-term profit in a longhorn beef program. She'd done a few preliminary sketches that morning. And John was due on the early evening train.

"Quill?"

"Sorry, Harvey. I did a couple of charcoal things." She set her sketch pad upright in front of her and flipped to the first page. "This is Leonid and Royal with Impressive, shaking hands over the bull's horns."

"That was my idea," Harvey said.

"Yes it was. And this is the other." She backed away from the sketch, letting it stand. She'd drawn a crowd of people, a little overfed, mouths slightly open, in strong aggressive strokes of the charcoal. The cows were in the background, the pencil strokes soft and indistinct.

"Those cows look sad," Leonid said. "Quite sad."

Colonel Calhoun was indignant. "Cows don't have feelings, Mr. Menshivik. Miss Quilliam? Would you go back to that first one? The very good idea Mr. Bozzel had? Yes. Thank you. I thought you knew that Impressive was my bull. Royal bought him from me, yes, but he is absolutely on the Calhoun side of the Calhoun Rossiter herd."

"That is an appropriate topic for discussion for our subcommittee," Harvey said.

"Subcommittee?" Lally said. "You've got a subcommittee? Let me guess. His subcommittee is you, the Russian, and this cowpoke here. Which is why the three of you are all over this agenda. I told you I wanted Meg to talk about the recipes, and I'm going to insist that Meg talk about the recipes. You can have her talk at the dinner, or not, it's up to you. If I don't catch her there, I'll catch her in the kitchen. I'm warning you, we're going to feature very little of this crap about genetics and Russian hoo-ha and village politics."

Harvey nodded as if he had it all under control. "Understood, Miss Preston. Is there anything at all you need from us?"

"The speeches. Copies of the speeches. We have to know what's going to be broadcast."

"I don't think you do," Colonel Calhoun said. "And I have to say that my speech on cow genetics reflects years of study on my part. Years. I do not allow copies in the hands of anyone who might take advantage of my research."

"You can bet your cute little butt I don't give a flying . . . hoot . . . about cow genetics. I do give a damn if you're going to bore the pants off my housewives in Peoria."

"I myself, speak from the heart. I have no written speech. In Russia," Leonid continued darkly, "it is sometimes not wise to write things down."

"Yeah, right," Lally said. "Then you're going to have to do it once for the crew and once for the camera. Otherwise, forget it."

Meg, who had ignored the wrangling, sat back with a gusty sigh and a satisfied wriggle of her fingers. "Got it. Now, Lally, you know you're locked into this program. We've already got the column slated to run in *New York* magazine next month, same time as the show will be broadcast. So don't be so hard on everyone, okay?"

"You have the menu?" Colonel Calhoun asked.

"I have the menu. Guaranteed heart-healthy and delicious as well." She wrinkled her forehead "I hope. I'm going to have time to practice. I've already tried out a couple of filets, Colonel, and I have to tell you, they were tough. I've devised a marinade that might work, and it's working away in my kitchen right now. We'll have to see."

"I admit that's always been a problem with the longhorn," Colonel Calhoun said. "I'm depending on you to come up with the answer. A longhorn marinade is crucial to success. We all are aware of that."

"I might have it. And I might not. Anyhow, here's the meal." Meg jumped up, grabbed the eraser, and vigorously swept the white board clean. Then she wrote:

### INTERNATIONAL DINNER
**Starters**
   **Filet by Quilliam—a variation on steak tartare**
   **Grapefruit broiled in mint sauce**
   **Longhorn pâté**

**Soup**
  Oxtail consommé
**Fruit sorbet**
**Entrée**
  **Stuffed bracciole à la Longhorn**
  **in a sweet potato nest**
**Vegetable**
  **Asparagus**
**Salad**
  **Basil, arugula, and iceberg lettuce**
  **with Longhorn vinaigrette**
**Sweet**
  **Mascarpone from Longhorn cream**
  **with raspberry sauce**

"And, of course, the appropriate wines to accompany each. I think I'm going to look for a full-bodied red, with some citrus overtones to go with the bracciole."

"Now, about my private wine label idea," Harvey said. "I have several wineries standing by."

"To make Cow-bernet and Moo-lot?" Meg said rudely. "I think not. And as much as I love the New York whites, there is no appropriate New York State red to accompany this meal." She wrote DONE at the end of the menu with a flourish of the Magic Marker.

Quill led the applause.

"And the recipes?" The colonel pressed. "The one for the marinade? That will be made available to the audience?"

"No," Meg said shortly. "It will not. A chef's recipes are like your . . . your whatever. Breeding papers. My recipes are my . . . my . . ." She waved her hands, searching for the right word.

"Net worth?" suggested the colonel.

"You could say that, I suppose." She exchanged a glance with Quill. "*Our* net worth."

"But what good are Longhorn beef recipes going to do for you? They could do so much good for people who love beef and have to give it up because of the cholesterol and the fats. It would be a genuine charitable act. A genuine charitable act."

Quill noticed that Meg flushed. Her sister had a generous heart, underneath the crabby expressions on her T-shirts. But she was right. Meg's recipes and her skill as a chef were the only thing that differentiated them from the competition. Quill cleared her throat and said rather loudly, "Would you like to choose the program cover? I'll need a few days to make the sketch camera ready."

"I myself find these cows in the circle too melancholy," Leonid said. "Much sadness in these cows. I prefer that as a program."

"I prefer the other one. Although I really don't think Royal would feel comfortable with his picture on the cover with my bull," said the colonel. "On the other hand, it is very important for people to realize that the genetics of these bulls is what makes the beef so healthy. We have a duty to use that first cover, the one that Harvey here designed."

"Well," Harvey said modestly, "I didn't exactly draw it. But yes, I admit the concept is mine, and more important, that it works."

"*You* sure as heck didn't," Meg snapped. "Do you know how much a gallery would pay for either one of these two working drawings? As is? You ought to be ashamed of yourself."

Harvey, who actually did have a modicum of taste in color and line, had the grace to look embarrassed. "Suppose Quill puts the colonel in place of Mr. Rossiter and we go with it that way.''

''All right I'll try to have a mechanical for you by Thursday, Harvey. You can get it scanned in and printed by Friday afternoon, can't you?'' Quill closed the sketch pad and tucked it into her capacious handbag. ''If you guys will excuse me, I've got to meet a train.''

She left them arguing amiably over additions to Meg's menu, which, if past such discussions were anything to go by, would escalate to an acrimonious squabble ending when Meg flatly refused to cook at all if she heard one more minute of uninformed hoo-ha.

The train station was five minutes away, half a block to the rear of the Municipal Building off Main Street. Quill had at least twenty minutes to spare. She'd parked right in front of Harvey's offices (flanked by Esther West's Best Dress Shoppe on the south and Nadine Peterson's Kottage of Kountry Gifts on the north). She decided to drive the long way around, up the hill to the Inn and down again the back way. The sun was almost gone, the sky a high ceilinged room stippled with patches of rosy light. Quill rolled the window down as she drove. Scents of evening flooded the car: the sharp/soft prickle-smell of damp grass, a handful of apple blossom perfume scattered on the current of the breeze, the odor of earth turned aside by the thrust of growing things. The Inn sprawled comfortably above her, like a gowned woman reclining on one elbow. The car climbed upward, and she heard the rush of the falls, muscular with the late spring rains. A pale moon drifted above the gorge, a fruit ready to burst into full silver as soon as the sun went down.

Quill braked in front of the metal gates that contained the cattle, got out of the car, and leaned against the bars. One by one, the heifers rustled up to the fence, almost silent, their mild eyes a little wary. The largest cow, speckled black and white, and almost invisible in the approaching twilight, moved to stand protectively in front of the calves.

"Kinda pretty in the dark." Marge rose from the garden bench in front of the koi pond turned water trough.

"Sorry, I didn't see you there."

"Brady come by a while ago to take that horse of his over to Laura Crest's. I watched him for a while and then was just sittin' here with Royal's cows. Hang on. I'll come on out." The cows moved aside for the short, stocky figure with an uneasy shaking of their horns. "They ain't used to me." Marge grunted as she climbed over the fence and thudded down next to Quill. "Not yet, anyways."

"Aren't you a little nervous around them?"

"Nah." The turret eyes swung toward Quill and back to the cows again. "Well, some, maybe. Royal says he's seen some bad holes poked in folks when they don't take care. They're animals after all." Marge scratched the back of her neck in an absentminded way. Quill inhaled Chanel Number Five.

"I've always liked that perfume, Marge. Chanel Number Five."

"Borrowed some off Nadine Peterson. You don't think it smells bad, then?"

"I think it smells great."

"What kind of perfume you use?"

This from tubby, stubborn, in-your-face Marge Schmidt? Quill kept the smile out of her voice. "It depends. Lavender cologne once in a while. Tea Rose, until Freddie Bellini said it smelled like funerals."

"Thing is, the sher'f seems to like it."

"You mean Myles?" Quill was silent. He was tied up

with this industrial espionage thing for another two weeks, he'd said. She wouldn't be able to call him for at least several days, either, since he'd decided to go undercover at the GM plant in Rochester.

"You think men like perfume, as a general rule?"

"Well, it depends. A lot of men want women to be different. So different that they can claim not to understand them at all. So they like high heels, frilly dresses, lots of makeup—things that are alien to them. Someone like—oh, Royal Rossiter—would like a woman to be herself. And that's the best kind of guy to have around, I think. Although I'm no expert, Marge."

"Best we got around here."

"Thanks. I guess."

Marge laughed. Then she said carelessly, "You remember old George Peterson."

"The car dealer? Gosh, he's been dead for five years, at least. He wasn't so old, Marge. Golly, Nadine's in her late forties and they'd only been mar—" She stopped. She'd forgotten. There was history there. "Yes. I liked George. I know that . . . you did, too."

"George liked this Chanel Number Five. Royal seems to like it, too. Said so today, anyways."

Quill took a deep breath. There were all kinds of reasons now to tell Marge of Royal's offhand interest in helping her buy the Inn. If she waited any longer, she'd be the worst kind of jerk. "Did Royal happen to mention that we'd talked about my buying the Inn back?"

Marge didn't say anything for a moment. Quill could see her chubby profile against the backdrop of cows and chewed up rosebushes. Her expression was hard to read. "Well," she said. "Well, well, well. He did, now, did he? Did he say why?"

"Why?" This caught Quill off guard. "Because it'd be a worthwhile investment, I suppose."

Marge laughed. It wasn't an unkind laugh, more of a heartily amused are-you-serious laugh. Quill was insulted. "I've learned quite a lot more about business since I've taken over the Palate, Marge."

"Any durn fool can run a business," Marge said. "No, I take that back. Any durn fool could serve successful dinners with Meg's cooking and you floatin' around looking like those long-haired wimmin in art history books. But real business, that's somethin' else. So, Royal's putting out a few feelers, is he? I'll have to think about that." She looked at her watch. "Train's about due."

This annoyed Quill profoundly. "How do you know I want to know when the train's due?"

" 'Cause you called that Muriel Sedgewick at the station to find out when it was comin' in tonight and she told me. Wanted to know if the sher'f was coming home for a while."

"He's out of touch for the next few weeks." Quill was afraid that her own careless tone would betray her the way Marge's had a few minutes before. But Marge had to know John was coming into town. First of all, he'd stop by to see her, since Marge and John respected each other a great deal, and secondly, Marge always found out what was going on sooner rather than later. She was worse than Doreen, since Doreen knew how to keep herself to herself. "No. Myles isn't due back yet. You remember John Raintree."

"Course I remember John. He's comin' back?"

"Just for a few days. He said to send you his regards."

"Well. Well, well, well." Marge's beady little eyes narrowed. "Royal give him a call? Or did you? Never mind. You prob'y don't want to answer that. Huh. You get on your way, Quill." She turned to leave, then threw over her shoulder, "You tell John I said hi. And you two drop around anytime you like. Anytime." She stumped away.

Quill got in the car and drove to the station.

In the days when wealthy New Yorkers summered in Upstate New York, train stations had been wonderful affairs, the promise of exotic otherwheres implicit in the wrought iron pillars holding up the roof, the granite tiles of the floors. Quill imagined the echo of porters, the ghostly circles of leghorn hats under the streetlights, the sweep of long skirts along the brick pathway. She'd never understood why the sound of a train whistle was such a lonesome call for so many; perhaps it was the minor key, or, more likely, the drawn-out trailing wail. She loved the sound of trains approaching, trains leaving, the *clack-clack-clack* of wheels on track. It was a staid excitement she felt, a nostalgic whisper of a slower past. For the long-dead people who had crowded this station in its heyday, it had been a place much like present airports; a crossing, a nexus, a place to go from, not a place to stay or a place to hold in memory, to think about while drifting off to sleep at night.

She walked up and down the concrete platform, hearing the train in the distance. The parking lot was deserted, except for a few cars waiting for late commuters from Syracuse, or the few students who'd hopped on the train at Ithaca after a day at the University.

John was first off, swinging lightly down the steps, backpack dangling from one hand. She waved and stood waiting for him, smiling to see the familiar coppery face, the black hair, the easy athleticism. She kissed him like she kissed Meg after a long absence, with a brief, hard hug and a brush of her lips against his cheek. "You *smell* different, John."

"You and your smells, Quill. It's the big city, I should think. And I use a different Laundromat. How are Meg and Doreen?"

"Fine. Meg said she meets you once in a while for lunch in the city."

"She's looking great. I caught one episode of *The Rusticated Lady*. She did her crème brûlée."

"Lally Preston's here now. They're going to tape this Russian-cattlemen dinner for the next show."

"Has anyone ever told Lally Preston what rusticated means?"

"I've never had the nerve to ask."

They turned and walked together toward the parking lot. John shifted his backpack from one hand to the other. "And Myles? How is he?"

"He won't admit it, but he enjoys this new job he's on."

"Set the date yet?"

Quill made a noncommittal noise. She waited until they were both in the Olds and she was driving to the Palate before she asked lightly, "And you? Have you set the date with anyone yet?"

"I've been seeing a very nice woman. A nurse at Caryn's hospital."

This was unusual. John hardly ever referred to his sister in the past. "How's Caryn doing?"

"The same. It won't change, of course. We've known since the beginning that the coma's too deep for recovery. But Taffy—the nurse—brought a portable CD player into the ward, and she plays the kinds of music Caryn used to like, before the accident. I think her face looks more peaceful now, hearing it.'' Quill pulled into the short driveway that led to the garage next to the restaurant. "So this is it. Looks pretty good from the outside.''

"Wait until you've seen the dining room. We should be just finishing up with the evening trade.''

He liked it all, the dining room with the Giverny colors, the small room paneled in basswood that they'd turned into a little bar, the guest room with the quilts Doreen had stitched hanging on the walls. "The bedrooms are big enough?'' he asked as he glanced into her room and then Meg's. "I did worry about that. The suites you two had at the Inn were pretty nice.''

"Only real problem is the bathroom. There's just the one, and the two downstairs for customers of course.''

He followed her downstairs and back into the dining room as she continued, "But then Meg isn't here that much anymore. She tends to be with Andy Bishop, or in New York. So far it's worked out really well.''

He gave her a sharp glance. "She'll be here tonight.''

"She's here now,'' Meg said, bouncing in the front door. She threw her arms around John and shouted, to the amusement of the few diners left at the tables, "It's so *good* to see you! Sit down. Right there. Best table in the house. I've got a nice wine chilling and a really superior pâté I want you to try. And *don't*,'' she scolded him, "tell me you're not hungry. You're looking way too thin for my taste.'' She dropped her menu and purse on the floor with a thump and bounded off to the kitchen.

Quill sat across from him at the little table. She adjusted the Dutch iris in the vase and moved the salt bowl. Then she moved it back again.

"Doreen's home already?''

Quill nodded. "It's been a struggle, but I've managed to get her to cut her hours. She won't admit it, but her arthritis is bothering her a lot these days."

"And Meg says Bjarne's doing well in the kitchen."

"To the point where I'm getting worried someone's going to hire him away. He's come along really fast."

"Meg yells a lot, but she's a good teacher."

"I do *not* yell a lot." Meg set a platter of grapes, pâté, and biscuits in front of them, then a wine bucket with a chilly bottle of Vouvray nested in ice. She sat down, poured wine for the three of them, took a long sip and sat back with a sigh of enjoyment.

John sipped his wine with a considering air. "That's the sparkling Vouvray we picked up from the Summerhill sale. It's good."

"It's good. I'm good," Meg said with a grin. "Quill, you missed out on the best part of that dorky meeting. Do you know Harvey wanted me to serve *hamburgers!*" She sipped more wine. "Texas longhorn *hamburgers!*" The second shriek made the elderly couple at table four wave frantically at Peter the waiter for the bill.

"And you said . . ." Quill prompted.

"I said . . ." She drew a big breath, then expelled it with a sigh at Quill's exasperated expression. "I said, hooey, I said. Over my dead body, I said."

"And there aren't any, are there?" John asked.

"What? Dead bodies?" Meg laughed merrily. The couple at table four scuttled out the front door, leaving a wad of cash on the tip plate. "Not so far. Although I wouldn't bet on Lally whacking that oily sneak of a colonel over the head with a branding iron. I almost," Meg rubbed her nose meditatively, "I almost did it myself. If he asks me for my marinade recipe one more time, I'm going to make up a big batch and drown him in it. Malmsey marinade, I'll call it. Be a big seller on death row."

"Meg!" Quill said. "For heaven's sake."

"Sorry. But, John, even *you'd* get manic around here. Do you know there are cows in our rose garden?"

That "our" again. Quill smiled hugely at both of them.

"Why don't you bring me up to date?" John said. "Quill asked me here to give some business advice . . ."

"And I'm paying him," Quill told her sister.

"You are?" Meg thought about this for a moment. John frowned. "I will not accept—"

"Yes, you will. It's like psychotherapy, Meg."

"You've never been in psychotherapy in your life."

"Well, it's like what they say about psychotherapy. You only listen to the advice you pay for."

"That's not what Freud said," Meg said loftily. "Not exactly."

"How do you know what Freud said? You've never been in psychotherapy either."

"Well, I'm dating . . ."

". . . a medical man. Spare me. Please."

"Spare *me*," John suggested, "and we'll talk about my fee later. Why doesn't one of you summarize what's going on here?"

The summary took all of the pâté, and most of a second bottle of the sparkling Vouvray. By the time John sat back with a "hang on and let me think this through" expression on his face, Quill was feeling flushed and tiddly. For a former innkeeper, she had a lousy head for spirits.

"Okay, let's get this straight." John held up one long finger and began to tick off the points. "Quill wants the Inn back. Meg and Doreen want the Inn back. Marge is making money." He stopped and shook his head admiringly. "Wish I'd thought of that. Booking fees. What a hell of a good idea. Money right from the customer into the bank account, with no expenses in between. Damn,

she's good. At any rate, Marge has found a way to make
the Inn profitable and she'll sell, all right, but to the highest bidder. And she wants a half a million, minimum.''

''For *our* Inn!'' Meg shrieked indignantly.

''It's not your Inn. Your Inn was putting you deeper
into the hole every month,'' John said bluntly, ''Marge's
Inn is in the black. Big difference. And she's right to
want to be paid the difference.''

''So where can we find half a million dollars?'' Quill
asked. She slumped back in her chair and looked despairingly at the second bottle of Vouvray. There was a
teeny bit left. She let it sit there. Then she brightened.
''Did I tell you Royal Rossiter wants to give us half a
million dollars? Did I tell you he is one of the richest
Texans in Texas?''

Meg snorted. ''He doesn't want to give us half a million dollars, Quill. He wants to invest half a million dollars in something that will pay him a lot of money back,
right, John?''

''That would seem logical. Both Mr. Rossiter and
Marge are going to expect a significant R.O.I.''

Quill had picked up enough business jargon along the
way to know that this meant Return on Investment. It's
significance as a term spoke for itself. This was a concept
of somewhat dubious ethical value as far as she was concerned. After all, a reasonable return on investment was
the eight percent interest you got on a CD. When John
talked significant R.O.I. he was talking forty percent or
more, which seemed rapacious, if not downright piratical.
''I've asked you here,'' she sobbed, ''for nothing.''

John grinned, and removed the Vouvray from her
grasp. ''Let's have some coffee, Meg.''

''Who wants to sober up?'' Meg demanded. ''I sure

don't. We are stuck with . . ." She waved her arm at the dining room, glowing yellow and blue in the dim night lights. Each of the tables was set with a vase of miniature iris. The old oak beams were hung with copper pans and dried hydrangea. It was beautiful. "All this," she said in disgust.

"You forget that 'all this' has quite a bit of value on its own. And there's something else, here."

"Cows," Quill said mournfully.

"That's precisely it. Cows."

"Cows?" Meg said. "You're kidding, right?"

"Not at all. How much of this nutrition information is verifiable, Quill?"

"All of it, I guess. You mean about the healthiness of the beef?"

"Absolutely. You know that America's consumption of beef has been declining year by year? And there's been a precipitous drop in consumption in Europe with the scare about Creutzfeldt-Jakob disease."

"Um, sure," Quill said. This was one of those things she ought to know and didn't. She made a mental vow to read more of the *New York Times* than the Tuesday and Sunday Arts sections.

"Creutzfeldt-Jakob disease is transmitted to humans by cattle that have been fed the brains and organs of diseased cattle. It's a virus that destroys the interstices of the brain. When cows get it, they act really goofy, which is why it's sometimes called mad cow disease." Meg shook her head despairingly. "I wish you'd read more of the newspaper than the Arts section. Anyway it's a big deal with the Board of Health. And John's point is that longhorn cattle are free-range. If they are fed any grain or supplements it's corn or oats in the last few months of the finishing process. The longhorns aren't carriers of Creutzfeldt-Jakob disease."

"Of course." Quill nodded knowledgeably.

Meg said, "Tch! Not 'of course.' It means that people can eat it safely. And because it's healthy they can eat it guilt-free."

"So you think we can make money raising cattle? We're going to be in the beef business? I don't want to be in the beef business. I look at those nice cows and I want them all to die peacefully in their sleep. I want Tompkins County's first cow cemetery."

"Oh, for heaven's sake, Quill," Meg said in a very annoyed way. "If you're going to go vegetarian on me, take off your shoes."

"What? Why?!" Quill regarded her Italian leather sandals with dismay. "Oh. I see."

"And give me your purse, and while you're at it, your belt and that nifty pair of leather jeans you picked up at Saks last month. In short, don't be a hypocrite."

"I'm disgruntled."

"You should be." She turned to John. "There's just one problem."

"It isn't Prime."

"That's right."

"You mean the F.D.A. won't rate the filets Prime?" Quill asked. "But Prime's all we use in the restaurant business."

"It's because there's not enough fat. But only the Feds equate fat with taste. The customer isn't all that aware of why Prime Angus cut tastes that good. If they were, they'd probably keel over from a cholesterol-related heart attack right at the table. But I think my marinade has solved the taste issue. I hope. I'll know tomorrow when I try the bracciole I've invited that bloody colonel and

Royal Rossiter to try. Sort of a preliminary menu tasting before I go gung ho for International Night. That hunky cowboy Brady, too, come to think of it. And the vet. She's supposed to bring me the back fat statistics from Cornell. So we'll know then whether we can make a longhorn beef retail operation a successful part of the Inn business. That's what you're after, John, isn't it?''

"That's what I'm after.''

"So. The proof's not so much in the pudding as it is in the bracciole.'' Meg yawned suddenly. When Meg became tired, it hit her as did all her other emotions: fast and hard. "I've got to go to bed. It's after one.'' She looked at her watch. "Yep. And Andy's on in the E.R. tonight so I was planning to go to bed early and get tons of sleep. Phuut!'' She jumped up, kissed Quill, then John, and clattered up the stairs to her room.

Quill's wine-induced giddiness ebbed. She got up to clear the table. John muttered something she didn't catch, and followed her into the kitchen, carrying the tablecloth, the wine bottles, and the glasses. Quill stacked the dirty dishes in the dishwasher, while he disposed of the bottles and the linen in the basement. She was standing at the sink when she felt him behind her. She reached for a dish towel, and felt his breath in her hair. She folded the towel, turned, looked into his face and touched his cheek. She went upstairs, leaving him there, in the kitchen.

That night, late, she heard a faint tap at her bedroom door. Or thought she did.

She didn't open it.

# CHAPTER 6

"Gee," Laura Crest said, "this is really nice." She stood awkwardly at the maître d' station, the faint odor of Betadyne surrounding her like Marge's Chanel Number Five. "Are you having a lot of people at this menu-testing thing?"

Quill and Doreen had pulled all the dining room tables into a large circle, preparing for that afternoon's test of Meg's Longhorn beef recipes. The tablecloths were bright yellow, the napkins a cheerful cadet blue. Quill had splurged on a large sheaf of freesia and maidenhair fern, and arranged the flowers to trail down the centers of the tables. The whole thing made the room look smaller.

"I'm sorry you missed lunch the other day," Quill said. "The room looks a lot better with everything in the proper place. Was it a real emergency?"

"It wasn't too bad. A pony with founder. You get a lot of it this time of year, with the grass being so rich. Sometimes no matter how careful you are grassing out, the pony will founder anyway. This was one of the here-we-go-again ones.''

"It's worse than Andy Bishop. At least he has some backup. You have to be on call all the time, don't you?''

"There's just a few of us this far south of Ithaca,'' she said. "Meaning vets, of course. The closer you get in to Cornell, the more there are. But right now, I pretty much handle forty farms and probably three hundred horses alone. Not to mention the cats and dogs. There he is.'' She bent forward as Max came loping into the dining room. He took one look, whirled, and disappeared back into the kitchen. She laughed ruefully. "That happens a lot. It's really bad when you go into being a vet because you love animals and you end up having most of your patients flee at the mere sight of you. Except Tye, of course.''

"Where is she now?''

"In the truck.''

"Max has a nice run outside. Why don't you put her there? Then we can go have a small sherry at the bar,'' Quill suggested. "I expect everyone will come drifting in about four.''

"And that's your nice way of handling the fact that I'm early. It's a great idea about the dog, if you don't mind. I'll be back in a few minutes.''

Quill went into the bar, set out the sherry bottle, and was waiting when Laura came back. "I'm glad you're a little early. I'd like to get to know you better. There aren't that many . . .'' She stopped and floundered a little.

"I know what you mean. Tompkins County is paradise as far as working conditions and the animals, but it's a little thin on people. And no, there aren't a lot of women our age around without three kids and a full-time job managing tired husbands.'' She sighed and sank into the one booth the bar space permitted. "Whoosh. I'm beat. I was up early with a case of mastitis at Harland Peterson's. Did you know he's registered for a permit for an . . . um . . . abattoir on the south side of his farm?"

"A slaughterhouse?"

"Yep. One of the reasons longhorn cattle aren't more widely distributed in the meat-eating population is that no one's really set up to handle horned cattle."

"I don't think I want to know a lot more about this," Quill said.

"You don't?"

"I don't. And don't ask me to give up my shoes either."

"Your shoes?" She grinned suddenly. "I see. We'll leave it at that. But you should think about a couple of things, Quill. Cattle are pleasant sorts of animals most of the time, but they are bred for a purpose. And most of the facilities . . ."

"Slaughterhouses," Quill said, in the mood to call a spade a spade.

"Right. Most of them are humanely run. The cattle aren't brutalized, rarely know what's happening, and they don't suffer."

"And if I don't believe it, I should stop eating beef . . ."

"Give up your shoes . . ."

"And generally move from hypocrite to hypercritic."

Laura applauded. "*Nicely* done. I'll have to see if I can top it."

"Let me pour you a small sherry. Dry?"

"Please. Thank you. Well, I got the information Meg asked for from my old sweetie professor at Cornell. These cattle are really neat." She dug into her chinos pocket with one hand, holding the sherry aloft with the other, then thrust the crumpled sheaf of papers in Quill's direction. "There it is. Now, some of the studies have been sponsored by I.T.L.A., that's the International Texas Longhorn Association, so you take those with a grain of salt if you like. But I've never known anyone at Cornell or Texas A&M in those departments to fudge data, and it looks as if the colonel's claims might be true. The beef is good for you."

Quill flipped through a stack of Xerox copies of articles titled "Percent Ratings of Back Fat in Longhorn Texas Cattle Carcasses" and "Hyperlipidity of Fats in Foreign and Domestic Cattle." She suppressed a shudder, and remembering her vow to focus, focus, focus, read as intelligently as she could for a few minutes. "Meg's interested in the taste tests. From these ratings, it looks as though the beef is pretty competitive with Angus and that lot."

Laura shrugged. "As a scientist, I can tell you that's subjective data. I plan to make up my own mind with this afternoon's . . . what is it, exactly?"

"You could call it a taste test, I guess. We've invited some of the people who're associated with the International Night dinner to try the beef with Meg's marinade. She doesn't want to risk a super public failure."

"I might be able to give her a little help with how to prepare the marinade if I can borrow the lab facilities at Cornell for a bit. Getting the right enzyme to break down the tougher meat fibers can go a lot faster if I can target the type of striated muscle in this beef."

"Hm," Quill said brightly.

"Now, papaya enzyme is one of the best organic tenderizers you can use. Has Meg had a lot of experience with that? Oh, hi. Who's this?"

"This is John Raintree," Quill said, sliding out of the booth. "Hey."

"Hey, yourself." He tossed a folder onto the stack of Xerox copies. Quill's stack of reading was now three inches high. "I ran some numbers for you. The lowball plan is A, the high end is B. All of it's predicated on the beef tasting as good as the usual supermarket stuff." He sat down next to the vet. "You must be Laura Crest, the vet. I talked to Royal Rossiter this morning about the hows and whys of shipping his beef from Texas. Can I verify a few things with you?"

Quill set a glass of club soda in front of John and took up her business plan with a resigned sigh. She'd let herself in for this. She'd demanded a plan to buy the Inn back and now here it was. Rows and rows of boring numbers, with jargon-filled labels to decipher like "5 yr. deprec. sched." and "debt carried forward." After a few minutes she said, "Hey."

"Hey yourself," John said.

"Sorry to interrupt, Laura, but John, none of the numbers at the bottom of the pages are in little parentheses."

"That means all these numbers in the profit and loss column are, like, profit," Laura said with an intelligent air.

"Positive profit," John said, "as opposed to the notorious negative profit. A term," he added, for Laura's benefit, "with which we at the Inn at Hemlock Falls are disconcertingly familiar."

"Don't I know it," said a familiar, truculent voice. "Well, John. How's Long Island treating you? We've missed you around here."

John held Marge's hands in a warm grasp. "You look just terrific. I'll bet that's a new dress."

Quill realized this was the second time she had ever

seen Marge in a dress; the first had been just yesterday. And she recognized it. It was the polished cotton number from the front window of Esther's shop. Marge pounded John on the back. "I have to say I missed ya." She gave his shoulder an affectionate punch. "Here. I came by because I want you to meet someone. Phil Barkin? John Raintree." John stood up and shook Barkin's hand. He wasn't from Hemlock Falls, Quill would have bet her best tube of cerulean on that. He was in a three-piece blue suit and looked like a banker. It would be just like Marge to bring a banker, uninvited, to a private party to which she hadn't been invited in the first place.

She said pleasantly, "How do you do, Mr. Barkin? I'm Sarah Quilliam. And this is Laura Crest."

"He knows who you all are," Marge said rudely. "Now." She rubbed her hands together briskly. "You got some beer for me, Quill? And maybe a martini for Mr. Barkin?"

"I'll get it," John said. "With an olive, Mr. Barkin?"

"Call me Phil," the banker said. "No olive." And, as far as Quill could determine later, when she reviewed the events of the afternoon, that was all that Phil Barkin had to say for the rest of the day. He settled back in the farthest corner of the booth, sipped his martini, and for all she knew, took a nap.

Quill sat down next to Laura Crest and beamed a mental message to Marge to go away.

"See you've got the tables set up for a party," Marge said. She accepted the dark beer John set in front of her, took a long drink, and wiped the back of her mouth with a satisfied burp. "You know," she said, apropos of nothing in particular, "I like beer. I like to burp. So what about the party, Quill?"

"It's just a few people, Marge, from the International

Night Committee. We're testing a couple of Meg's recipes.''

"Sounds good," Marge said. "Harland and Royal? Both of them sort of let it drop that they were invited. Told 'em I'd probably be there, except that Phil here was comin' in to talk over a few things. So I wasn't sure I could make it."

Quill bit her lower lip firmly, so she wouldn't ask Marge and her silent pal to come to the menu testing.

"Sounds kinda exciting. Phil, here, he's only in town for a few days, and he asked me this morning: Where are all the Texans and Russians going, Marge? Some event in the village I don't know about?"

"Have you tried the wine tours, Mr. Barkin?" Quill asked.

"Wine!" Marge snorted. "I guess Phil knows enough about wine."

Quill refused this offer to inquire further into the mysterious Phil's knowledge of wine, and from there, his undoubted preference for spending the afternoon drinking it at her expense.

Marge turned her beady little eyes on the vet. "You goin', Dr. Crest? To this menu-testing thing?"

Laura shifted uncomfortably in her seat. "Well, Marge. I may get called away suddenly. You know how it is in early summer."

Marge nodded. "Harland got the mastitis up to his farm, I hear."

"Just a touch," Laura said, unsuspecting. "One of the older heifers."

"So if you go, there might be a place or two extra at the table?"

Laura looked alarmed. Quill gave up. "There's more than enough room, Marge, for you and Mr. Barkin both."

"Oh, I don't know," said Marge, suddenly affable. "I wouldn't want to put you out."

"In that case . . ."

"But seein' as how you insist, we'd be happy to come. When's the feed?"

"Four o'clock. I thought," Quill said with a determinedly innocent look, "that you knew that already."

Marge swallowed the rest of her beer and cocked her head alertly. "Sounds like they're filing in. I'll go get 'em seated for you, Quill. C'mon, Doc, Phil. I'll put you right by the kitchen door. Meg always serves that side first."

"Marge! There're name tags . . . oh, never *mind!*" Quill rolled her eyes helplessly at John, then followed him into the dining room. Everyone seemed to have arrived at once, and Marge, with the temerity of a MacArthur to Quill's unwilling Truman, began reorganizing the seating arrangements to her own satisfaction. "Harland, you sit over here, on this side of me, and Royal, you sit here on the right. Brady, you get on the other side of Royal." Peter, in the best tradition of Cornell School of Hotel Management trained waiters, was unperturbed by the extra two guests, and placed the extra settings with deft efficiency.

Quill, focusing hard on resisting the impulse to run her hands through her hair and scream, jumped when Colonel Calhoun touched her arm.

"Would you have a few minutes to escort me into the kitchen, Miss Quilliam? I wanted to ask your sister a few things." He had removed his Stetson for the occasion but added a bolo tie and a red brocaded vest to his black suit.

Quill assumed this was cattleman-formal, and told him he looked very nice. "And I'm afraid I never take guests into the kitchen when Meg's cooking. You've probably heard how temperamental she is."

"No, ma'am, I have not. But I have some ideas about the marinade that I wanted to ex—"

Quill took him by the elbow. "Now, I think you mentioned to the mayor that you're going to try out a version of your speech, so that Lally Preston can hear it before the dinner. Is that right? So I placed you right here, at the head of the table." She drew out his chair and pushed him firmly into it.

He rose back up, like a sea lion through sheet ice, with purpose and oblivious to Quill's icy glare. "I have visual aids," the colonel said. "Where can I use my visual aids?"

"What kind of—"

"Slides." His lower lip jutted out. "I have my briefcase, as you see, with my computer. The computer will project my slides on any appropriate bare space. Like right there." He pointed at the far wall, where a collection of Quill's watercolors was arranged. "You can remove those, if you please." He sat down, clutching his briefcase. Quill smiled, hoping he couldn't hear her teeth grinding. She asked Peter to remove her paintings, shook hands with the Russians and the mayor, and air-kissed Lally Preston.

She cast an expert eye over the tables: water in place, wineglasses lined up; small baskets of bruschetta fresh from the oven and wafting garlicky odors into the air; everyone seated and being sociable over the preliminary glasses of dry sherry. She went into the kitchen and nearly tripped over Max, who was lying with his head under the prep table and his hindquarters sprawled on the rubber matted pathway.

"How come he's not in his pen with Tye?" Quill asked.

"He thinks he's hidin'. " Doreen said. She slid lemon slices deftly onto the platters of rare beef. "Vet must be out there."

"She is."

"We on time, or not?"

"On time so far. We can serve the steak tartare."

"Steak Quilliam," Meg said crossly.

"Sorry. At any rate, we can serve it while the colonel drones on."

Doreen scowled at her.

"Sorry again. I'm sure it'll be a wonderful speech. He's just so determined to get the recipe for Meg's marinade that I'm cross with him. Anyway, we should be ready for the entrée in about half an hour. How's it going, Meg?"

Meg shook her head. She leaned over a pan of crisply roasted bracciole, a paring knife in one hand. "I'm scared to try it."

"Let me try it."

"Right. I don't *think* so. Bjarne. Here. Try it. And, damn you, tell the truth."

Bjarne the Finnish chef was tall, thin, as pale-eyed as winter and as honest as cold air. He nodded solemnly and delicately cut a slice of the bracciole from the roast. He ate it. He chewed silently. Thoughtfully. He smiled. "Papaya enzyme?"

"You can *tell!*" Meg shouted.

"No, no. Of course I cannot tell, it does not affect the flavor of the beef at all. Merely, this is what we use with the reindeer, you know."

"It's not the same," Meg said sulkily. "Reindeer's bloody *tough!*"

"This is not. This . . ." Bjarne rolled the food around in his mouth one more time. "This is superb. The beef flavor is real. True. And very, very good. I would not know this is not prime."

Meg exhaled with a long sigh. "Fine. I want to let it stand, then seal the juices with a quick sear. Okay, Doreen. Tell Peter we'll be ready to plate entrée in twenty minutes, with service in thirty."

"Gotcha."

"Now can I try, Meg?"

"Help yourself."

Quill tried the beef. It was beautifully seasoned, tender, the stuffing in the bracciole a triumph of mushrooms, wine, cream, and something else. She cut a small slice of the rare beef, squeezed a little lemon on it, and that, too, was meltingly tender. John's business plan had been for a small, specialty retail operation like the Angus beef sold by catalogue and over the Web. The recipes would be showcased at the (reclaimed) Inn at Hemlock Falls. The plan would work only, as John had said, if the beef could command the same prices as prime. And that depended solely on the taste. "Well, I love it," she said to no one in particular. "We'll see what the others think."

"Let me know," Meg said intensely. "Right away."

"We'll do the gourmet night thing, shall we?" This was a plan they'd discussed, but never tried, in the days when they were attempting to come up with ideas to put the Inn in the black. Meg had designed a series of cooking seminars/gourmet dinner weekends, where the guests would learn new cooking techniques during the day, then eat Meg's professional version of them at night. Meg would appear at the table after each course (in her toque and tunic) to answer questions with the appropriate demure modesty. They'd never had a chance to offer the weekend package, and the Palate had been so successful off the regular dinner trade, that they hadn't needed to.

Quill went back into the dining room and sat down next to John. The bruschetta was gone. Peter removed the sherry glasses and began to pour the Pinot Noir John had suggested to accompany the rare beef starter. Everyone seemed happily occupied: Laura Crest looked almost pretty, sitting between Jack Brady and the taciturn Phil. Harvey, the mayor and his formidable wife Adela had their heads together and were chatting sociably. That is, Adela was chatting and Harvey and the mayor were nodding dutifully.

Quill stood up, her wineglass in her hand. "Ladies and gentlemen? I would like to welcome you all to the Palate, and to this late afternoon test of the menu for International Night. Mayor Henry? Would you like to say a few words?"

"I would and I will. You all know how high our hopes are runnin' for the success of this bidness between the cattlemen of Texas and the Russians of Russia."

"Hear! Hear!" Harvey shouted.

"In anticipation of the real thing, Colonel Calhoun will give you a brief summary of his remarks on the genetics of that true American breed of cattle—the Texas longhorn!"

The Russians shouted. The Hemlockians cheered. Lally Preston rolled her eyes and signaled Peter for more wine.

The colonel got slowly and pleasurably to his feet. He switched on his PC slide show function, and the first of what turned out to be forty-six longhorn cows appeared on the Palate's wall. "The Texas longhorn cow is a pure breed," the colonel said. His high-pitched voice carried remarkably well. "And although I will go into this more on the actual night, I will tell you that I have devoted my life to determining the best genetics needed in breeding this cattle. You breed pure and you breed to the line. All you true longhorn lovers will know what I mean when I say that if they'd been dealin' with cattle instead of people, the Nazis had the right idea.''

Quill's mouth dropped open. Somebody gasped. John coughed into his hand and winked at her.

The colonel smiled happily and turned his attention to the brown and white cow pictured on the wall. "Now this here little lady is a fine example of what you are goin' to taste tonight. Her name is Calhoun's Caddy. She's by Cadillac Star out of Baby Driver. She's got a real straight top line, a good feminine expression, which is what we want in a heifer, and she's thick. She's real thick. This is what you're lookin' for in your basic beefy longhorn.''

There were forty-six fine examples of heifers with straight top lines. All of them were thick. Real thick. And all of them just as soft-eyed and appealing as the real cows Marge had corralled at the Inn.

Quill pinched her knee, hard. She'd been dubious about serving wine at a meal where the reactions of the diners to the entrée were essential. She'd instructed Peter to pour sparingly, and to save the heavier wines for toward the end of the meal, when the salads and the sorbet would be stimulating jaded palates, but now Quill began to regret her decision to go easy on the wine. In fact, she wished she'd served whiskey. Doubles. Straight up.

When she checked her watch, Quill discovered that the actual slide show had lasted just under fifteen minutes. It had seemed interminable. Peter and Doreen swung out of the kitchen one after the other, the plates of rare beef Quilliam held aloft, and began to serve.

"Now, what's this, then?" the mayor asked, poking dubiously at the plate of beef. "We're supposed to squeeze this here lemon on it?"

"For heaven's sake, Mayor," Adela said. "That's Chef Quilliam's version of steak tartare."

"Quite a Russian dish, in this country," said Leonid. "Although, I think it is more like pizza, which has never been Italian."

"It's raw beef, Mayor." Adela, stern in a flowered hat, wrapped a piece around her fork and took a delicate nibble. "Delicious," she pronounced.

"I don't think I'm up to eatin' raw beef, Adela."

"Shut up and eat, Mayor."

"And this black stuff? What's that?"

"Caviar," Quill said brightly.

Elmer frowned.

"Eggs. From fish," Leonid said. He swallowed a large spoonful. "I am sad to say that this is the only thing I do not like about this country."

"Fish eggs. I thought so." The mayor put his fork on the table, folded his arms, and looked mutinous. Harland Peterson winked at Marge. Both of them began to laugh. Neither of them ate either the caviar or the beef.

"What do you think of the beef, Colonel?" Quill asked hastily.

"Reasonably tender," Colonel Calhoun said thoughtfully. "I say it's reasonably tender. If I knew what went into the marinade I might feel a little more comfortable. You say it's raw longhorn?"

"I will have more," Leonid announced. "And so, too, will Vasily and Alexi. And perhaps some vodka? It is permitted to serve vodka in this country?"

Quill, who agreed with Nero Wolfe that a guest was the jewel on the cushion of hostility, signaled Peter to bring some vodka. "Stoli," she added, hoping she didn't appear too resigned. Vodka would kill the taste of anything dead flat, unless it was baked potato, which had no taste to begin with.

"I think it's great," Laura Crest said. "It's just . . . I hadn't really thought of raw beef before. You sure your parasite control program is all that efficient, Colonel? I mean, roundworms, especially, are pretty resistant, and if you're only worming the cattle twice a year . . . Not that this looks infested," she added hastily. "Not a bit."

This put an effective stop to everyone's consumption of the beef Quilliam except the Russians, who not only ate the beef, but the lemons, onions, and chopped caviar, too.

Peter placed chilled vodka glasses in front of the Russians, and carefully poured the Stoli. "And *thank you,* very much," Leonid said. He shook Peter's hand, grabbed the bottle, and put it by his plate.

"Here," said the mayor, "lemme have some of that."

"I will trade you," Leonid said graciously. "Is good capitalist thing to do, vodka for your beef? We Russians do not mind worms."

"In the interest of good trade relations," Adela said nicely, "I will offer mine as well."

At least Meg will see only empty plates coming back to the kitchen, Quill thought. Because Brady and Royal have eaten theirs, bless them.

"Psst," Meg said, opening the kitchen door a crack and raising an eyebrow at Quill. "Are you ready for me yet?"

"Excuse me," Quill said. "Peter will serve the rest of the starters. I'll be back in a moment."

"Well?" Meg demanded when she entered the kitchen.

"I think maybe steak tartare was a bit—um—flighty to start with."

"Flighty?" Meg's voice rose. "What do you mean, flighty?"

"These are basically cattlemen, Meg, Harland and the Russians included. They'd be more familiar with a nice thick steak. Thinly sliced rare beef, no matter how well marinated, is sort of a feminine thing."

"Oh, it is, is it?"

"Not to the Russians, of course. They loved it. Ate every bit and clamored for more."

"That's something, anyway. What are they going to think of the bracciole?"

"They are going to love it," Quill announced. "And then you can let them know how long it takes to pound out the filet in those little thin strips, create the stuffing, mince all the mushrooms. That should impress the heck out of the meat eaters."

"Huh." The flush in Meg's cheeks receded.

"And this is a sort of bratwurst?" the mayor asked some minutes later, poking at the bracciole with his salad fork.

"Braseeoley, Mayor," said Adela. The cabbage rose in her hat dipped forward in a gracious nod. "Isn't that right, Quill?"

"Um," Quill said, "what do you all think of it?"

"I'd know a *sight* better what I thought if I knew what was in it," Colonel Calhoun said.

"It's great," Brady said, his mouth full. "Knew a fellow in San Antonio could cook up squirrels as nice as this."

"It's very, very good, Quill," Royal said. "As a matter of fact, I could use another helping, if your sister would be so kind." He put the last bite in his mouth, and drew breath. "It's pret—" He clutched his throat and coughed. He coughed again, a hacking, spitting choke. Bracciole stuffing flew across the table.

"Here, boss," Brady said, and pounded Royal on the back. Royal, his face red, tears starting from his eyes, shook his head desperately and pointed at his hat. He made a cawing sound.

"John," Quill said.

But John was already there. He stood behind Royal and put his arms around his chest, then pulled upwards, sharply. Royal wheezed. His face turned blue. He fell forward into an appalled silence.

"I told you," Colonel Calhoun said after a minute. "I told you I wanted to know what was in this stuff."

Meg huddled in a chair in the corner of the kitchen, her back to the crowd of people there. The state police were in the dining room; the trooper in charge, a surly man in his late thirties with a beer drinker's potbelly had directed the guests into the kitchen, leaving only John to answer questions. Since he'd refused to let anyone else leave, either, Quill felt as if she was waiting for the subway at rush hour.

Between the guests at the menu testing, the kitchen crew, and the wait staff, she counted eighteen people. No one was eating or drinking anything except Bjarne, who was finishing a plate of bracciole with a defiant expression on his face. Marge, her face set, her cheeks pale, stood by the window and looked at nothing. Outside, Quill heard Max bark once in his pen, then fall silent. Tye was too well-trained to bark at all.

Quill edged her way past the Russians and over to Meg. She put her hand on her shoulder.

"Go away," her sister said in a small voice.

"Meg . . ."

"This is the second person to die after eating my food." Her whisper was urgent, flooded with tears.

"He didn't die after eating your food. He choked to death. And that other case was murder." Quill's voice was pitched low, but she felt the word reach out and float around the room. The Russians muttered and moved closer together. Brady, arms folded, backed against the sink, jerked his head back like a startled horse.

The door to the dining room opened and John looked in. "Quill?"

"Over here."

"Bring Meg out here for a moment, will you?"

"Mr. Raintree!" Adela Henry's voice was commanding. "How long are we going to remain in here?" She was standing between the mayor and Leonid. In her effort to keep physical distance between herself and the Russian, her considerable bosom was pressed into the mayor's ear.

"That's up to Trooper Harris. But I don't think it will be long."

"The poor man choked to death," Adela boomed. "If there are any questions to be asked about the death, it would seem that you should be the one to answer them. After all, you were the one with your hands around his throat."

"That's enough, Adela," Quill said, her voice deadly.

John's face was impassive. "Never mind, Quill. Bring Meg out here, will you?"

Meg shoved her chair violently, got up, and pushed her way to the door. Doreen detached herself from the space between the refrigerator and the ice machine and plowed after her. Quill followed them both.

Royal Rossiter's body was still in position over the

table where he'd been sitting. His hands and feet were in plastic bags. Andy Bishop, Hemlock Falls best-looking (and only) internist, was kneeling at his side, peering into Royal's throat with a scope. The Tompkins County forensics team was busy photographing parts of the dining room that didn't hold any bodies at all, as far as Quill could see. Trooper Harris stood in the middle of the room, thumbs hooked into his belt. He jerked his head at John. "Bring the women over here."

"I'm gonna call Mr. Murchison," Doreen said loudly. "I don't like the look of this bozo."

"That your lawyer, Miss Quilliam?" Trooper Harris had muddy brown eyes and a mottled nose. He smelled of dry cleaning fluid. "Heard his name before."

"He's the family lawyer," Quill said a little nervously. "I could give him a call, if you think it's necessary."

The brown eyes slid over her like a water moccasin. He shrugged. "Up to you."

"Well," Meg said tightly. "What happened?"

"Massive heart attack," Andy said. He got to his feet and came over to stand by Meg. They didn't touch, although his gaze rested on her face like a caress. "I won't know for certain until the autopsy, of course, but it looks like a heart attack at this point."

Harris's eyes moved from Meg to Andy and back again. "I want it done by the Tompkins County coroner, Bishop. Heard about you two."

Meg adjusted the diamond on her ring finger. "If Dr. Bishop says it's a heart attack, you can bet it's a heart attack." She shrugged off Quill's cautioning hand with an angry jerk of her shoulder. "How dare you, you . . . you . . . *slime.*"

Trooper Harris snapped his gum and raised an inquiring eyebrow. Quill had never seen such an insolent expression on anyone's face. "Slime," he said amusingly. "A-huh." He turned his back to them. "Burton?"

A young trooper with lank brown hair jumped a little. "Yessir?"

"Team about finished in here?"

"Yessir."

"Move the body on out, then. You get all the names of the witnesses?"

"Yessir."

"Get statements. Then let 'em all go." Without looking around, he added, "You run background checks on these three, Raintree and the sisters." Then he swiveled his head halfway round. "Stick around, folks. Especially you, Raintree."

Doreen carried the news back to the kitchen that Royal's death had been a natural one. With the others, Quill gave her name, address, phone and social security numbers, and a brief statement of the activities that had led up to Royal's death. By midnight, the Palate was empty except for Quill, Meg, John, and Doreen. Andy had accompanied the body to the coroner's office in Ithaca. Quill sipped a hot cup of chamomile tea and closed her eyes. She was exhausted.

"You called him yet?" Doreen demanded.

"Called who? Myles?"

Meg yawned. With Andy's assurance that Royal's death had been a natural (if untimely) occurrence, she'd cheered up almost immediately. "It was a natural death, Doreen. I mean, I'm really sorry the poor old duck passed away here. It was a frightful end to the dinner."

"And Marge's hopes," John said quietly. He avoided Quill's quick glance.

Meg didn't seem to hear this. "But Myles is in the

middle of a real case. You can only call him in an emergency, Quill, right?''

''He'll call me at some point,'' Quill said. ''He always does. I'll talk to him then. I'll see you guys in the morning.''

''What I wanta know is, what good is somebody when he ain't around when you need him, anyways?''

''Good night, Doreen,'' Quill said firmly. She went up to her room, showered away the day, and got into bed. Her suite at the Inn had been large compared to this, and at first she'd been delighted with the small, self-contained space. The room was only sixteen by sixteen. Two narrow windows fronted Main Street. Two windows on the adjacent wall looked out at the narrow side yard and the garage. The phone didn't ring.

What good is somebody who ain't around when you need him, anyway?

middle of a real case. You can only call him in an emergency, Quill, right?''

"He'll call me at some point," Quill said. "He always does. I'll talk to him then. I'll see you guys in the morning."

"What I wanta know is, what good is somebody when he ain't around when you need him, anyways?''

"Good night, Doreen," Quill said firmly. She went up to her room, showered away the day, and got into bed. Her suite at the Inn had been large compared to this, and at first she'd been delighted with the small, self-contained space. The room was only sixteen by sixteen. Two narrow windows fronted Main Street. Two windows on the adjacent wall looked out at the narrow side yard and the garage. The phone didn't ring.

What good is somebody who ain't around when you need him, anyway?

middle of a real case. You can only call him in an emergency, Quill, right?''

"He'll call me at some point," Quill said. "He always does. I'll talk to him then. I'll see you guys in the morning."

"What I wanta know is, what good is somebody when he ain't around when you need him, anyways?"

"Good night, Doreen," Quill said firmly. She went up to her room, showered away the day, and got into bed. Her suite at the Inn had been large compared to this, and at first she'd been delighted with the small, self-contained space. The room was only sixteen by sixteen. Two narrow windows fronted Main Street. Two windows on the adjacent wall looked out at the narrow side yard and the garage. The phone didn't ring.

What good is somebody who ain't around when you need him, anyway?

# CHAPTER 7

Quill was up early, despite the fact that Trooper Harris had kept them all till almost midnight. She'd left a message for Myles on his voice mail, telling him briefly what had happened, then sat in the rocking chair at the window and looked out at Main Street. She could see a few pickups parked in front of the Croh Bar. The breakfast crowd, loyal to Marge's Diner for years, had finally settled on the new place to drink coffee, gossip, and generally hash over events past and to come in Hemlock Falls. She wondered if Marge missed it, the gossip, the liveliness. Breakfast at the Inn was an altogether quieter affair. Royal Rossiter's death would be a hot topic at the Croh this morning.

Max nudged her knee. "No early escape this morning. Good boy." She thought a minute. There wasn't a great deal to do. Breakfast was in the hands of the kitchen staff, and there were at most a few tourists late in the morning. She was too tired to paint. "What I ought to do, Max, is reward you for staying in last night. Do you want to go for a walk?'' Max barked. ''If we walk, we might run into Andy. He could tell us a bit more than he was willing to tell that trooper last night. What do you think, Max?''

Max really wanted to walk in Peterson Park. Andy usually jogged there around six o'clock, and she wanted to ask him what he really thought about Royal Rossiter's death.

Apple blossoms scented the air around the statue of General C. C. Hemlock, and late flowering peonies attracted a few enterprising bees. Summer mornings like this one put a favorite hymn in her head, and she sang, ''Morning has broken, like the first morning, blackbird has spoken, like the first bird,'' over and over again (she couldn't remember the rest) until Max sat down, flattened his ears, and barked. ''It's not nearly as awful as Aunt Meg's singing, is it?'' she asked the dog.

''It's pretty enough. Just repetitious.'' John rose from his seat at the foot of the statue and joined her on the sidewalk. ''Is anyone else in your family tone-deaf? Or is it just Meg?''

''Our father was. He always told us he got kicked out of the choir when he was a kid for doing it on purpose. He couldn't even tell a major from a minor key, much less the difference between two notes. Are you out for a walk?''

''I thought I might run into Andy Bishop. I've got a couple of questions to ask him.''

''Me, too. He usually does the circuit, so if we keep going, we're likely to run into him.'' They walked in silence for some time. The air was fresh, with a hint of the heat to come. Quill took a deep breath; she caught the faint odor of cows. ''Did Meg tell you about the Zoning Board meeting?''

John nodded.

"You want to know the unworthiest thought I've had all week?"

He shot her a glance and grinned.

"That CarolAnn gets these dolts from Q.U.A.C.K. to picket the cows and Marge is so embarrassed by the publicity that she *begs* me to buy the Inn back." She sighed happily. "I'm going to sit down and go over that business plan right after breakfast, John."

"Have you talked to Meg about it? Are you really sure she wants to take all this back on?"

"Of course she does," Quill said. "She's all excited."

John didn't say anything.

"Well. Okay. She's happy because I'm happy."

"What did she say?"

"She said it didn't matter where she cooked, as long as she wasn't cooking for people who preferred McDonald's, or words to that effect. What did she say to you?"

"That you were using the Inn as an excuse to hide from getting on with your life. And that touched off the worst quarrel you two ever had. Which," he added reflectively, "must have been some fight, given the way you two wrangle with each other. She said you haven't talked about it since. That she's going along with what you want to do because, as you say, she can cook anywhere. And," he added reflectively, "we've got a real treasure in Bjarne."

Quill noticed the "we" and smiled at him.

"Do you want to talk about it now?"

Max veered off to investigate the leg of a park bench. From there, he cocked his head alertly and charged into the stand of old oaks which were the pride of Peterson Park. Quill whistled. Max ignored her, scrabbling frantically at something in the dirt. She watched the dog for a long moment then asked, "What do you think? Do you think I'm avoiding real life by wanting the Inn back?"

"That depends. On how you handle it this time." He sighed. "You don't have to let everyone in, Quill. You spend a lot of time responding to the guests, the employees, to whomever plants himself in your path. That hasn't changed since you've downsized to the Palate. Instead of using your free time to paint, or spend time with Myles, you joined the Zoning Board, which has given you a whole new set of people and causes to worry about. I agree with Meg that you're neglecting your own life so you can live someone else's. But I don't think your desire to repurchase the Inn has anything to do with that."

"So you think I'm a cuckoo?"

John seemed unaware of how icy her voice was. "You mean as in the bird that borrows someone else's nest?"

"That's what you said, isn't it?"

"It's not what I said at all. I said that for whatever complicated reasons, you're putting off making decisions about your own life by becoming involved with other people's. Here, let's sit down." He pointed at the bench. Quill sat, her temper ebbing as fast as it had come. He stood in front of her. His gaze was direct, unchallengingly friendly. "What did you like least about running the Inn?"

"Worrying," she replied promptly.

John waited a bit. Then he said, "About the food?"

"Meg took care of that."

"About the rooms?"

"Doreen took care of that. And you generally booked the guests, and Mike took care of the gardens—and, come to think of it, what *was* I worrying about?"

She needed to move. She got up, walked around the bench, and sat down again. Max cocked his head in a puzzled way. "Well, I worried about money when we didn't have any."

"That was a legitimate concern."

"I told you on the phone what Marge was doing. Charging a booking fee. Why didn't we think of charging a booking fee?" She held her hand up and said hastily, "That may sound as if I think you did a bad job. You know I don't mean it that way."

"It must have crossed your mind that if Marge thought of it, I could have." He smiled and sat down beside her. "Marge's tactics work very well in an economy like this. You'll remember that we hit bottom when the economic cycle was down. It's likely to turn down again, that's just in the nature of things."

"So you're saying Marge will go broke, too?"

"I'm not sure what Marge is up to. She had enough resources to pay off the debt. That's cut her carrying costs a lot. But Marge isn't about to lose the money she took from other funds on the Inn. I'd bet my last dollar on that."

"Then what's going on?"

"I have an idea. I'm going to make some phone calls. But let me ask you this. Are you absolutely sure you want the Inn back?"

"I'm sure. Doreen's sure. Meg will agree if . . ." She hesitated.

"If she's sure that it's not going to overwhelm you. *You've* got to be sure it's not going to overwhelm you."

She'd asked him here for his advice. She hadn't asked him here to see if he would take his old job back. She wouldn't ask him now. He hadn't brought up Myles. And if she did, she knew him. He'd talk with her calmly, objectively, as he always had. Her friend when she needed him most, he would always back off when she needed the room.

She couldn't ask him now. Not until she knew, herself, what she really wanted to say. The *pad-pad-pad* of rhythmically running feet jerked her from her absorption. "Here's Andy," she said unnecessarily. Max shot out of the brush under the oak trees and raced toward the sound, head up, tail wagging happily. Quill dashed forward and grabbed Max by the scruff of the neck. He liked Andy, but he liked chasing joggers more. She took her fingers away from his ruff and frowned. "SIT, Max!" she said in a ferocious tone. "Leave Andy alone!" There was sticky stuff all over her fingers. Another dead raccoon. Ugh. She knelt to clean her fingers on the grass.

Andy Bishop bent forward and rumpled Max's ears. "Are you out recapturing him?"

"No, he's legal; this time," Quill said absently. "Yuck. This darn dog gets into more messes."

Andy shook hands with John, slapped him on the back, and said, "Good to see you again." Andy was of medium height, with the well-muscled but lithe build Quill always associated with tennis players. His reserve balanced Meg's volatile nature, and although she'd never tell her sister this, he was very like her young first husband, who had died in a tractor-trailer pileup on an icy night in November ten years ago. "Sorry about last night," he said. He jogged in place. "Meg was pretty upset."

"I don't know why she should be," Quill said a little tartly. "Bodies seem to follow us around everywhere we go."

"Speaking of the . . . er . . . body," John said. "What's your take on Rossiter's death?"

"His wife's coming up from Dallas this afternoon,"

Andy said. "So I'm assuming I'll be able to get more of a medical history. His cattle manager Brady worked for Royal for almost twenty years. Says he's never known him to be sick a day in his life, but then, Royal may not have mentioned any heart problems to Brady. Some middle-aged guys can be in denial about illness. But it looks like a massive coronary occlusion to me, and I've seen a few. What *is* that smell, Quill?"

"Max got into something under the trees. He knocked me into a dead raccoon the other day. Why is it that dogs have a thing for carrion?"

Andy inhaled sharply. The breeze was from the west and came from the trees. There was a sweetish odor of decay. "Wait here a minute, Quill," he said. "Hang on to that damn dog. John, can you come with me?"

Quill watched the two men jog to the oaks. From the sudden stillness in the set of John's shoulders, the intent curve of Andy's back as he bent over the ground, she knew it wasn't a raccoon, that it was much, much larger than a dead raccoon.

"Right." Trooper Harris rolled his tongue behind his lower lip, increasing his resemblance to a gorilla. "How long you say the body's been here, Doc?"

Andy pulled the plastic gloves off his hands with a snap. The forensics team was back, cameras flashing strobelike in the shadows under the oak trees. Quill stood back a little. Max roamed the path to the far side of the statue. A crowd of people stood behind the yellow police tape Trooper Harris had used to cordon off the area: the breakfast crowd from the Croh Bar.

"Forensics is not my specialty, Harris." Andy adjusted his wire-rimmed glasses. "Three or four days, at a guess. Decomposition wasn't much advanced. I would suspect that the wounds on the neck are the result of insect activity; I also suspect that he died of that stab wound to the chest. But these are guesses, Trooper. Not facts.''

Harris spat on the ground. "We got any idea who this fellow is?''

"I don't think he's from around here," Quill said hesitantly. "The Texans might know.''

Harris swung around and glared at her. "And why is that?''

"He ... it ... the body was in snakeskin boots and jeans, and a Stetson was found a few feet away. No one in Hemlock Falls dresses like that.''

"Had quite a tan on his face and neck," Andy offered. "And from the shape of the femurs I'd say the man was a horseman.''

"Bunch of them staying up to the Inn," Harris said. "Burton?''

The trooper with the crew cut who had leaped to Harris's demands the night before stepped forward. "Yessir.''

"Go on up to that big stone inn on the hill, the one with a big plaster cow in front. Get what's her name—Marge Schmidt down here.''

"That's Marge now," Quill said in some surprise. "In that Izuzu Jeep thing.''

Marge's tangerine-colored Jeep bounced down the road winding from the park and came to an abrupt halt. She flung herself out of the vehicle and came stamping across the grass. Her lower lip jutted out. Her forehead was wrinkled in a fierce scowl. Her lantern jaw was set. "Not *here*," she roared at the sight of Trooper Harris. "Up at *my* place. Where'n the heck is that Dave Kiddermeister when you need him?! I didn't call the flippin' staties, anyhow, I called the flippin' sheriff!''

"Sheriff Kiddermeister is away at traffic school,''
Trooper Harris said. "I told you that last night. And your
flippin' call can wait, Miss flippin' Marge Schmidt. We'll
get to it when we've taken care of this business, understand?''

"What business?'' Marge's expression was no less
truculent as she took in the ambulance, the evidence bags,
the yellow DO NOT PASS POLICE tape surrounding the
oak tree. "What the hell. Not another body, Quill.
What'd you, poison this one, too?''

Trooper Harris surveyed Quill like a lizard considering
a bee. He blinked once, slowly. "We don't know that
yet,'' he said slowly. "No, we don't know that yet.''

"Who is it?'' Marge asked.

"We were hoping you could take a look and tell us,''
Harris said. Quill wondered if he practiced sounding rep-
tilian when he was shaving. She could just see him, like
Travis Bickle in *Taxi Driver: You talkin' to me? You
talkin' to me?* "Some guy about sixty, Bishop says. Farmer's tan on him. . . .''

Marge's cheeks paled. "Not—not anyone I know? Not
Harland Peterson?''

"It's not Harland,'' Quill said quickly. "My goodness,
Marge, he's right over there with the mayor and the rest
of the breakfast clubbers. Harland!'' She waved. "Harland!''

Harland ducked under the tape and walked awkwardly
across the grass toward them. "Marge thought it might
be you!'' Quill greeted him.

Marge gave her a malevolent glance.

"So was you worried?'' Harland asked in a low,
pleased voice.

"Yeh," Marge said shortly. Harland's hand crept out, grappled hers briefly, then withdrew.

"I've got a body to identify here!" Harris said loudly. "You going to take a look?"

"You watch your mouth, young fella," Harland growled. "Stay here, Margie. That's not something you want to see, I expect."

"Oh, I dunno," Marge said. "Might as well take a look. As long as you're comin' with."

"I'm comin' with."

The whole party moved to the trees. Quill came along unwillingly; she didn't want to look at the body again, but she did need to know who it was.

The med tech looked at Andy, who gave a short nod. "Just the face," he said. The tech zipped the body open down to the neck. Quill took a deep breath and looked at her feet. "Huh," Marge said in a speculative tone.

"You okay, Margie?" Harland asked in a low voice.

"Hell, yeh. I mean, as long as you're here."

"Will you cut the *crap!*" Trooper Harris exploded.

"Pull that zip down a little bit more, Calvin," Marge said to the tech. "Yeh. Lookit that. See that belt buckle?"

Quill peeked. The silver buckle was huge, four by five inches at least, and heavily inscribed.

"That's a championship rodeo buckle." She leaned forward, seemingly indifferent to the odor. "Southwest Texas Bull Riding, 1998."

"So you know who this is?" Harris demanded.

Marge narrowed her eyes at Harris. Since they were little and beady anyway, this added a malicious sparkle to her complacent tone. "Says so right on the belt buckle, Trooper. That's Candy Detwiler, the colonel's cattleman. Now that I've done your job for ya, you wanna do your job for me? Seein' that I'm a taxpayer in this county? Those damn vegetarians are all over my place up there, carrying signs and hooting and hollering fit to bust. I want those bums outta my rose garden, and I want them out now.''

"Two bodies," Quill said to Myles. "This isn't looking good." She adjusted the phone against her ear. She was sitting up in bed. Max snored in the corner of the room. The lace curtains at the open windows fluttered in the nighttime breeze. Charles Sheffield's *Aftermath* lay open on her knee. She'd found the story of a postholocaust earth oddly soothing after the events of the day. "And how's *your* day been going?"

Myles's deep voice was amused. "Just fine. Surveillance is a pretty tedious job, but I'm hoping things will break tonight or tomorrow."

"So you won't be back for a while?"

"Not for another week, at least. Are you holding up all right?" His tone was tender. "I miss you."

"I miss you, too. I'm holding up fine. But this Harris, Myles. What a jerk." Quill found her indignation returning. "He herded those poor vegetarians off in a county sheriff's bus. I talked to Howie Murchison about it. He said they have a right to protest if they want. And I told you about the scuffle."

"You told me about the scuffle."

"Vegetarians are peaceful, nonviolent. I mean, their whole lives are dedicated to everyone living together in a nonaggressive way. That wispy bearded guy—Normal Norman I think his name is—had this whole belt of implements just for freeing caged animals, he said. Pliers, wire clippers, knives, that sort of thing. And he *told* Harris that's what the tools were for, and Harris had two of his goons put Norman in a headlock . . .'' Max woke up and barked. Quill made a conscious effort to lower her voice. "Anyway, I'm surprised there wasn't any bloodshed. So can you check out this guy Harris? He's scary, Myles. I'm afraid something's going to happen."

"Such as?"

"I don't know. Someone getting hurt. Harris is convinced these two deaths are related, *why* I don't know, because Andy *told* him poor Royal died of a heart attack."

"What does Rossiter's medical history say?"

"You mean did he have a history of heart trouble? I don't know. Mrs. Rossiter was supposed to be here this afternoon, but her plane was diverted and she got in late. She's staying up at the Inn. I think I'll mosey on up there tomorrow morning, as the Texans say, and see what's going on."

"Quill."

"Don't 'Quill' me," she said crossly. "All poor Meg needs is another suspicious death. And things were going so well, Myles. John says the Palate is showing enough of a growth curve to command a pretty good price from an outside buyer. And if I get a good price for the Palate, I may be able to afford to buy the Inn back. I will NOT let some bozo of a hotshot state trooper screw things up because he wants to make a name for himself."

Silence on the other end of the phone. Then, "You're sure about that?"

"Why does everyone ask me that? Of course I'm sure!"

"Easy, easy. I was just asking."

"I'm not a horse, Myles."

"Why do you think you're a horse?"

"Don't say 'easy, easy' like that."

"This conversation is getting ridiculous," he growled.

"Sorry," she said after a moment. "So. Do you think your guys can check out these names for me? Both of the men who died."

"I'll put someone on it. But I doubt anything will turn up."

"I know Harris is checking them out," she said mutinously, "and I want to know what he knows."

"Just a moment." Myles put his hand over the receiver, and she listened to the cupped quiet. He came back on suddenly. "I'm needed. I'll call you." And was gone.

Wide awake, a little cranky, Quill put the phone back on the nightstand and got out of bed. She needed something to eat. Meg had bounced off again, and wouldn't be back from New York until tomorrow afternoon, which meant there wouldn't be anything good in the refrigerator. Bjarne was very economical (another reason for the financial success of the Palate; Meg was prone to throw out any produce that was over a day old, and make more than was needed for the week's bookings) and there was usually nothing left in the coolers from the evening trade. She went downstairs to the kitchen in her bare feet, Max clicking along behind.

No desserts. A bowl of dough, chilling for tomorrow's muffins. Strawberries and cantaloupe, clearly portioned for tomorrow's breakfast customers. Unopened cartons of Devonshire cream. Quill thought about it. If she took one strawberry from each parcel, slit open the cream container and repasted it, Bjarne might not notice he was shorting his customers. She pulled out a colander and gathered half a dozen strawberries to rinse under the faucet. She jumped a foot when John came into the room.

"Now, *that* looks great."

Quill smiled at him. He was wearing pajama bottoms, a dark blue robe, and his hair was tousled from sleep. She went back to the fridge and gathered a second set of strawberries, some from each serving.

"What are you doing?" He was curious, not challenging. John, she realized suddenly, was never anything but kind.

"You never intrude, you know that?"

One black eyebrow rose.

"Meg would want to know what I was doing so she could argue about it. Bjarne would want to know what I was doing so he could give me a lecture about the food budget. Doreen would want to know what I—"

"I get the picture." He sat down at the prep table and yawned. "With all due respect to Bjarne's management style, I think you should take as many strawberries as you want."

"I don't know, John. He's been very firm about raiding the refrigerator."

He held up one coppery finger. "One—he can buy more from Peterson's farm market before we open. And two—" he leaned forward and whispered, *"it's your restaurant."*

"Oh. It is, isn't it." Recklessly, she grabbed two bowls of the fruit and an entire container of Devonshire cream. "This is definitely one of the great all-time midnight snacks."

They ate at the prep table, perched on the stools, a comfortable silence between them. Quill scooped up a last bit of cream, then said, "So who do you think killed Candy Detwiler?"

"I haven't the least idea."

"It had to have been an outsider. I mean, no one who lives here even knew him."

"Didn't they?"

"Colonel Calhoun said Detwiler hadn't been north of Texas since he was in the Army forty years ago. There's just no connection that I can see."

"There's the cattle."

"True. But all the cattlemen are from Texas, as well. And one of them is dead, too. John, do you think that Royal Rossiter's death is connected to this?"

"There have been stranger coincidences, Quill."

"Does that mean yes or no?"

"It means that I haven't a clue. We really don't have enough facts." He got up and took his bowl to the sink. "What we might do is some discreet information gathering tomorrow. If the cows are the connection, then perhaps we should find out all we can about the cows. Didn't you say that Laura Crest had quite a bit of information on them?"

"She left a lot of stuff for Meg. She can probably get a lot more, if we asked. But what would we need to know?"

"The estimable Harris is investigating the usual avenues concerning Detwiler's death. But he'll be stymied until the forensic autopsy's finished. He needs to establish the tie between the two deaths, retrace Detwiler's movements before he got to Hemlock Falls, discover who talked to him and what about before he died. It's even possible that he wasn't killed here, Quill, but that the body was dumped here, which is going to make solving this particular case all the more difficult.

"We won't know if Rossiter's death is at all suspicious until that autopsy is done, either. I have a suggestion, if you want to hear it."

"You mean, you want to help me investigate this case?"

"Sure. Why not?"

"Well." Why not, because Myles always gets porky when amateurs butt into official police work. Why not, because Meg is too busy to be Watson, and thinks I'm the Watson, anyway. More seriously why not, because even a peripheral involvement in Rossiter's death might rebound to the discredit of Meg's cooking and the financial worth of the Palate. On the other hand, this last "why not" was a compelling reason "why to." She knew her sister, and there was no way that she or her cooking could have been responsible for Rossiter's death. And if the death were suspicious, then the sooner the perpetrator was found, the better.

"That's a lot of ifs, though," she said aloud. "What do you think we should do first?"

John grinned. "I know you, Quill. You're just being polite. Let's try this. What are you going to do first?"

"Follow the cows," Quill said promptly. "You're right about that, just as you were right about 'follow the money' in the Peterson case. And that's the big connection here, isn't it? The cows. First, we have the two rivals, Colonel Calhoun and Royal Rossiter. Both of them have been wrangling over who owns the right to what bull, have you noticed? Second, we have Harland Peterson, the slaughterhouse zoning problem, and the horrible CarolAnn Spinoza. Third, we have the people from Q.U.A.C.K., which also involves the awful CarolAnn. And finally, there's the Russians. Who are suspiciously eager to corner the cattle for themselves, in my view."

"They haven't behaved suspiciously, have they?" John asked.

"Ha," Quill said. "They're capitalist Russians. What could be more suspicious than that?" She wriggled her eyebrows. "I la-hove thees kontree."

"Very funny. So, what's your game plan?"

"Interrogation," Quill said promptly. "We ask questions of anyone who'll answer them. First, I want to talk to poor Mrs. Rossiter tomorrow morning. Then I want to speak to Colonel Calhoun."

"And you'd like me to talk to Laura Crest."

"To find out more about the cows. Yes!" Quill was delighted. With this kind of partner, her investigation could go very well. "Now, we need some background searches on both the—um—deceased. So when Myles called, I asked him."

The name fell like shrapnel between them. John's face closed up. Quill looked at her thumbs. There was a bit of artist's charcoal under her nail. Max nudged her knees and barked for the rest of the Devonshire cream.

"When is he planning on coming back?"

"As soon as this case is wrapped up. He's not sure. A week. Maybe." John took her hand in his. The engagement ring Myles had given her was elegantly simple, two sapphires on either side of a small diamond. John drew his finger down her palm. Quill clasped her hand convulsively.

"Why did you call me?"

She forced herself to look at him. "Partly because I was in a temper. Marge changed the Inn. It's her right to change the Inn. I hadn't realized until I saw it, talked to her, examined what it was that I really want out of life, how much all the work that went into the design and running the place had meant to me. I just lost it." He touched her red hair. She took a deep breath. "Partly because I can't believe how much I've missed you these last two months."

"What does that mean for me?" He looked away. "I can't stand it if you're frivolous, Quill."

"I've never felt less frivolous in my life." She needed to move. She got up and walked restlessly around the kitchen. Max followed her for a circuit or two, then went back to sleep on the floor. "You were always there, John. You were always so much a part of the Inn and the fabric of life. Then you were gone." She snapped her fingers. "Poof. Like that. At first, I didn't think I minded. At first, I told myself that in any event, this job, this opportunity, was the best thing that could have happened to you. Your career at the Inn wasn't much. Even I knew that, as much as I love the place. And Meg told me I was responsible for keeping you here, even though I didn't know it. Or rather," she added, her voice low, "I knew it and didn't admit it. So. I began to realize that you weren't there to talk to. And that it was a great grief to me. I remember exactly when it hit me. This perfectly awful family of three came in for lunch. A preppy kid who must have been on his way to Cornell and his carefully well-dressed parents. They complained about everything. The table, the temperature of the ice water. Anyway, they sent back Bjarne's sour cream grapes, you know that dish he does with caramelized brown sugar. First time Bjarne's ever had that happen, even though it happens in the life of every chef—even Meg. The grapes were sour, they said. Not at the peak of perfection. Besides, they were Thompson grapes and oh, I don't know. Anyway they didn't want to pay for the meal. That type, you know? Maxed out on the credit cards and don't realize until halfway through the wine how expensive the bill is going to be. But what capped it was, well, Doreen was heading up the wait staff that day."

"Uh-oh."

Quill began to giggle in spite of herself. "Bjarne came out and started to yell in Swedish. Or maybe it was Finnish. *I* don't know. The woman, skinny, face-lift, that sort of streaky frosted blond hair, said that they should have known the minute an old lady waited on them that this wasn't a top of the line place. So they threw her two pennies for a tip and left in a huff. Or started to leave in a huff.''

''And?''

''Oh, dear. Oh, *dear.* I wish you could have seen Doreen.''

''The mop and bucket?''

''She hadn't emptied from washing the floor that morning. I had to pay for dry-cleaning that kid's double-breasted navy blue blazer, but my gosh it was worth it.'' She stopped laughing. ''And I thought, John will get such a kick out of this. I turned to tell you. And you weren't there.'' John didn't say anything for so long that she began to blush. ''What? That is, what's your job like? Is it satisfying?''

''A lot of meetings. I dress in a three-piece suit. I'm working with a team on an international acquisition now.''

''And this nurse?''

''Very nice woman.''

''So you've made a life for yourself.''

''I have, Quill. I'm not a fool. I'm not self-destructive, not in the way I was when I was younger and drinking. Of course I've made a life for myself.''

And what is this, then? The knock at my door last night. The tension I felt in you when we walked together this morning. She didn't say this aloud. She couldn't. She didn't know what it was, either.

''If there's a chance for me, Quill, you must tell me now.''

''There is,'' she said, and went back up to bed.

# CHAPTER 8

"My Royal. My Roy!" the widow cried. She was surrounded by a respectful circle of Hemlockians in the Tavern Lounge. Or what used to be the Tavern Lounge. It was just after ten o'clock, a respectful time of day, Quill thought, to call on the grieving Mrs. Rossiter. She'd brought freesia and white roses. Esther West, who had diversified into flowers, suggested the tasteful addition of a tiny cowboy Stetson in the bouquet. Quill had declined.

"Hit me again, Nate." Mrs. Rossiter pushed a beer and shot glass across the bar. "And pour for my friends." The mayor demurred. Mrs. Mayor had a frozen look on her face. A sheaf of daisies lay in her lap. Harland Peterson and Marge looked at each other, shrugged, and held out their coffee cups in front of Nate.

The widow, a healthy brunette in her mid-forties, exhibited that curious phenomenon known to Quill and her sister as "big hair." She wore it long, past her shoulders, and it was pouffed and sprayed at right angles to her face. She resembled a chrysanthemum. She wore a white denim top decorated with sequined spurs, saddles, and pistols. Her feet were small, in bright red strappy shoes that wrapped around the ankle. Her white jeans were so tight that Quill could see where she might want to lose a few pounds.

"Yo, Quill," Harland said.

"Harland, Marge."

"Please join us, Quill," Adela Henry said. "*Please.*"

"As a matter of fact, Mother," Elmer said, "I think you said you had to make that call on your sister."

"You are correct, Mayor, I did." Adela rose to the full majesty of her five-foot-three. "Good day to you, Mrs. Um."

"Good day to you," Mrs. Rossiter sobbed. "But it's not a good day for my sweetie."

"No, indeed." Adela adjusted her hat. "Come, Mayor. Marge, are you and Harland joining us?"

"Hell, no," said Harland, who was gazing at the widow in frank fascination. "I want to see if she falls off that bar stool after that third shot and a beer."

"Me, too," Marge said.

Quill sat carefully on the stool vacated by the mayor's wife. She laid the freesia next to the daisies. Mrs. Rossiter regarded them mournfully, then broke off a fragrant stem and stuck it behind her ear. She had big earrings, too, Quill noted. Copper cows with gold horns.

"Shirley Rossiter." The brunette extended her hand. Quill took it. Shirley curled her fingers around Quill's hand and drew it to her bosom. "You knew my Royal?"

"Just for a short while," Quill said, reclaiming her hand. "I met him while he was walking his . . . while he and Impressive were out for a . . ."

"Dumb bastard spent more time with that bull than he

did with me.'' She wiped the back of her hand under her eyes. ''Dumb bastard,'' she repeated.

Quill, assuming that dumb bastard was a term of affection in Texas, patted her shoulder. ''I'm very sorry.''

''Me, too.'' She sighed. ''Everyone here's been just fine to me. Just fine. Marge here? All this beer and a shot is free.''

Marge opened her mouth, then closed it with a snap.

''In honor of my Royal. My Roy . . .''

''Had he had any heart disease?'' Quill asked hastily, since subtlety would be wasted on Mrs. Rossiter.

''Roy?'' She furrowed her brow. ''*Heart* disease,'' she said flatly. ''That's what that cute young doc told me carried him off. It isn't,'' she added suddenly, ''the cough that carries you off, it's the coffin they carry you off in.''

''Ha,'' Harland said.

Quill, emboldened by this foray into doggerel, said, ''I suppose poor Roy left a pile.''

''A pile,'' she repeated. ''Well, I don't know that I'd call it a pile. Where's that lying son of a sea biscuit, Calhoun?''

''The colonel? Went out somewhere this morning,'' Harland said. ''He was over to my place early on, checking out the slaughterhouse. We gotta get a couple of squeeze chutes that'll handle the horned cattle, and he was looking the land over.''

Shirley blinked. Her mouth opened and closed like the koi that were (undoubtedly) no longer in Quill's pond. Eaten by cattle.

''Do cattle eat fish?'' Quill asked.

''Sure they do. Fish meal. Good for them,'' Harland said. ''Shirley, the colonel'll be back to pay his respects. Seems like the kind of fella that will do the right thing.''

Marge nodded sober agreement.

Do cattle make a meal out of fish, or did he mean fish meal? "Harland," Quill began.

"Colonel!" Shirley said. "Colonel of what, I may ask."

"Well, what is he a colonel of?" Marge asked. "Thought it was the Army, myself."

"Army!" Shirley snorted. "Army!" She subsided into her beer.

"He wasn't in the Army?" Quill leaned forward and placed her hand on Shirley's arm. Her head dropped forward onto her chest. She began to snore.

"Thought that last beer'd do it," Harland said. "Out like a light. Margie? You, Nate, and I better get her to bed."

Marge rose off the bar stool and dusted her hands together. "Hell, Harland. The two of us can get her. You grab the feet."

"Done. Then we'll go check out the herd. Thought we'd move 'em down to my place rather than have 'em up here with you. When Shirl comes to, we can discuss how much she wants for 'em."

Shirley, slumped over the bar, stirred and murmured. Marge grabbed her shoulders with rough expertise, swung her around, and Harland lifted her feet with a grunt. Quill watched them carry Shirley off, and when they were out of hearing, said, "Nate, did Harland make arrangements with Mrs. Rossiter to buy the cattle?"

Nate took off his captain's hat and ran his fingers across his bald spot. "Bought them from Rossiter yesterday, far as I know. They were discussing the deal over a beer or two. You know how these things go. . . ." His fingers stopped moving. "Do you think I've been losing more hair?"

Quill craned her neck to look. "Yes," she said ruthlessly. "Since you took this job, especially. Stress will do it, you know. What were the terms of the deal?"

Nate sighed. "You think Rogaine might work?"

"Nate?"

He leaned forward.

"I like you bald. Forget the Rogaine. Answer my question. What were the terms of the cattle deal? I had the impression that ownership of the herd was shared by Roy and the colonel."

"I don't know about that. I do know that CarolAnn Spinoza has been raising holy heck about the permit for the slaughterhouse."

"She has?" Quill thought a moment. "It hasn't come up before the Zoning Board. Although come to think of it, those space cadets from Q.U.A.C.K. mentioned it. CarolAnn must have told them about that, too." She didn't ask why CarolAnn was sticking her nose into the permit for the slaughterhouse. CarolAnn stuck her nose into everything. "Who has she been talking to?"

"The mayor. Harland. Augustus, too. And since he's the one who issues the permits, he's the one she's been harassing most. He's scared shi—I mean green whenever CarolAnn opens her mouth, so who knows whether Harland will get that permit or not?"

Quill took out her sketch pad, wrote down *LEADS,* and under that, *slaughterhouse.* Then she wrote: *Cardiac history, Rossiter? Ask A. B.*

"Who's A. B.?" Nate asked, craning his neck for a better look at the notepad. "Oh. Andy Bishop." He grinned at her. "Off on a case again, huh? I thought Mr. Rossiter's death was natural."

"You heard his wife—widow, rather. Royal was never sick a day in his life."

"She didn't say that, Quill. She said 'heart disease' like she was surprised. But she didn't say he was never sick a day in his life."

"Brady did," Quill said. "Somebody told me Brady did. Where is Brady?"

"Checked out this morning."

"He's gone?"

"No. He went down to that Motel 48 near the vet's place. Said he wanted to be near his horse."

"I think I'll go and see him. I'll either be there, or at the vet's, if anyone's asking for me. And, Nate, could you leave a message for the colonel? I'd like to invite him to dinner at the Palate tonight. About seven-thirty, if it suits him."

"Will do."

Quill went out the front door feeling as though she was accomplishing something. Max lay curled up in the front seat of the car and wagged his tail lazily as she got in. "What do you think?" she asked. "Do you want to go with me? Or do you want to stay home?"

Max barked.

"Okay. You can go with me. But you can't hang your nose out the window. It looks like rain." The sky was threatening a shower, if not a downpour. She reconsidered her decision to take Max; there was nothing worse than a car filled with wet smelly dog. Max barked and put his paw on her knee. "Okay. But you'll have to stay in the car. All right?"

Max cocked his head. Quill made an unsuccessful attempt at getting him to go back to his nap. She even relented on keeping the window open, and as she drove down Route 15 to the Motel 48, it began to rain.

The Motel 48 was one of the many cheap, well run places that had sprung up at the end of the eighties, when occupancy of luxury hotels was down, and business travelers needed inexpensive places to stay overnight. Quill pulled into the parking lot. She didn't see Brady's truck among the vehicles parked in front of the two-storied structure. She dashed through the rain to the door marked OFFICE. The motel had forty-eight rooms, named for each of the contiguous forty-eight states. Brady, appropriately enough, was in Texas. "But he was up early this morning. Went out before six o'clock. The night manager told me." The clerk was young, with that kind of uniform prettiness that Quill saw in kids under twenty. She fervently hoped this observation wasn't a function of her own age.

"He didn't tell the night clerk where he was going? For example, to see his horse?"

"No, ma'am." The clerk sighed. "If I knew, I think I might have followed him. Is he married, do you think, Ms. Quilliam?"

Quill left a message for Brady, just in case she missed him at the vet's.

The rain was off-again, on-again as she drove a little farther down Route 15 to get to the Paradise Veterinary Practice. As soon as they turned down the familiar road, Max began to whine.

"No vet, Max. No vet."

Max barked, jumped into the backseat, then into the front seat and into her lap. She caught a sudden flash of hooves, cream, and a booted leg. She heard a shout, and slammed on the brakes. Through the windshield, she saw a horse down in the graveled yard, and a figure lying beside it. She jumped out of the car and ran toward the horse. The animal snorted, rolled its eyes at her, and heaved itself to its feet. The figure on the ground got to its feet, readjusted its hat, and gave her a level look.

"Brady! I'm so sorry! Are you all right?"

"I'm fine." He ambled over to his horse, who blew out with an angry sound. "Scooter's fine but you look a little pale, Quill. Here. Sit down and put your head between your knees."

Quill sat. It started to rain again. Brady left her alone, went to his horse, and methodically began to remove the strap under its stomach, the bridle around its head. "Dang," he muttered. He hiked up his jeans leg and pulled out a slender knife. It looked wickedly sharp. Quill's breathing slowed. Her head cleared. She watched as Brady sliced through a snagged buckle on his saddle with the knife. He stuck the knife back in its sheath in his boot and removed the saddle.

"I'll just put her back in the stall. Too wet to ride today anyhow. Didn't bring my slicker."

Quill leaned her head against the Olds' quarter panel. Did all cattlemen carry knives? Long and thin, Andy had said. Sharp enough to slice through bone. Or wet leather.

Brady led the horse into the vet's barn. Quill got to her feet and followed him.

The barn was more of a giant, three-sided shed than what Quill knew as a horse barn. Back home in Connecticut, horse barns had been gabled, shingled, fancy affairs that were sometimes better kept than the houses of her friends who owned them. This place had a highly utilitarian, no-nonsense feel. The building was perhaps one hundred and fifty feet long and about forty feet wide. The door to the yard and clinic was on the short wall to the east. As Quill entered, she saw a row of pens on her left, and hay and supply storage on her right. The lights were on. It smelled of horses, cows, and the omnipresent Betadyne. Laura Crest was standing about halfway down, in a well-lighted area that had an arrangement of metal bars about waist high. A horse stood placidly between the bars, its foot in a rubber bucket. Brady led his horse past them, and Quill heard her say, "You all right, Jack? I heard you shout."

"Yeh. No problem." He paused by her. "Sarah Quilliam's here." Was that a cautionary note in his voice? He put the mare into a stall and came back toward Quill. He brushed the vet as he recrossed the aisle toward Quill; Laura was bent over the horse, but Quill could see her smile.

They'd met before. She was sure of it. The tone of voice, the brief physical contact, the intimacy of Laura's smile. Friends of long standing at least, if not more. Quill tried to remember what had happened the day she, Royal, and Brady had come out here to get Max's rabies shot. She'd been worried about Max, about whether he'd bite Laura, or whether she'd be rough with him. But she was darn sure that Royal had introduced the two of them to each other. And they had behaved with the politeness of strangers.

"The dog okay?"

Quill jumped. Brady bent slightly toward her. She edged back a little. "Max is fine. I mean, I'm not here because of Max." She smiled ruefully. "Although I suppose I should ask Laura if she runs obedience classes."

"Just have to let them know who's boss." He raised his voice. "Dr. Crest? You mind if we use the office for a talk?"

"Not at all." She stepped back from the pipe pen and spoke to the horse. "You just stand there for twenty minutes. Let that sucker soak." She wiped her hands on a towel as she came on through to the front door. "It's nice to see you again, Quill. Is Max okay?"

"Max is fine."

She darted a brief look at Brady. "Then, can I help you?"

"Actually, both of you probably could. You heard about Candy Detwiler's death yesterday?"

"I sure did." Laura's face sobered. "I understand you found the body. I'm sorry."

Quill considered several responses to this. I'm used to it, seemed too flip. I'm sorry, too, seemed insincere, for some reason. "Yes," she said. "I did. I thought I'd ask Brady a little bit about him, and then ask you about the Texas longhorn cattle. So if you both have some time, I'd appreciate it."

Laura looked back at the horse with its foot in the bucket. "I've got twenty minutes while that abscess soaks. And there's coffee on in the clinic."

"You don't have patients waiting?" Quill asked as they crossed the yard to the office.

"Not until five o'clock on Fridays. I allow this time for farm calls and work in the hospital." She blushed. "Not that you'd call the shed a hospital, really. But I always thought as soon as I got the practice built up a bit, I'd put in a real operating room, something like the arrangements they have at Cornell." She unlocked her office door and switched on the lights. "Here we are. And there's the coffee. Can I get you any?"

"No, thanks. But if I could sit down?"

"Sure." Laura cast a distracted glance around the office. The three-cushion vinyl couch was stacked with journals, newspapers, and manila folders. So was her gray metal desk. She shoved the pile on the couch onto the floor. Quill sat down. The whole place smelled of wet dog.

"I'll take a cup, Doc." Brady eased himself into a vinyl and chrome chair next to the desk. Laura poured coffee for the two of them, then leaned against the far wall. There was an ease between her and Brady that was unmistakable. He propped one booted ankle on his knee. "So you found Candy? Yesterday morning?"

"Did you know him very well?"

"Well enough. Been in a few bars together."

"In Texas?"

"Mmhm."

Terrific. Grade for interrogation of laconic cowboy: F. Quill braced herself to try a different tack. "Andy Bishop's our local G.P. He took a look at Candy. He's pretty sure that the bo—that Candy had been there three or four days based on the way the wounds clotted. But he died within twenty-four hours of my coming across him."

Brady took a sip of coffee. "That right?"

"So he lay there, for God knows how long . . ." Quill trailed off.

Laura, pale, asked, "How did he die? I heard he was stabbed."

"Yes. Although they can't be sure until the final autopsy."

"Met Candy way back. Maybe twenty years ago, when I was riding rodeo. He was a clown. You know about rodeo clowns?"

Quill shook her head. "Just that they divert the dangerous animals."

"That's right. It's a hell of job. Lot more dangerous than what I did. Bull riding," he explained briefly. "Candy put his life on the line for me more than once. You want to know how well I knew him? Well enough to be a little disappointed when he went to work for that lyin' sack of shit Randall Calhoun."

"You don't like Colonel Calhoun?"

He gave her a considering stare. "Like him? No, I can't say as I like him. Does he know his cattle? You bet. Is he a lyin' sack of shit? You can bet your life on that, too."

Quill wanted to pound her fist on the couch and scream with frustration. Instead she said, "Shirley Rossiter's checked in at the Inn. Have you seen her yet?"

"Hell, yes." He laughed. It was a hayloft kind of laugh. A Tom-Jones-at-the-chicken-dinner kind of laugh. Suddenly, Quill wasn't so sure that Brady had moved to the Motel 48 because of his horse. "Sorry," he said, "didn't mean to sound impolite about Mrs. Roy. Not with Candy lyin' dead as a doornail and Royal the same."

"Had she ever spoken to you about Mr. Rossiter's heart problem?"

"Heart problem? Roy didn't have no heart problem."

"Did he have any kind of health problems at all?"

"No. Not that I can think on. If you will excuse me, Quill, I'm going to go check on the horse for the doc, here." He drained his coffee and left. Quill sat back on the couch. She bit off a nail in sheer, screaming frustration.

"Is there something you wanted to ask me, Quill?" Laura smiled at her. But not with her eyes, Quill thought. Not at all with her eyes.

"Just a little more about the cattle. Was there anything special about Royal's herd? He and the colonel seemed at odds over them."

"Do you know much about the beef industry? Or about how beef is raised?"

"No," Quill said, very much afraid she was going to find out.

"Bear with me a bit. Basically, there're two reasons

to raise cattle. One is to establish a championship stock, like Royal's, that has a lot of value as a foundation herd. In other words, the heifers and the bulls from a breeding herd are sold to guys who raise beef as the herd sires and herd dams.''

''They don't get eaten.''

''They don't. From a beef cattle point of view, you want a steer that's . . . well, beefy. It's more economical to get a lot of beef from one carcass than a little beef.''

''Yes,'' Quill said, a little impatiently.

''Now. Royal was breeding foundation stock for the beef industry. So he was trying to get a heavier steer with more beef on it. All that stuff about longhorns is true. Their body fat is remarkable. It's actually healthier for you than lean chicken. And you can get more money per carcass if this carcass is taller.

''The colonel, on the other hand, is a sentimentalist. And there are a lot of them in the agricultural world. The original longhorn that came from the old West is a small scrawny specimen that's built to survive in the wilderness. That's where the genetics of the low fat beef comes from. So Calhoun despised Rossiter's efforts to change the look and heft of the breed. He's a fanatic, Quill. And fanatics don't care much about money, or profit. They care about the cause. Look at those dolts from Q.U.A.C.K., or whatever they call it. Ready to slaughter human beings to protect animals.''

''Gosh,'' Quill said, startled, ''I don't know that Skye and Normal Norman would go that far.''

''Oh, no? Have you seen today's paper?''

''The *Gazette*?'' Doreen's third husband (or maybe it was her fourth, no one knew for sure) was Axminster Stoker, publisher of the *Gazette*. Quill always felt guilty when she admitted that she didn't read it.

''*The Syracuse Herald.* They covered that little fracas yesterday. Read this.''

Q.U.A.C.K. QUELLED, the headline blared. There was an excellent photograph of Marge, looking like a Berserker, grabbing Skye by her long gray hair. CarolAnn smirked for the camera in the background. The article beneath reported on the demonstration (CarolAnn was not quoted, thank the gods of news) and then gave a brief history of the organization itself. ''Norman's been in jail? For battery? My goodness, Laura. He pulled a boning knife on a chicken farmer and . . . ugh!'' Quill put the paper down with a shudder.

''Protesting castration techniques,'' Laura said. ''Which don't hurt the chickens all that much, I assure you. And the chicken farmer survived to have two more kids, it says later on.

''Candy Detwiler's death is on page one.''

Quill paged to the front of the paper. There was an excellent photograph of a round-faced man in his late forties and a story headlined, BODY FOUND IN RURAL PARK. The article was brief. Trooper Harris was quoted: ''Extensive leads are being followed up.''

''Golly.'' Quill folded the newspaper up. ''Do you mind if I keep this?''

''Not at all. Anything to keep the chaos in here to a tolerable minimum. I'd better go check on that gelding, too, if you don't mind.'' She shoved herself away from the wall. ''Unless there's anything else?''

''I don't suppose you know Brady well enough to get him to open up about Candy.''

''That's the cowboy way, you know. Yes, ma'am. No, ma'am. And then they spit . . .''

''. . . and walk off into the sunset with their horse.''

She gazed at Laura steadily. "You haven't met him before this?"

"Me? Not a chance. Guy that good-looking I'd remember." She opened the door and waited for Quill to pass through. "You tell Max hello for me, okay?"

"Sure," said Quill absently. "No problem."

"And I don't believe her for a minute, John. They're hiding something. I just know it." They were at the train station, waiting for Meg and Lally to arrive. It was raining again, this time a hard steady downpour that was good for the lawn but a pain in the neck to walk around in. Quill lowered her umbrella to protect herself from a gust of wet wind.

"Why would it matter if they knew each other or not?"

"I don't *know*." Quill stamped her foot. Water splashed into her shoe. She stood on the other foot and shook the water out. "Something's funny about this whole business. Does anyone know when Candy Detwiler came into town?"

"I checked with Marge. The colonel was expecting him four days ago."

"And Calhoun wasn't worried when he didn't show up?"

"Apparently not. Said Candy would show up in his own good time. He wasn't going to be needed until the colonel's bull arrived anyway."

"And when's that supposed to happen?"

"Today. On this train, I think. That's what the colonel said at the Palate night before last."

"Do you know if Candy drove in from the Syracuse airport? Or if he took this train? It stops at the Ithaca airport."

"No one's found his personal effects yet. And as far as I know, no one's reported an abandoned rental car. But there are things the police will find out eventually, Quill."

"Yeah, well, good luck getting any information from the horrible Harris. If the train gets in, will you guys wait for me? I want to ask the ticket clerk if she saw Detwiler get off the train four days ago." She showed him the folded up newspaper. "Picture," she said proudly. "I may be a lousy interviewer of true Texans, but I did get a picture of the poor guy."

The ticket clerk, Muriel, was somehow related to the Peterson clan (almost everyone in Hemlock Falls was), Quill wasn't precisely sure how. She had to wait in line for a few minutes while Muriel dealt with a couple trying to get to Albany, then stepped up with the newspaper article in her hand.

"Hello, Quill. Heard that new restaurant of yours is doing well."

"Thanks, Muriel."

"Your sister is sure keeping us in business these days. My goodness," she chuckled, "you'd think she'd get tired going back and forth like that. Now, are you going to New York with her this time?"

"No, I just wondered if you'd seen this man in the station a few days ago. His name is Candy Detwiler."

"The poor guy you found in the park." Muriel shook her head, tsk, tsk. "Trooper Harris asked me the same thing. Although not," she added, "in as nice a way as you. Yes, I saw him." She nodded cheerfully, and said over Quill's shoulder, "Next."

"Excuse me," the man behind Quill pushed forward.

"Muriel!"

"Yes, Quill."

"When and where did you see Detwiler?"

"Do you *mind*?" The man elbowed Quill aside.

"On the four-thirty from Syracuse, same train as this one coming in now. Got off with a green duffel bag. Waited around for a few minutes, then some guy with a . . . just a *minute,* sir!" (this to the shover) "wispy beard met him and they went off together."

"Guy with a wispy beard?" Quill, well to the rear of the line now, had to strain to hear her.

"In the picture. The other picture. Those animal rights people—okay, mister. I'll get you your consarned ticket!"

"Hey!" Meg said, poking her in the back with her umbrella. "How's by you?"

Quill gave her a quick hug and greeted Lally.

"Sweetie!" Lally said. "Another murder! How lovely!"

"She thinks it's going to boost ratings," Meg said glumly. "I say, yuck. So, other than the odd dead body or two, what's been happening around here?" The four of them moved off to the Olds. Quill explained her latest discoveries on the short drive back to the Palate. "And it looks," she said, "as if the vegetarians are implicated after all."

"Oh, no, cookie," Lally said as Quill slowed in front of the restaurant. "I'm going up to the Inn. Just drop me off there, please."

"You're not staying with us?" Quill turned to look at Meg. Meg gave her a sarcastic wiggle of the eyebrows.

"Not this time, dearie. You're not going to make me walk, are you?"

"Of course not," Quill said hastily. "Is Marge . . . that is, do you have reservations?"

"Marge offered her a free week," Meg said. She

snapped her fingers and began to hum "Mack the Knife" in a tuneless falsetto. At least Quill thought it was "Mack the Knife."

"I'll drive you up, Lally," John said. He, too, recognized Meg's storm signs. "I wanted to talk to Marge anyway. You two go on in, I'll be back in time for dinner."

Quill got out of the driver's seat, then grabbed Meg's backpack while she disentangled herself from the backseat safety belt. John got in the driver's side, Lally got in the front passenger side, and Quill felt she was in a Chinese fire drill. As John drove away, she shouted, "The colonel for dinner!" which later, Esther West told her, made the whole town think she and Meg were going to eat fried chicken.

Quill followed Meg up the stairs into her room. "So what's going on?"

"Marge is trying to steal Lally."

"Steal her? You mean get her to do a show about the Dew Drop Inn? Get serious, Meg."

"I am serious. Marge has got some of the best diner food in the United States."

"That's true."

"And there's nothing really wrong with a name like the Dew Drop Inn except that it's a little . . ."

"Cutesy."

"Cutesy," Meg agreed, "and you wouldn't think twice about it if she hadn't renamed our, I mean, your Inn."

"Lally's still going to do the TV show, isn't she?"

"Yeah." Meg threw her duffel bag onto the bed. "But she says a place with the historic associations of a Laundromat isn't half as fascinating as a place dating back to the seventeenth century and Leaky Peg the trapper's friend.''

''She's got a point.''

''Sure she does. But dammit, Quill. My food...'' Meg's voice rose in a familiar sirenlike shriek. ''My food is ART! Marge's food is CRAFT! And Marge doesn't even COOK IT HERSELF! Betty Hall does.''

''Is Betty going to be on TV?''

''Betty Hall is so shy no one's heard her say more than three words in the forty-two years she's lived in Hemlock Falls. *Sure* she's going to go on TV. She'd sooner die. Those are the three words she's uttered, by the way, and she uttered them to Adela Henry, of all people.''

''Adela Henry? When did you talk to Adela Henry? You've been in New York for three days.''

''Well, somehow Marge got my number, and Betty Hall got someone to give Adela my number.''

''Doreen!'' they chorused at the same time.

''Where is she?'' Meg demanded.

''Five o'clock?'' Quill said, checking her watch. ''The kitchen, poking her broom into Bjarne's business.''

They clattered downstairs together. Doreen was at the sink, scrubbing potatoes. ''So where you two been?'' she greeted them.

Meg glowered. ''Where have we been? Why did you give my phone number to Marge Schmidt so she could get Lally Preston to put her on the TV show instead of the Palate? So, where have *you* been, Doreen? Looking for your mind?!''

''Meg!'' Quill said sharply.

''Marge is the competition!''

''Settle down.'' Doreen, her hands full of potatoes, indicated the two stools at the prep table with her chin.

"Siddown there. And keep out of Bjarne's way. He's in the middle of salmon filets."

"Tak," Bjarne said absently. He flipped one filet onto a chilled platter, and turned the gutted fish over with an expert turn of his wrist.

"You're welcome," Doreen grunted. "You two, on the other hand, are not. What d'ya mean coming in here shrieking like a pair of banshees? I gave Marge the number so that Betty Hall would quit."

"Oh," Meg said.

"Durn right, 'oh.' Most of the success of that place is Betty's cookin'. Betty don't cook, Marge don't have half the business she has now. And she knows it, too."

"And?" Quill said. "Has Marge called, agreeing to sell the Inn?"

"Nope. But she and Harland Peterson are goin' to the International Night together. And that's the second good sign. Harland thinks Marge is goin' to be on TV, he's gonna pop the question a whole lot faster than he might of."

"You think so?" Meg was skeptical.

"I durn well know so. Where d'ya think I was this lunchtime, Miss Meg?"

"I don't know, where?"

"Down to the Croh Bar with that there CarolAnn Spinoza."

"Ugh. Why?!" Quill, revolted, reached over for a handful of capers and onions. She ignored Bjarne's glare.

"Because," Doreen explained, with the patience one uses toward a toddler who has to be told one more time why you can't play nude in the rain, "CarolAnn wants to be in the middle of everything. Glory hound. Mean as a pig, but a glory hound. If she thinks that Marge is gonna be on TV, she's gonna be nice to Marge. If Marge is gonna marry Harland, she's gotta be nice to Harland, too, and,'' Doreen took a deep breath, ''CarolAnn's gotta get her nose out of Harland's business and let him have that permit for a feedlot, or he's gonna be too hacked off to marry Marge. So that,'' Doreen dumped the peeled potatoes into the colander with a thump, ''is how come I gave Marge and Adela your phone number in New York.''

''It makes a weird kind of sense,'' Meg admitted. ''But that doesn't change the fact that Marge is going to take my place on Lally Preston's *Rusticated Lady* show.''

''Maybe once, she'll be on it. But you ast me, once is goin' to be enough for Marge. Now you two think about it. You got Lally. You got Marge. How are they gonna get along?''

Quill thought of Lally's laser-resurfaced complexion, her expensive New York City haircut, and her twice-a-week manicured nails. Of her habit of air-kissing everyone she met. Of Marge and her manure-covered overalls. She grinned. ''Okay,'' she said. ''I'll put a quarter on good old Marge socking Lally right in the kisser.''

''I'll put fifty cents on good old Marge bootin' her in the butt. Now.'' Doreen turned off the tap water and turned to face her two employers, arms folded, jaw at a decisive angle. ''What are you two gonna do about buying back the Inn?''

# CHAPTER 9

"I thought we agreed we'd buy back the Inn," Quill said.

"*You* talked about it," Meg said. "We listened. But we haven't even begun to figure out how it can be done."

"We are going back up the hill?" Bjarne said.

"I hope so." Quill ran her fingers through her hair. "I've done some planning. That is, I've asked John to figure out a way we can finance it."

"And?" Meg's eyebrows rose. "I thought Marge said she wouldn't sell."

"She'll sell," John said. He came through the back door. His hair was wet with rain. Quill threw him a towel, and he rubbed his head vigorously. "The problem is the price."

"I thought the price of the mortgage," Quill said. "Three hundred thousand dollars."

"That business plan I gave you was predicated on two things. The three hundred thousand cash—which is fair, Quill, since that is the amount of debt that you left, plus a two hundred thousand one-time payment for the name of the business itself and to reimburse Marge for the work she's put in. The other was the success of the Longhorn beef retail business. That end of it appears to be fine. You could work out a deal with Harland to buy the beef from the herd he's bought from Rossiter. I've already phoned Laura Crest and asked her to do some back fat sampling on the herd, so you can use specific statistics from Cornell to advertise it.''

''We're not goin' to eat that Impressive, are we?'' Doreen asked.

''He's a herd sire. So no, he'll have a long and productive life, Doreen,'' Quill said. John's eyebrows rose, and she smiled at him. ''I've been doing a little research myself,'' she said modestly.

''The beef hasn't been aggressively marketed in the U.S. You should be able to charge a premium for it, and that's where, frankly, quite a bit of the projected profit will come from. But.'' He paused and tapped his thumbs together. For John, this was a sign of significant agitation. ''The price has been upped.''

''Upped?'' Quill asked hollowly. ''Upped by whom? And by how much?''

''By the gentleman that came to the menu testing two nights ago. Phil Barkin.''

''He didn't say a word all night,'' Meg said indignantly. ''He was here to buy the Inn? What is he, another rich Texan?''

''No, he's from the Marriott.''

''The Marriott!'' Quill's heart lurched. ''But they have money. A lot of money.''

''So they do. He's taken a look at the healthy beef angle, at the way Marge handles the cash flow and pricing—which is brilliant, I'm chagrined to say—and he's talking a million, a million and a half.''

''A million dollars?'' Meg said faintly.

''He's crazy,'' Doreen said belligerently. ''He's outta his mind.''

''Crazy like a fox,'' John said ruefully. ''I'm sorry, Quill.''

''I'm not giving up,'' Quill said. ''I don't want any of us to give up.''

Doreen went ''t'uh!'' and then said, ''A million *bucks*!''

''I should,'' Meg said thoughtfully, ''have put ipecac in his fruit salad.''

''We didn't serve fruit salad,'' Quill reminded her. ''So, what now, John?''

''You mean you're interested in carrying that kind of debt load?''

''I'm not crazy about it. Do you think we can do it?''

''It depends. If we can match the Marriott's offer— and based on the beef plan, I believe it's finance-worthy, yeah. It's doable. But there's a hitch, and it's a major one. The Marriott's pockets are a lot deeper than ours. It's a well-run business, but if they really want this deal, we've got to be prepared to say no. All we're going to be doing if we get into a bidding war is make Marge Schmidt rich. Which,'' he added, ''she already is.''

''Maybe she doesn't need to be richer?'' Meg said hopefully.

Doreen went ''t'uh!'' again.

''So what do you say?'' John folded his hands.

''What D'Artagnan said to the Three Musketeers.'' Meg clasped her hands and shook them over her head. ''One for all and all for one.''

"It's not a game, Meg," John spoke softly, but his eyes were on Quill.

"We know it's not," Quill said. "Let's talk to Marge, to the bank, to Harland and the colonel. It doesn't cost anything to move ahead at this point, does it, John?"

"Just my consulting fee."

"Hi! Anyone at home?" Andy Bishop tapped lightly on the screen door to the back porch and stepped inside. Meg jumped up and flung her arms around him. He gave her a kiss. "See your train got in on time. I'm sorry I wasn't there to meet you and Lally. . . . Is she here?"

Meg scowled. "She's up at Marge's place."

"So that's still simmering, huh?" He gave her a quick hug and released her. "Well, don't worry about it, Meg. I'll back you against the Tiny Tank for audience appeal anytime." He dragged a stool up to the prep table, which was, Quill thought, getting crowded. "Anything to eat?"

"Two seconds." Meg went to the cooler and began to pull a variety of items from the shelves.

"I came by because I've got the results of the autopsies on Detwiler and Rossiter," Andy said. "You still interested?"

"Yes. But let's get you settled first." Quill got up, put a napkin, cutlery, and wineglass in front of him. John disappeared to the closet that held their wine cellar, and reappeared with a bottle of California Chardonnay. Meg placed a plate of cold salmon, homemade mayonnaise, and pickled asparagus down for him, settled into the stool next to his and said, "Shoot."

"Rossiter first. He wasn't in terrific shape for a man his age. Muscle tone was a little flabby, liver somewhat enlarged, so he had a bit of an alcohol habit. But his ticker was fine. At least, fine for a man in generally poor shape at sixty-two. There was more than an average degree of arteriosclerosis. Which is to say, an aggressive event could have triggered a fatal heart attack. And I think it did."

"You don't mean my food was an aggressive event," Meg said.

"Of course not. But he'd been drinking fairly steadily all day, it was hot for July, and he'd had a heavy lunch. My guess is he was feeling off-kilter most of the afternoon. Perhaps he complained to someone. In any case . . ." He paused to take a healthy bite of salmon, and then a swallow of wine.

"In any case, what?" Meg demanded.

"He was dosed with DMSO."

"With what?"

"Dimexyethodie. It's a stimulant and a vasoconstrictor. It triggered a cardiac spasm that in turn triggered a full-scale heart attack."

"Where did the DMSO come from?" Quill asked.

Andy shrugged. "It's illegal for human use, precisely because of what happened. It's a veterinary drug, though, used to relieve muscle aches in horses, I'm told."

"He did mention that Impressive had strained a shoulder muscle," Quill said thoughtfully.

"Well, when you apply it to animals, you're supposed to wear rubber gloves, since any contact with the skin means instant absorption. I didn't find any on his hands, so if he did use it to massage the bull, he was careful."

Meg fiddled proudly with the collar of Andy's shirt. "Where did you find it?"

"Down the right side of his forearm. Which means he may have brushed up against the bull accidentally, I just don't know. Problem is, the timing's a little screwy."

"A little screwy?" Quill asked. "Why?"

"Because most of the value of DMSO is in how fast

it is absorbed. It's almost instant. I looked it up in the Desk Reference which said that it takes less than three seconds to flare through the system. Now, there had to have been at least an hour's time lapse between wherever he was and the time he died, because he was here at the restaurant for a while. It's possible that he was feeling ill, ignored the symptoms, and just keeled over. Was he that kind of guy? Not one to complain?''

"He was trying to impress Marge Schmidt, that I know," Quill said. "So if he'd been feeling awful, he might not have said a word."

"Do you remember what he had to eat or drink that night?"

"Vodka," Quill said positively. "The Russians made everyone drink a toast. He tossed it back, then died."

"Could have been the proximate cause." Andy still looked doubtful. "Anyway, that's what we found. It's up to the coroner to establish whether or not it's been a suspicious death, so I expect Trooper Harris will be around to interview you, Quill, and you, Meg."

"Andy?" Quill asked slowly. "Who has access to DMSO? On a regular basis?"

"It has to be prescribed by a vet. Most vets have it, as a matter of fact. And Laura Crest confirmed that she gave a supply to Rossiter for use with his bull. So the whereabouts of the drug have been established."

"And what about Detwiler?" John asked. "Did you make any progress with that?"

Andy sighed. He pushed away the plate of half-eaten salmon. "Yeah. You sure you want to hear about it?"

"Yes," Quill said.

"It's not pretty. Detwiler wasn't stabbed in the park. He'd been in the trunk of a car—forensics is establishing the make right now, and then dumped under the oaks about seventy-two hours before he died.''

''Oh, no!'' Quill felt as if she'd been hit in the stomach. ''You mean he *was* alive all that time in the park? For three days?''

Andy nodded grimly. ''I'm sorry. It's pretty horrible. He died of a combination of dehydration and exsanguination. Blood loss.''

Nobody said anything. Quill closed her eyes for a moment.

''Proximate cause of death was a knife wound to the sternum. It was a long, thin, very sharp blade, like a boning knife, as I mentioned at the scene. Whoever delivered the blow had above-average strength. My guess is that it would be a very fit male, but that's a guess.''

''My goodness,'' Meg said. ''There's a horrible story.''

''It is.'' Andy got up. ''Thanks for the meal. I've got to get back to the hospital.'' He bent to Meg's ear. ''Will I see you tonight?''

Meg nodded. ''I refuse to sleep alone after a story like that.''

Quill ran her hands through her hair and looked at her watch. ''Rats. I've got to make a phone call. Oh! Doreen! Did Nate call and confirm my dinner with the colonel?''

Doreen nodded. ''Said he'd be bringin' a guest. Didn't say who.''

''Then I've got about an hour to call Myles and change.''

She went upstairs and dialed the number Myles had left her in case it was urgent. She hesitated a bit beforehand. She didn't know whether he would think this was important or not. When she had first fallen in love with him, she'd found his detachment, his remoteness from her own life as a painter, as an innkeeper, to be a restful thing in the chaos of her life. But things were righting themselves. It was as if she had been looking at life through an out of focus camera lens. Somehow, she was tuning it, and the way was sharper, clearer, than it had been before.

He answered the phone himself.

"Hey," she said.

"Quill." He sounded tired. She knew better than to ask him why.

"Are you all right?"

"Fine."

"You'd say 'fine' if you were staked on top of an ant hill in the broiling sun."

"Mhm. Some interesting background showed up on Rossiter."

"No kidding?" Quill hadn't known the man very long, but she felt sad. She didn't buy the old bromide. "At least it was quick." Dead was dead.

"First of all, he wasn't a Texan."

Quill sat up. "No! With that drawl?"

"And his first name wasn't Royal, it was just plain Ronald. He had it legally changed when he moved to Texas in the early eighties."

"Where did he come from?"

"Long Island."

"Long Island?!"

"Graduate of Columbia, Ph.D. in genetics. Made quite a bit of money when he patented one of the mediums used to filter genetic material in research, sold out to Pfizer, and became a cattleman."

"For heaven's sake," Quill said faintly. "He seemed so . . . so Texan. Is there anything about his wife?"

"Diane Rossiter, also a graduate of Columbia. Royal

was married in 1965, divorced in 1988. Two children, Joshua and Jennifer. Married again in 1992, to a Shirley Backus, occupation: housewife. Divorce pending.''

"Shirley and Royal were getting a divorce?" Quill's mind was racing now. "Myles, how much was Mr. Rossiter worth?"

"In the area of one hundred million."

"Good grief!"

"One hell of a motive," Myles agreed. "Has there been any substantive evidence that his death was—shall we say, encouraged?"

"Andy promised specific autopsy results as soon as they came in. And, Myles. Brady, that's Rossiter's cattle manager, implied that Shirley was, um, a little free with her favors." She heard the *tap tap tap* of his fingers on the computer.

"Nothing here about the bill of particulars. But I can put someone on it."

"If you're not too busy."

"No. I'm not too busy. Christ, surveillance is boring. Nothing much came up on Candy Detwiler. He was a rodeo clown for a number of years, retired with some fairly impressive injuries, and went to work as a cattle handler for Randall Calhoun."

"I don't suppose you have any information on the colonel."

"Well, he's a real colonel. National Guard, but that counts. He's from Oklahoma, a widower, very active churchman. He's been a cattleman all his life."

"He's the real thing, at least," Quill murmured. "Thank you, Myles. I know you don't really approve of my . . . my . . ."

"Meddling?" His voice was teasing, but it stung.

"I was about to say detective work."

"Just keep out of Harris's way."

"Oh." Quill thought a moment and dredged up some jargon. "Is he dirty?"

"Good God, Quill. No, if anything, he's a little too enthusiastic about his job. There're a couple of things I've heard I don't like at all. So don't ask him for anything, avoid him if you can, and manage not to be alone with him."

"He can't be *that* bad, surely."

"Might be. I don't suppose you'll wait until I get home to get involved in all this."

"When are you coming home?"

"Hard to say. A couple of weeks."

She took a deep breath. "Myles? I gave John a call. You know, John Raintree."

"Of course I do. How's the job in Long Island working out?"

"All right, I guess. But I've hired him. As a consultant. I've started talking with Marge about buying the Inn back, and I wanted John to tell me and the bank if there was any way it could be done. I won't go into all the details right now, because you sound so tired, but . . . Myles? Are you there?"

"Still here." He was quiet a long moment. She thought she could hear him breathing. "It's what you want to do."

"I, yes. It is. I've worked out a whole new way to handle things, Myles. So I won't get so involved with irrelevant things."

"I see. Well. Good luck."

"That's it? Good luck?"

"What would you like me to say? That I think you're doing the right thing? I can't answer that for you, Quill.

All I can tell you is that it isn't the right thing for the two of us.''

"And why is that?" she asked, her voice cool.

"Because no matter how you handle it, it's a full-time job."

"And my relationship with you should be my full-time job, is that it?"

"You know that's not it." He controlled his impatience with an effort that came clearly over the phone. "Both of us will be involved in work that fully occupies our time. In very separate areas."

"Well, why don't you become an innkeeper?"

No response.

"Okay, then why don't I learn to do what you do?"

"It's too dangerous, dammit."

"I don't care."

"I do. Because I love you. And I'll tell you this, Quill, bottom line, if I'm worried about you, it's going to be a lot more dangerous for me."

And that was the bottom line. The whole of it. Quill said good-bye, I love you, because she did, then she hung up the phone.

She sat on the bed for a moment, thinking of the feel of Myles's chest against her breasts, the strength of his cheekbones, the power in his hands. She'd never painted him. She wondered why she'd never painted him.

"Quill?" Meg tapped at her door and stuck her head inside. Max poked his nose through the crack in the door and shoved inside. "The colonel's here."

"Is it that late already?" Dismayed, Quill looked at her watch. "Damn, I wanted to change."

"You'd better change pretty fast. He's brought the Russians with him, and Bjarne's mad as fire."

Quill could hear loud, quarrelsome voices floating up

the stairs from down below. "Meg, go talk to them."

"What in heck am I going to say to a bunch of Russians and a teed off Finn?" She narrowed her eyes. "Hey." She stepped into the room and sat beside Quill on the bed. She put her arm around her. "What's the matter? Are you okay?"

"I just need a minute, okay?"

"Sure." She brushed Quill's hair back from her forehead. "You tell me about it later."

"In a while."

"Okay. I'm always around, you know?" She kissed her ear and jumped up. "C'mon, Max, let's go amuse the Russians."

"Just don't *sing*!" Quill called after her. She got up, grabbed her bathrobe from the back of the door, and went down the short hall to the bathroom. She didn't think it would bother her to have to share a bath with Meg and whomever happened to be staying with them that week, but it did. She always felt as if she should hurry, although she had a good reason to hurry now. She stared at herself in the mirror, wondering if she could see what Meg had seen in her face. Her red hair was a mess, as usual. Her eyes were still hazel. Maybe there were lines at the corners of her eyes and on her upper lip. She hadn't noticed that before. She showered and changed into a long gauzy dress with a deep V neck. She brushed her hair as fast as she could, wondering for the thousandth time if it would be more convenient to cut it short and have to wrestle with a curling iron. She swept it up onto the top of her head in a knot and raced downstairs.

The colonel hadn't just brought the Russians, he'd brought the Widow Rossiter, too, who looked none the worse for wear after her boozy morning. They were seated at the center table. The other diners, more soberly dressed, cast sidelong glances at the colonel's hat, Shirley's matching jeans and button-down shirt in gold lamé, and the Russians sweating in their dark three-piece suits. It wasn't particularly warm for July, but Quill wondered if she should turn on the air-conditioning. If she did, the other diners in their summer wear would freeze.

Leonid jumped to his feet as she came into the room and grabbed both her hands in his. "How I love you when you arrive like this!" he shouted. "You are a wonderful part of this country."

"Thank you," Quill said. She gently withdrew her hands and smiled at everyone in turn. "I'm sorry I wasn't here to greet you when you came in. If you'll excuse me, I'll just let the chef know you're all here."

"The Finn?" Leonid's thick eyebrows came together in a scowl. "It is not such a good thing, that a Finn cook for Russians. He has already come out to see us."

"And what happened?" Quill asked, in spite of herself.

"He goes, 'Phuut!' " Leonid made an "o" with his mouth.

"Here, now," the colonel said in alarm.

Leonid shrugged. "I am thinking. It is not against the law in this country to have Finns in the kitchen. Is it?"

"No."

"And if he goes, 'Phuut' in our soup? The thing is, I was not even born when we in Russia were maybe a little rude to the Finns. So why should this Finn be mad at me? Or at Vasily? Or Alexi? Me, I am trying to explain to this Finn that we are young, we are not of the same prejudices as our fathers, but you know," he leaned forward and whispered, "Finns are funny that way. Most of them . . ." He twirled his finger around his ear. "Crazy. Very crazy. It is well known in . . ."

"Stop," Quill said. "I'll go check on the meal. In the meantime"—she beckoned to Peter the waiter—"please order yourself drinks." She stalked back to the kitchen. "Bjarne!"

He didn't answer. He was at the stove, stirring something. It may have been black bean soup with sour cream, which was on the specials menu.

"Bjarne?"

"Yes!"

"Don't spit in the Russians' soup. You look guilty." She advanced on him. "Did you already spit in the Russians' soup?" Her gaze fell on three filled bowls that had been set to one side. "Throw them out," she said.

"They are . . ." and there was that bad Finnish word again. Or maybe it was Swedish.

"Probably," she agreed. "But we'll have the Board of Health after us in two seconds flat if you spit in the soup." She looked around the kitchen. "Where are Meg and John and Doreen?"

"Doreen went home," Bjarne said sulkily. "The others are out back."

Quill stepped outside onto the back porch. Meg and John were sitting on the steps leading to the small little excuse for a vegetable garden, heads tightly together in deep discussion. Max was asleep in his pen. "Meg?" Quill said.

Her sister jumped as if she'd been stung by a bee. "What!"

"I thought you were going to pour balm on troubled waters in there."

"I did. I made Bjarne go back to the kitchen."

"But then you left, too."

"So!?"

"So it would have been better if you'd sat down and chatted them up a bit."

"That's your job. It's my job to make sure we have enough food on hand when a reservation for two turns into a reservation for five."

"I don't know why that happened."

"And," Meg continued remorselessly, "it's all on the house, right?"

"Um. Well, I did invite the colonel to be my guest. So I suppose it is."

John groaned. "You know, Quill . . ."

"I know. I know. Free food costs us. I'm sorry. But," she brightened, "we may get some inside information on this deal the Russians and the cowmen are cooking up. Not to mention the murder of poor Candy Detwiler."

"And what possible use could this be to us?" Meg asked, her eyebrows raised.

"I won't know until I sit down with them, will I?"

But dinner proved to be less than satisfactory for either detective work or business plans. Quill sat down next to Calhoun. "I like the hat," she said. "Is it a Stetson?"

"No, Miss Quilliam, it isn't. This is a quintuple-nine Texas beaver. With an Oklahoma crease."

"My goodness," Quill said. Peter set soup in front of the party. Quill squinted at the bowls in front of the Russians. They looked spit-free, but you never knew.

"An Oklahoma crease?" She picked up her spoon, then set it down again. What if Peter had gotten the bowls mixed up?

"Something wrong with the soup, Miss Quilliam?"

"No, no." She swallowed some. It was excellent, even if it did have Finnish spit in it.

"You can tell where a man is from by the crease in his hat," the colonel said. "When I'm running a cattle auction, I can look across the room and tell where every single soul is from by the crease in his hat.''

"What sort of crease did Candy Detwiler have?''

"Candy? West Texas. Fold on the right brim, half dent at the crown.''

"His death was a terrible thing,'' Quill said soberly.

Shirley was having a high old time with the Russians. She was drinking vodka. She tucked one forefinger behind Leonid's lapel and shrieked, ''Darlin', *where*'d you get this ole suit?''

"K-Mart,'' Leonid said. ''Part of the reason why I love this country.''

"It was.'' The colonel nodded slowly.

"Did he leave any family?''

The colonel shook his head. ''I was his family. My sons and my wife and I. Although I do believe there was a daughter somewhere.''

"Do you have any idea who would want to hurt him?''

"It wasn't Candy they wanted to hurt. It was the breed.''

"The cows?''

"Cattle, ma'am. Cows are female cattle.''

"I don't understand.''

He turned to her, his eyes bright. There was a bit of black bean soup on his upper lip. ''The purebred Texas longhorn is the greatest breed of cattle on earth. Have you heard my lecture on genetics?''

"Yes,'' Quill said shortly. ''But I fail to see why anyone would want to murder Mr. Detwiler because Texas longhorns are the greatest breed on earth.''

"He was a heck of a cattle handler, Miss Quilliam. The best. Why, he was the one that broke my bull Impressive to saddle. Rounding up a herd of steers to go to the slaughterhouse, there was no one like Candy. He could get those cattle in the trailer just as sweet as you please. He was killed because whoever did it knew that it was one of the worst possible blows I could take. The only thing worse would be losing my bull.''

Quill took a moment to collect her thoughts, and more important, control her tongue. The guy was squirrelly. ''About that bull. I thought Royal Rossiter owned the herd.''

''It's my bull,'' the colonel repeated.

''But did Royal pay you for it?''

''Of course Roy paid him for it,'' Shirley interrupted suddenly. ''Crazy old coot. That's a Rossiter herd. It's *my* herd now.''

''This I must ask you, then,'' Leonid said. ''Your poor husband . . .''

''Roy!'' Shirley wailed. ''My Royal!''

Leonid poured her a glass of vodka. ''In Russia, this is what we do when we are sad. We drink vodka. Also when we are happy.''

Shirley gulped the drink. Peter set the wild greens salad in front of her. She poked at it. ''Looks like hay before it dries.''

''I must ask you this,'' Leonid said, as if there had been no interruption. ''We are very interested in sending these cows to Russia. I have spoken with your—with Mr. Rossiter, who says, he will think about it. He is not so sure that he wants his cows to leave this country. But these cows, these cows can survive on our land like no other cows can. They are tough, these cows, I think maybe these cows are from Russia to begin with, and perhaps they got over here by mistake.'' He smiled. ''And, of course, now Mr. Rossiter is dead.''

''Excuse me, sir.'' The colonel stood up, attracting the attention of everyone else in the restaurant. ''Royal never

would have sold American cattle to a bunch of Russkies.''

''That's for damn sure,'' Shirley said. Then, ''You all
are Russians?''

''So he may have said. At first,'' Leonid said. ''But
he—ah! Died. Right here in this restaurant not two nights
ago before he could change his mind.''

The well-dressed couple at the table adjacent to Leonid's chair exchanged alarmed glances. Quill made a face
at Peter, who nodded and quickly left the room. The colonel leaned across the table, his face red in the candle-
light. ''Royal Rossiter may have been a lot of things. He
may not have been the cowman he thought he was. But
I'll tell you this, you Commie, he never would have
agreed to sell those Longhorns!''

''He would,'' Leonid said.

''He would *not,* sir!''

''He would. He would, he would, he would.''

''Gentlemen?'' John put a firm hand on the colonel's
shoulder. Peter, who was standing behind him, gave Quill
an interrogative grin: Was I right? Quill nodded a fervent
yes! The colonel sank back into his chair. Peter, carrying
a bottle of cabernet of exceptional quality, moved lightly
over to Vasily and began to pour. ''This is a French
cabernet from the north of that country,'' John explained
smoothly. He went on to describe the year, the vintage,
the fact that a few thousand of the bottles from that press-
ing had landed on the bottom of the Atlantic Ocean after
a shipwreck the year before. Quill knew him well enough
to sense the wince when Shirley upended her glass and
drank it all at once. But the wine served as an effective
diversion, and the topic of the longhorn sale was
dropped.

Quill ate the rest of the meal with half a mind on the

desultory conversation, the other half occupied in speculation.

Who had killed Candy Detwiler? The colonel's claims that the murder was directed at him were ridiculous, but then, who knew?

Except, of course, that Candy had been knifed several days before he'd died. A powerful arm, with a lot of muscle behind it, Andy had said. Rossiter was sixty-two, thin, and hadn't seemed particularly fit to Quill, as indeed, the autopsy results had borne out. He'd even had trouble dumping the manure bucket over the side of the pen when Marge was helping him clean out the corral.

Should she throw out the assumption that Detwiler had been killed by another cattleman, jealous of the colonel's success with the breed? Quill wished she had her sketch pad to make a note. There was a very significant clue that bothered her: the DMSO. Brady had access to it, of course, since he took care of the cattle. And Laura Crest was the supplier. Quill would take an oath that the two of them had known each other well before they had met in Hemlock Falls.

But why would Brady kill his employer? Why would Laura kill for Brady? Quill eyed Shirley Rossiter. One hundred million was a lot of money. Suppose Brady was having an affair with Mrs. Rossiter, Royal discovered it and filed for divorce, and Laura Crest and Brady, who were also having an affair . . . Quill tugged at a strand of her hair in frustration.

"Spray it," Shirley Rossiter advised loudly.

"Beg pardon?"

"Your hair. I noticed you were lookin' at my do, and I'm tellin' you unless you have a hairdresser right on your little ole tail all the time, it's hell to keep up. I mean, just look at yours, all over your face like that. I got some spray right here in my purse, it'll fix you right up.'' She narrowed her eyes. '' 'Course, you'll have to comb it first. Y'all got a ladies' room here?''

''Dessert, I think, Peter,'' Quill said firmly. ''And coffee.''

It was another forty-five minutes before Quill could (tactfully, she hoped) edge the Calhoun party out the door and back up the hill to the Inn. She came back from the farewells and thanks to a table littered with empty vodka bottles, crumbs, spilled food, and a wine stained tablecloth.

''Just throw it out,'' Peter advised, as he began to clear. ''You can't bleach that color primrose, or so my mom tells me.''

''Um. Is everybody in the kitchen?''

''If you mean Meg and John, yeah. And the cleanup crew.''

John and Meg were not in the kitchen but outside on the same back steps. Quill joined them, locking her arms round her knees and gazing up at the sky. The moon was high and white. The air had cooled from the heat of the day, and mist trailed pennants under the trees.

''What a meal,'' Meg grumbled. ''And all for . . .''

''Don't say it,'' Quill warned.

John chuckled. He rarely laughed, and the sound was pleasing.

''So did we learn anything of note, oh, great detective?''

''Just shut up, Meg,'' Quill said amiably. ''As a matter of fact, we did.''

''Yeah, from Andy. And I don't mind feeding him for free.''

''Not from Andy.'' She pursed her lips. ''Did you hear how agitated the colonel got over the Russians buying the cattle? And did you hear how insistent Leonid was that they get them?''

"So do you think it was the Russians or the colonel with the candlestick . . .''

". . . in the library,'' Quill finished for her. "I don't know what to think. I'm going up to bed so that I can think.'' She peered into the gloomy backyard. "Where's Max?''

"Escaped again,'' Meg said. "And he's your dog, so you go look for him.''

"He comes when you call him, you look for him.''

"I'll look for him.'' John got to his feet. "I could use a walk after tonight.''

"I could, too, actually,'' Quill said casually. "You going on to Andy's, Meg?''

Meg yawned. "Yeah. I'll see you in the morning. There's another flippin' Chamber meeting, right? At one? I'm supposed to be there?''

"Yes. I've got the proofs of the program for International Night. But it should be a short one, Meg. I don't think it will go on and on.''

"Ha! They always do.'' She gave Quill a sleepy hug. "You have time to talk tomorrow?''

"Sure. We'll have lunch after the meeting. Just the two of us.''

"We'd better get out of Hemlock Falls, then. Every time you sit down to eat or talk to me, some bozo comes bursting into the kitchen or the dining room or wherever.''

"Hey,'' John protested.

"You're not a bozo,'' Meg said affectionately. "Have a nice walk.''

Quill and John gave the yard a brief search to confirm that Max wasn't there, then set out in the cool and the dark. "He usually heads for the Park, and then the Gorge," Quill said. "Actually, he usually comes on home by himself, but I suppose it'd be irresponsible to leave him out."

He took her hand, lightly, as a friend does. Quill curled her fingers around his palm, squeezed it, and let it go. "Max!" she called. "Max!"

A bark in response.

"What do you know," John said, "his master's voice."

"Max! Here, boy! I've got some liver for you, boy."

"You do?"

"No, but by the time he gets here, he'll have forgotten all about it. He doesn't have much on his little doggy mind, John."

The barks escalated in volume.

"He's never sounded like that before," Quill said. "You don't suppose he's hurt?"

"You don't suppose he's found another body?"

"You know, John, that really bothers me. Max has been in the Park every day since poor Detwiler was put there, and he never came home and . . ." She trailed off. John took her elbow and guided her to the sound of the barking. "I know he's not Lassie, but . . ."

"He's a dog," John said briefly. "Max!"

Max dashed out of the darkness and danced urgently around Quill. His ears were up. His eyes were anxious. He dashed back into the brush and crouched there, tail wagging frantically.

Quill's heart contracted. John knelt down and shoved his way into the brush. "John?" She cleared her throat and said more loudly, "John! It's not another . . . it's not a body, is it?"

"No. Not a human one. It's Tye. Laura Crest's dog."

# CHAPTER 10

"The dog's hurt," Quill said. She knelt beside John in the bushes.

"Don't touch her. She may bite."

Quill shuddered.

He put his hand on her shoulder. "Are you all right?"

"Just remembering that German shepherd when we went to investigate the Thermo King truck way back when we had our first corpse."

"This is a good dog. I don't think we'll run into that kind of problem here. Here, steady, girl." He probed along her ribs, her jaw, then each of her legs in turn. Tye lay on her side, her brown eyes rolled trustfully up at him. There was blood on her hindquarters. Quill bent next to John. She could feel his skull, the silkiness of his hair.

"I think she's been kicked." He eased the dog up into his arms, then got to his feet. Tye whined, but didn't bite.

"Is she going to be okay?"

"I don't know. But we'll get her back into the kitchen and give Laura a call."

They walked back to the house, not speaking. In the kitchen, Quill spread several large dish towels on the prep table. John laid the dog down. She waved her legs feebly, licked John's hand, then closed her eyes. Quill went to the phone on the wall and dialed directory service for Laura Crest's number, both the emergency and the clinic number. "No answer at the clinic," she told John. The answering service promised to call the vet's private line, and no, they wouldn't release the number to Quill. "It's extremely urgent," Quill said into the phone. "Please have her call right away. Tell her we've found her dog Tye, and she's seriously hurt."

Minutes passed. John kept his hand on Tye's head, which seemed to quiet her. Quill paced restlessly up and down the kitchen. "I'm going to try again."

Sorry, the answering service said. Her line was busy.

"Then will you interrupt, please?! And call me back right away." Quill left her number and hung up the phone with a frustrated snap of her wrist. "What if we try Andy? She doesn't look good, John." Tye's tongue lolled from her mouth. She panted heavily. Quill called Andy at home and her sister answered.

"A what?"

"The vet's dog."

"But Andy's a people doctor. He doesn't know a thing about animals."

"He must know something, Meg. Please. The poor thing."

"Oh, all right." Meg banged the phone down. Moments later, it rang.

"That phone is off the hook," the answering service operator said.

"Laura Crest's phone? Off the . . ." Quill's breath came short. "All right, thank you." She hung up for the final time and turned to John. "We'd better call the police."

"How did you know she was dead?" Trooper Harris demanded, several hours later.

"I didn't know she was dead. I just knew that something must be wrong." They were seated in the semi-darkness of the dining room. It was three o'clock in the morning. John had taken Tye to a vet in Syracuse, where they had a 24-hour emergency service. Andy had said he wasn't sure, but he thought that, at worst, Tye had a ruptured bladder.

"A kick, probably," he'd said sadly. "If I'm right, she'll just need a week or two off her feet."

Max was asleep in his pen in the backyard.

"You must have had some prior knowledge to call the police at that hour for a phone off the hook. Why didn't you go out there first, before giving us a call?"

Quill didn't like his tone of voice at all. She kept her temper and said calmly, "The biggest problem with running a restaurant this size is that there's no place to really sit. Would you like to go into the kitchen and have a cup of coffee there?"

"No."

Quill raised her eyebrows. She got up and flipped on the dining room lights. She felt better, with the darkness at bay.

"You were telling me why you called us and didn't go out to take Crest's dog to her."

"I was afraid to transport the dog, John told you that. I told you that. And that dog meant the world to Laura. It just seemed very suspicious that the dog would be here, ten miles from the clinic without her, and that her phone should be off the hook. She's a vet, Mr. Harris.''

"Sergeant Harris."

"Sergeant. And a good one. Responsible vets don't leave their phones off the hook. They're on call twenty-four hours a day.''

"Right.''

The sarcasm in his voice raised her temper. She controlled it with an effort. "What did you find? Do you think it was a burglary?''

"Maybe. Maybe not.''

"How . . . how did she die? I understand that it must not have been a natural death . . .''

He leaped on that. "Why?''

"Because you're asking me all these questions.'' You idiot, she added silently.

"It's enough for you to know that the circumstances weren't by the book.'' His eyes slid up and down her face. He got up, placed both his hands on the table, and leaned into her. "Now. Let's go through this one more time.''

"Let's not," Quill snapped. She shoved herself away from the table and went into the kitchen. She could feel him behind her. "Sergeant, can't we continue this in the morning?''

"You have some reason you don't want to talk now?'' His hand caressed the gun at his belt.

"It's three o'clock in the morning. And you're a by-the-book kind of guy, aren't you? That's what Myles McHale said tonight. And a by-the-book kind of guy should really have another person present when doing . . . whatever it is that you're doing.''

"You know McHale?''

He was standing so close to her that she had to bend

back from his breath in her face. She put her hands on his chest and gave an angry shove. He didn't even flinch. "I said, you know McHale?"

"She knows McHale. And she knows me." John came through the back door, face impassive with anger. Harris backed off.

Quill stood up straight and took a deep breath. She felt sixteen different kinds of a fool. Make that twenty. It could have been worse. She could have thrown herself on John's chest and squealed, "John." "Coffee anyone?" she said brightly.

Harris left, with a silent glower in John's direction. Quill covered her face with her hands and counted to ten.

"You okay?"

"I'm okay." She took her hands away. "Did you find out what happened to Laura, John? And how's the dog?"

"The dog's fine. Or will be. Andy was right about the kick. She'll be at the clinic for a couple of days, and then she can come home."

"And Laura?"

"I don't know any more than you do."

"The whole town will know by morning. All we have to do is wait."

"I'll see you in the morning then." He hesitated, then went upstairs. Quill heard the quiet tread of his feet, the closing of his bedroom door. She waited for a long while before she went to bed herself.

"Quill?" Someone was pulling her out of water. "Quill!" Quill woke up. Doreen stood over her, a scowl on her face. "*I* didn't want to wake you up. John said you didn't get to sleep till after four. But you better come downstairs."

Quill rolled over and looked at the bedside clock. Ten-thirty. "Good grief, Doreen, I slept past the breakfast trade." She sat up. "What's going on?"

"Hear that?" Doreen gestured toward Main Street with one scrawny arm. There was a thud of marching feet and a rhythmic chant.

"What in the heck is it?" Quill pulled her robe from the rocking chair and went to the window. "Who are all those people?"

There was a crowd on Main Street. All ages. All sizes. All genders. Some of them were carrying signs: DON'T SEND OUR FRIENDS TO SLAUGHTER and ONLY CANNIBALS EAT MEAT. The chant was loud, if uninspired: "No! No! No! No!"

"Oh, dear."

"What'ya goin' to do about it?"

"What am I supposed to do about it, Doreen? And why should I get involved in what looks to be perfectly peaceful . . ." She gazed out the window again. It was an oddly ragged crowd for a vegetarian demonstration. Quill didn't know a great deal about vegetarians, but she hadn't noticed that they dressed any worse than anyone else. ". . . if somewhat disreputable demonstration." An old yellow school bus was parked directly across from the Palate. The sides were painted with slogans such as FREE THE INNOCENTS and STOP THE SLAUGHTER! The whole was dominated by the picture of a pitiful-looking calf squashed into a carrying crate. Quill saw Sky and Normal Norman talking to CarolAnn Spinoza. CarolAnn was nodding her head so vigorously Quill hoped her hair would fall off.

"Jeez," Meg said. She came into the room without her usual bounce. "What are you going to do about this, Quill?"

"Me? Why me?"

"Because it's our restaurant they're picketing." Meg pressed close to her and peered over her shoulder. "See? They're protesting the Russians coming here to buy cattle to ship back to Moscow or the Gulag or wherever. They want to close down International Night. Sky and Norman want to talk to you."

"Oh." Quill considered this.

Meg nudged her. "Well?"

"Well, what?" she said crossly. "Where's John, anyway?"

"Went over to talk to that bozo from the Marriott," Doreen said.

"Besides, you're in charge of public relations," Meg added.

"Right. Yes. I am. Okay." Quill threw off the robe, pulled on a pair of jeans and a T-shirt, and smoothed back her hair. "I'm ready."

"Shoes," Doreen said briefly.

"Right. Shoes."

They followed her downstairs. The dining room was totally empty. Half filled cups of coffee, uneaten food, and pushed back chairs told Quill that at some point the diners here had made a hasty departure. And without, she suspected, paying the bill.

She walked out onto Main Street and surveyed the situation. Esther West stood in front of her store, arms folded over her chest. Marge stood beside her. Both of them were glaring in the direction of the Palate. Quill crossed the street and went up to them. "Hi, guys."

"What are you going to do about this, Quill?" Marge demanded. "These are the same damn fools what picketed the Dew Drop day before yesterday. I thought that Harris ran them out of town, but hell, no, here they are back again. Harland,'' she added with a slight blush, ''is all upset. 'Fraid they'll be out to his place next. And if they are''—she hitched up her chinos with a determined hand—''they're gonna know what hit 'em.''

''Why aren't they going to know what hit them right now?'' Quill said. ''You're good at this sort of thing, Marge. Why don't you tell them to go?''

''She can't go near them,'' Esther contributed nervously. ''Trooper Harris served her a restraining order after she clobbered that bearded guy up at the Inn the other day. She's not allowed to go near them.''

The protesters had formed into a ragged circle smack in front of the Palate's teal blue door. Quill could see Doreen and Meg staring at them through the large plate glass window. Suddenly Max bounded around the edge of the stone building and joined the group. Tail wagging, he attached himself to Sky (who apparently had the lead, although since it was a circle Quill wasn't sure).

''I hope,'' CarolAnn Spinoza said sweetly, coming up to her, ''that you aren't contemplating the disturbance of a peaceful protest.''

''CarolAnn,'' Quill said, ''why are you doing this?''

''I don't know what you are talking about.''

''You know perfectly well what I'm talking about. You got these protesters here. Why are you stirring up all this trouble?''

CarolAnn grew sullen. ''You'd better watch it, missy.''

''Now, CarolAnn,'' Marge said, ''Quill didn't mean what you think she means.''

This was the last straw. Rough, tough Marge groveling in front of this person? ''Now, you *look* CarolAnn Spinoza . . .''

''Hang on,'' said Marge, grabbing her arm.

Quill threw it off. "Hang on yourself, Marge. It's about time somebody . . ."

"No. Hang on. Somebody called the cops."

Two state police cars drove slowly through the crowd (half Hemlockians and half protesters) and stopped in front of the Palate. Trooper Harris got out of the passenger side and swaggered up to Sky and Normal Norman.

"Down!" Sky screeched. The circle promptly collapsed onto the pavement. Sky lay flat on her back and resumed her chant, "No! No! No!"

Trooper Harris said, tight-lipped, "Norman Francis Smith? You have the right to remain silent. You have the right to counsel to represent you, and if you do not have counsel, one will be appointed . . ."

Quill, Marge, and Esther edged closer.

"That little snot," Marge said two decibels lower than her usual bellow. "Whyn't the heck he arrest them when they was up to my place?"

Harris jerked Normal Norman upright. Two troopers from the second car put handcuffs on him. Harris droned, ". . . for the murders of Laura Crest, and Bruce Detwiler, known as Candy Detwiler. The charge is murder one."

"I don't believe it for one minute," Quill said, astonished.

Harris shot her a glance that would have wilted kudzu.

"I do." CarolAnn was loud, as usual. "I guess you didn't hear about what happened up at the vet's?" She smirked at Harris, who smirked back. "They were up there yesterday afternoon, trying to free those poor test subjects in that so-called clinic."

"Trashed the place," offered a fair-haired trooper, as he pushed Norman into the patrol car. "Trashed the vet's office, too, and then . . ." He made a sharp thrust with his hand.

"She was knifed?" Quill said.

"Same as Candy Detwiler," CarolAnn said. "The O.M. was exactly the same, which is why they're arresting Norman for the both of them."

"M.O.," Marge said sourly.

"Huh?"

"M.O., not O.M.," Quill said. "It stands for *modus operandi*."

"Now look at *that.*" There was such smarmy glee in CarolAnn's voice that Quill's palm itched to smack her. A van marked THE RUSTICATED LADY, HGTV squealed to a halt behind the trooper's car. "Lally Preston's good for something, I guess." CarolAnn sprinted toward the car.

"That's her TV crew, innit?" Marge said.

"Yes." Quill glumly returned Lally's wave. Lally's cameraman got out of the back and looked vaguely around, his camcorder in hand. Lally herself grabbed his shoulders, pointed him in the direction of the protesters still milling around the Palate, then trotted over to Quill and Marge. She had the grace, at least, to look embarrassed. "Sorry about this, but we make an extra dollar or two when the networks call for footage. They'll cut in the national anchor later, I guess."

The cameraman ran alongside the protesters, who broke happily into their chant. One of them turned the sign that read: CLOSE THE PALATE! straight into the camera lens.

"Gee, Quill," Marge said with a grin, "that can't be good for the price of that business now, can it?"

So the truce was over. In several minutes the protest was over, as well. Lally's cameraman shot a few more feet of tape, got back into the car, and gestured to Lally.

"See you, bye," Lally said. "We all set for tonight?"

"I guess so," Quill said. "You mean the banquet's still on?"

"Of course. Time and TV wait for no man. Dead or alive."

"Uh, Lally," Marge said. "We talked about maybe serving Betty's lemon custard pie tonight? Instead of that puddin' thing Meg mixes up out of a bag."

"It's NOT out of a bag," Quill said indignantly. "It's crème brûlée, which is eggs, sugar—"

"Well, the sugar's out of a bag, innit?"

Quill slammed the door on her way back into the restaurant.

"Wow," Meg said. She was sitting at a table, her feet propped up on a chair. She was drinking lemonade. "Want some?"

"I just made a record," Quill said. She shoved Meg's feet off the chair and sat down.

"What's the record?"

"For the shortest amount of time between wanting to smack two people ever."

"CarolAnn I can understand. Who else?"

"Marge, of course. Where's Doreen?"

"Went to chase Max and bring him home. I told her it was her turn." Meg set the lemonade on the table. "So they arrested that poor geek Norman."

"Q.U.A.C.K. was up there yesterday, and Trooper Einstein must have put one and one together to get five. Those people didn't kill Laura. And I'll bet they didn't kill Candy Detwiler, either."

"I don't know, Quill. Norman's got a record."

"I can see them maybe clobbering a human over the head," Quill admitted. "But, Meg, would animal rights people kick a dog? With as vicious a kick as laid out poor Tye?"

Meg's eyes widened. "Jeez," she said.

"CarolAnn let something drop that didn't make sense. She said that Q.U.A.C.K. was at the clinic to free test animals."

"Test animals?"

"You know. Lab animals. Rabbits. White rats. The sort they use in labs to test cosmetics."

"Laura Crest didn't have test animals at her clinic."

"I know who can tell us if she did. Jack Brady."

First, they drove out to Motel 48, where the hopeful little desk clerk said she hadn't seen him all night, and if they found him, would they tell him they could have a drink some other time. Then they went to the Inn. Marge, in charge of setting up the conference room for the Chamber lunch, said belligerently she hadn't seen Brady, and would they please get their keisters outta there, unless they had a couple million in their pockets to drop into her bank account.

They finally found Jack at the Croh Bar, slouched over a table in the corner and listening to Patsy Cline's "Walkin'." He looked awful. The skin under his eyes was purple. He hadn't shaved. He sat like a man defeated. He didn't notice either one of them at first. Quill signaled Ben Croh for another round of whatever Brady was drinking with a circular sweep of her finger.

"It's beer," Meg whispered.

"So we'll drink beer."

"At eleven-thirty in the morning? I think not."

"Ladies." Brady raised his head. Quill was shocked at the expression in his eyes. "Y'all have a seat."

They sat down on either side of him. Ben set three beers down. Quill took a sip, then remembered she hadn't had any breakfast. Meg gave her glass a disgusted shove. Brady drained his, took Meg's with a courteous crook of his eyebrow, and drained that. Quill pushed her glass toward him. He wrapped his big hands around it. "What can I do for you two?"

Quill hesitated. "It's about Laura Crest."

He ducked his head once.

"You knew her before, Brady? Before you came to Hemlock Falls?"

He ducked his head again.

"In Texas?"

"At Cornell." He drank half of Quill's beer. "I brought up some steers from San Antonio. Fellas in the research lab wanted to study 'em, I guess. Laura was just gettin' herself out of school."

"She was a resident in the lab?"

"Ahuh."

And Brady, being Brady, would have seduced the young resident with no problem at all. "Brady, why would the animal rights people protest against the clinic?"

His face was bleak. "I think it was my fault. They killed her. And it was my fault." He rotated the beer glass between two palms. "I was shootin' off my mouth. In here. Laura was with me. She keeps a couple of those horses for blood serum. You know, you can make a decent buck collecting antibodies from them couple of times a week. She supplies Cornell. She needed the money. It don't hurt the horses none, to have blood drawn every once in a while. But I was kind of raggin' her about it, and that fella Norman was sitting right over there. By the jukebox. He comes up, all goofy, starts hollerin' about how animals have souls, too, Jesus." He expelled his breath. "I'm a horseman myself. You think I'd . . . anyhow, I just kind of egged him, just to tease Laura."

"It's not your fault, Brady." Quill laid her hand gently on his arm.

He didn't say anything.

"It's not your fault because they didn't kill her."

"What d'ya mean? They tore the place up."

"Who told you that?"

"Harris."

"You think they kicked Tye hard enough to put her in intensive care?"

He thought about this. "Hell, no."

"And Harris is a dolt," Meg said. She began to tap her foot on the floor in an impatient rhythm Quill recognized. She was beginning to think about having to cook that night, and she was beginning to get nervous.

"You got that right." He eased back in his chair. A little color had come back into his face. "So who tore the place up?"

"I don't know. But as far as I can gather, Q.U.A.C.K. doesn't do anything more than walk around in circles, literally, and wave their signs around. The most damage they've ever done is to let those turkeys out on Interstate 90. And they didn't even mean to do that. I know because I asked Sky about it, and she said she thought the turkeys would just fly off. To their home in the wild, she said."

"Turkeys can't fly."

"I know that. You know that. But how much do animal rights people really know about animals?"

"Jack shit."

"Yes. So. I'll tell you what I think we should do. I think we should go on up to Laura's clinic and poke around and see what really happened."

"We've got to get to the Chamber meeting, Quill, and then I have to get back to the kitchen." Meg drummed her fingers on the table. "I know this is important, but so's the bloody meal."

"In a minute," Quill soothed.

Brady said, "Harris'll have a man on point. I know, because I'm tending to the stock up there until I can ship them off to another vet."

"Not at night, he won't. That's just to keep sightseers away. I know because Myles told me once . . ." She bit her lip and stopped.

"Who's Myles?"

"Just someone I knew."

Meg raised her eyebrows at that.

"So what do you think, Brady? Shall we do a little investigating? Tonight? After the International Night Dinner?"

"Yeh. I think we should. Do you want me to bring my gun?"

"No!" Quill said, horrified. "I do not. We'll leave from the Palate."

"It's quarter to one, Quillie. We've got to GO!"

"Hang in there, Meg. We'll see you tonight, Brady." They left him there, still brooding over his beer, and got into the Olds to drive to the Inn.

"I like this," Meg said as Quill navigated the hill. "This is the first time I get to do the dangerous stuff. I mean the visit to the clinic tonight. Not the cooking. I can handle the cooking. I think. I'll concentrate on the dangerous stuff, instead. Then maybe I won't get so bummed about having to cook."

"That's not the dangerous stuff." Quill parked under the DON'T EVEN THINK OF PARKING HERE sign and sat looking at the Inn. "The Chamber meeting's the dangerous stuff. Fasten your seat belts, sweetie, it's going to be a bumpy ride."

• • • •

". . . disGRACE!" Adela Henry was saying, as Quill and Meg walked into the dining room. Since Marge had cut the menu prices (a move which had baffled Quill, until she learned about the infamous booking fee) the Chamber had resumed its monthly lunches at the Inn. The tables were arranged in a U, with the mayor and Adela at the head. Meg and Quill took seats near the end, and Meg poked glumly at the appetizer. "Peaches. Fresh peaches."

"They look great."

"I know they look great!" She bit her lip. "Maybe I should do something with fresh peaches tonight."

"The menu will be fine, Meg."

"The menu sucks. Look what happened the last time I served it. The guy croaked."

"There you are, Quill," the mayor said. "I guess we can start now that the secretary's here." He beamed around the room. "Everybody's here," he said. "Good turnout. Should be a good meeting." Quill scanned the room. Colonel Calhoun was seated to Elmer's right, as guest of honor. The Russians were lined up to Adela's left (appropriately enough). The four of them were politely attentive. The citizens of Hemlock Falls, however, were not. Most ominous was the fact that CarolAnn Spinoza was there, looking pious. Everyone else looked mad. Seeing the cross faces, Quill wasn't as sure as the mayor that it was going to be a homey, feel-good meeting. She'd seen the expressions on the faces of the villagers caught up in the morning's brouhaha, and she was fairly certain the mayor was about to get an earful.

After Dookie Shuttleworth's invocation, he did. Norm Pasquale, principal of the Hemlock Falls High School (and coach of their unsuccessful football team, the Hemlock Highballers), raised his hand to be recognized.

"Yeh, Norm," the mayor said.

"A deputation of parents came to me last night, Mayor, and expressed concern for the safety of our children. Between the bulls and the bodies, this town's not safe for anyone."

And then, Quill reflected later, the dam busted. She abandoned taking the official minutes, letting the cacophony wash around the room like a surge down a storm drain. The complaints resolved themselves into three categories, which Quill recorded in numerical fashion in the minutes book.

1. The cows, most especially the manure, and the danger implicit in having a bull on the loose. Quill noted parenthetically that the focus of the protest was CarolAnn, who seemed to have a positive thing about manure, and those townspeople unacquainted with the day-to-day routine of farming.

2. The Russians, or more colloquially, the Commies. Quill found it of less than compelling interest that these fears emanated primarily from those Chamber members over sixty-five. She hoped that Leonid's English was as good as she thought it might be. Adela was positively rude.

3. Q.U.A.C.K. and the demonstration that morning. This dispute resolved itself into two factions: villagers who thought the Commies were behind it, and those who had sympathy for the cause.

4. The murders: Everyone was against them.

Meg listened to the furor with bored patience that turned rapidly to irritation. She began a tuneless hum (overture to *The Magic Flute*) which segued into bombast (*The 1812 Overture*). Then she yelled, "Shut UP!"

which astonished Dookie Shuttleworth into speech, and the rest of the room into silence.

"Now, now," Dookie said.

"For heaven's *sake,*" Meg stormed. She shot out of her chair and waved her arms like a windmill. Her face was red. Her teeth were clenched. "I have a dinner to cook tonight. The dinner's going to be televised to forty million people! If we don't get to my part of the agenda pretty damn soon I am WALKING out of here and catching a bus to Detroit!"

"Why Detroit?" somebody asked.

"Because it's the last damn place anyone would think to look for me, that's why! I'm going to dye my hair black, wear lifts in my shoes, and no one will EVER BE ABLE TO FIND ME! If you don't want the Wednesday night menu testing to be the last meal I ever cook in this town, GET ON WITH IT!"

"Motion to discuss the menu for International Night," Howie Murchison called out.

"I second," Quill said.

"Great!" Meg stomped up to the mayor, grabbed the gavel, and whacked it on the table with all her one hundred and three pounds behind it. "This is the menu. Texas longhorn beef. I'm cooking it any way I damn please!" She handed the gavel back to the mayor, and the temper tantrum was gone as swiftly as it had come. She saluted the company with a cheerful forefinger and walked out of the room.

"Well, I *must* say," Esther West muttered.

Betty Hall, who as far as Quill could recall had never opened her mouth in a Chamber meeting in the past eight years, said loudly, "Let her alone! Cooking is hell!"

"Can we have a review of the minutes up to now, Quill?" the mayor asked a little desperately.

Quill looked at her notes in bemusement. "Actually, we never got to the official agenda. Except for Howie's motion to discuss the menu. And that's been discussed, sort of. I guess since the Chamber is sponsoring International Night, we ought to vote on the menu." Quill read the menu off, a vote was called, and the motion passed.

"The next order of bidness, Quill?"

"Um. That would be to vote on the program for tonight. On Tuesday, the subcommittee for International Night met and approved program design and the agenda for the evening." Harvey, who had picked the programs up from the printer that morning, passed them around. Murmurs of approval swept the room.

"And the agenda for the evening?" Adela Henry asked. "I understand that the mayor is scheduled to speak."

"If you'll open your programs you'll see the order of events. Harvey Bozzel will do the introduction, followed by the mayor's welcome speech. Mr. Menshivik will give a talk, titled, 'Why I Love This Country.' Then the colonel will deliver a short address on the longhorn cow."

"Hm," said the mayor. "Harvey, you got fifteen minutes for the introduction."

"Well, yes," Harvey said nervously, "but an order of business has come up. It's the visual?"

"Come again?" asked the mayor.

"Lally Preston doesn't want to use the colonel's slides."

"I must protest." The colonel rose to his feet. "All my speeches are illustrated with the right sort of slides. It is not possible to do justice to the longhorn cow in the time allotted without visual aids."

"I thought," Harvey said in a sprightly way, "that you

would feel that way. So if you wouldn't mind, Colonel, you can deliver the illustrated part of the speech now. I have the slide show all set up for you and everything.''

The mayor was clearly annoyed. The colonel looked baffled, but already had his hand on the slide remote. Clearly any opportunity to bore his audience with six thousand slides of identical-looking cattle was not to be missed. Quill, who knew very well that Harvey was attempting a diversion from a discussion of the length of his introduction—or even the fact that he should be allowed to give it at all—settled back in her chair with a sigh and took a forkful of chicken à la king. It was delicious. She smiled appreciatively at Betty Hall, and tried unsuccessfully to shut out the more explicit parts of the colonel's slide show. This consisted of slides of cuts of beef, statistics about back fat, more slides of cuts of beef, and a paean to heart healthiness, purity of the line, and once again, the fact that when it came to breeding, the Nazis had the right idea. (Except they shouldn't have tried it on humans, of course.)

Quill got sleepy. This frequently happened to her in Chamber meetings, especially if she'd slept poorly the night before. She pinched her knee. This didn't help. She bit the inside of her lip, but didn't have the nerve to bite really hard. Finally, she decided that after all that iced tea, no one would question a foray to the ladies' room. If she didn't get outside into the fresh air, she was going to fall face forward into the rice pudding Betty Hall had prepared for dessert. She picked up her purse, smiled apologetically to no one in particular, and headed into the foyer. The Ladies' Lounge was under the stairs to the left. Quill took a sharp turn to the left and was out into the warm July afternoon. She took several breaths of air, then walked briskly down the path to the rose garden.

There were four heifers now, in the metal pen. Quill winced, knowing the reason for the absence of the fifth. Meg was probably unwrapping parts of the poor thing even now.

Impressive stood quietly with his hindquarters back to her, and his nose pointed to the far side of the fence. His head was down, and all Quill could see was his muscular back and two feet of horn sticking out either side. She walked around the fence to face him, and found Sky leaning over the fence, scratching his nose with a stick. The bull's eyes were half closed. Slobber dribbled down his nose. He looked blissful.

"Hello, Sky." Quill stood next to her and also leaned against the metal bar. "How's it going with Norman?"

Sky shook her head. "I don't know. That terrible trooper transferred him to the sheriff's office in Ithaca. They wouldn't let me go with him."

"Do you guys have an attorney?"

"Oh, yes. He's a volunteer. Of course, he's more used to defending animals' rights than people's rights, but I think it will be okay."

"I hope so."

"You don't think Norman killed anyone, do you?"

Quill didn't know if she was prepared to answer this question. "Sky, why do you think Laura Crest died?"

The little woman blinked at her. "Why? I don't know."

"Was it because she was—um—torturing lab animals?"

Sky flushed. "Oh, no. Actually, I kind of liked Dr. Crest."

"You met her?"

"Yeah. After CarolAnn told us about the lab animals."

"CarolAnn Spinoza?"

"Right. Well, this is a big part of our mission, you know. To free these poor tortured creatures. So we went on up to the clinic, and Dr. Crest was there, and she showed us around and explained everything. Those horses were nice. The ones that help save babies with their blood. Dr. Crest showed us how she drew blood, she even," Sky said proudly, "drew it from me, first, so I could feel that the needle didn't hurt much at all. So she served us all some herbal tea and we went home."

"You didn't—ah—trash the place?"

"Of course not." Sky's face turned pink with indignation. "We only trash the place when the torturers deserve it. Dr. Crest loved animals." Her face softened. "You could tell from the way she got on with that wonderful dog."

"Tye."

"That one. The Australian kelpie. She showed us all the tricks Tye can do. That dog's amazing. I wish I had a dog like that."

Quill patted her arm. "When this is all over, maybe you will."

# CHAPTER 11

It was a glittering evening for Hemlock Falls. Main Street was lined with cars. Excitement was in the air. Everyone attending International Night was dressed in clothes used only for special occasions such as funerals, weddings, and the Christmas gala. Lally Preston's TV crew was wandering in and out of the restaurant, steady cams on their shoulders, their faces inexpressibly bored. The two most vividly dressed were Adela Henry, resplendent in the sequined purple and gold mother of the bride dress she'd worn on the Henry girls' weddings, and Shirley Rossiter in scarlet lamé with a back cut so low she had a second cleavage.

The line of people waiting to get into the Palate stretched all the way to Esther's dress shop. Quill, in a sleeveless white dress with ruffles at the ankles, her hair swept up, long gold earrings and gold sandals, watched the crowd through the plate glass window as she waited for the stroke of eight o'clock. She'd left off the primrose tablecloths for the dinner, and gone to starched white

linens. Doreen (who'd been taking flower arranging classes at the Tompkins County Junior College) had exhibited an unexpected restraint with the centerpieces:
bluebonnets (for the Texans), red roses (for the Russians), and white statis. The blue bonnets had already
begun to show signs of wilt. The color, at least, should
last the evening.

John, handsome in his tux, unearthed from goodness
knew where, made a last-minute inspection of the tables.
"I sprang for the Piper Hediseck," he said. "Just for the
toast. You've had a good month, Quill."

"I never thought I'd hear you say that again." She
smiled at him, conscious of looking pretty and of the
perfume she'd sprayed around her shoulders. "It's nice
to be in the black again."

"How's the time?"

She looked at the clock over the discreet sign that read
"Occupancy by more than sixty people is strictly pro-
hibited." "Another twenty minutes. Meg will have a fit
if I let them in early. I hope it's not too hot out there."
She turned back to the plate glass window. Adela (who'd
arrived shortly before and unapologetically inserted herself at the head of the line) nodded majestically. Quill
nodded solemnly back, and then felt like an idiot. She
shivered suddenly and rubbed her bare arms.

"What is it?"

"What if we're going to serve dinner to a murderer?"
She bit her lower lip. "What if one of the people standing
in that line killed Laura Crest, Candy Detwiler, and Royal
Rossiter? And what if one of them plans to kill the colonel tonight?"

"The police think they've got the murderer in custody.
I've got Howie Murchison seated next to the colonel, and

he's keeping an eye on him. Nothing's going to happen tonight, Quill."

"I don't believe Q.U.A.C.K. is behind these deaths or the threat the colonel sees to his cows."

"Quill, look at the evidence. Norman and the other Q.U.A.C.K. members were all in Hemlock Falls the day that Candy arrived. They protested Royal Rossiter's beef raising methods, confronted Royal himself. They even had an opportunity to obtain DMSO. They raided Laura's clinic. Norman has a record involving assault with knives. As a member of Q.U.A.C.K., he has a motive. Fanatics are just that: illogical, narrowly focused, irrational. It makes perfect sense to a fanatic to kill the human beings who are killing their animal friends, just as it makes perfect sense to the abortion protesters to bomb clinics."

"CarolAnn has a motive, too. She hates those cows. She's squirrelly about the manure. And she was the one who got Q.U.A.C.K. here in the first place and told them Laura Crest was doing experiments on lab animals." Quill frowned. "But there's no real motive to kill Laura, is there? Unless she stole the DMSO from Laura's clinic and Laura found her. And she admitted to seeing Candy Detwiler the day he arrived and hassling him about the cattle."

"You can guess what I think."

"You've said it before. And you've been right before. Follow the money. Which would make Shirley Rossiter a logical suspect in the death of her husband. But why kill Candy Detwiler? A jealous rage? And what about Laura Crest? Jack Brady knew all three of them, but he was genuinely fond of Royal and Laura both. Did he kill Candy out of revenge on behalf of his boss?"

"Royal may have paid Brady to do it."

"I can't believe Brady would have killed Laura. As a matter of fact . . ." She bit her lip. John was easygoing, but if he knew that she, Meg, and Brady were planning to search Laura's clinic for evidence linking the crimes together he'd insist on going along. And three people involved in breaking and entering was two too many. Four would come close to being a crowd, and they would be sure to be discovered.

Outside the windows, Leonid, Vasily, and Alexi milled about the head of the line uncertainly. Then, reacting to the turned backs and stern frowns of the villagers, the Russians meekly walked down the block to the end of the line. And if one or more of them was behind the murders, then the colonel's life was definitely in danger. Nah. There was a kinder, gentler Russia now that the country was splintered into separate states, if only because they couldn't get it together enough to make war on each other. But the Russians' dogged mission to take the cattle back with them one way or the other was sinister, if not fanatic in its intensity.

Quill scribbled for a few minutes on her sketch pad and announced, "There are three bodies, but only two murders confirmed. There are five suspects, but none for whom we've satisfactorily identified means, motive, and opportunity."

"And it's eight o'clock, with a lot of impatient people to feed," John said. "Why don't we talk about it later tonight?"

"In the morning," Quill said, adding hastily, "We're all going to be whipped after this is over."

John unlocked the door, and the crowd poured in. Peter sorted everyone into the proper seat with his customary aplomb. The colonel was seated safely between Howie on his right, and the mayor on his left. Lally Preston signed autographs. Doreen was in black toreador pants and a red velvet top. Her husband Axminster Stoker darted among the crowd like a gaily dressed goldfish, taking pictures for the *Hemlock Falls Gazette*. Lally's TV crew shot footage of the milling crowd, the crowd seated and ready for the appetizer, and Quill herself, shaking hands with the Russians. In the confusion, Quill didn't notice that one of the two cameramen had taken his steady cam into the kitchen until she was seated with Miriam Doncaster and Esther West. Peter tapped her gently on the shoulder.

Quill smiled at him. "Everything seems to be going well here." Her smiled faded. "What? I don't like that look on your face. What?"

"They're trying to interview Meg while she's cooking."

Miriam stifled a giggle.

Quill sighed. "Oh, dear. I *told* Lally that wouldn't work. Tell John where I am, will you? And keep your eye on this lot."

"For what?"

Another body, Quill thought. That's what. She eyed the colonel nervously. He'd taken his hat off, thank goodness, and was talking nineteen to the dozen to a visibly bored Howie. About cows, no question. Quill, lingering a moment, briefly considered the colonel as a suspect. He was going to benefit enormously from Royal's plans to market the beef, so it didn't make sense for him to murder his partner. By all accounts, he keenly missed his cattle manager, Candy, and if he had wanted to kill him, why now, and not before this? And for heaven's sake, why kill the vet whose unique knowledge of the longhorn was so important to him?

No, she could definitely see why the colonel with his

high-pitched voice, his annoying mannerisms, his endless slides, and his ghastly politics would be a candidate for murder. Maybe she should have called the Horrible Trooper Harris for more protection.

"Quill?" Peter's voice was urgent.

"Um? Oh. Meg. Cameramen. Kitchen. Right." She excused herself and hurried into the kitchen. Bjarne, his back eloquent with disapproval, was standing at the vegetable sink, mixing the vinaigrette with testy clanks of the egg whip against the stainless steel bowl. The cameraman was rolling tape. Meg, at the stove, was yelling at Lally Preston.

Lally made ineffectual soothing motions, hands waving in the air like semaphores. "But we want to see you in the heat of the moment, Meggie."

"DON'T you call me Meggie!" She stamped a frustrated jig on the floor. Since she was wearing her ratty Nikes, this didn't make any noise, which made her madder. She picked up a wooden spatula and whacked the stove. "GET (*whack*) THAT PERSON (*whack*) OUT (*whack*) OF (*whack*) HERE!" (*whack-whack-whack*) She brandished the spatula over her head and advanced on the cameraman, who, tape still running, backed into the steel shelving, knocked a twenty-gallon stockpot off the top shelf, and narrowly missed a concussion when it fell with a *CLANG!* to the floor.

"What brought it on?" Quill asked Lally.

"The beef." Lally shrugged. "The weather. The fact this is America. Who the hell knows?" She reached out and grabbed the cameraman by the scruff of the neck. "And where do you think you're going?"

"You wanna add fifteen percent hazard pay to my fee, Miss Preston?" He eyed Meg, who'd turned back to the stove and was muttering over the beef. Suddenly, she whirled and threw what looked like tenderloin across the room and into the wash-up sink. "Make that twenty. Union rules." He shook his head. "We can't use this footage anyhow, unless we sell it to Jerry Springer."

"You wouldn't dare," Quill said. "Lally . . ."

"All right. Mark, take the damn steady cam out there and get a few establishing shots of the front of the restaurant. And *don't* bother with that twerp Harvey or that dolt the mayor."

"Lally," Quill said. "You can use them as background for the voice-over, can't you? Please?"

"You are too softhearted to be in business, Quill."

"And you put Meg into a genuine fit. She hasn't been this mad since the Board of Health shut us . . . never mind," Quill amended. "Just go out and do your thing in the dining room, Lally. I'll join in as soon as I've settled things here."

As soon as the kitchen was empty of all but the paid Palate staff, Quill got her sister's attention. "Anything I can do?"

"No."

"What's the problem?"

"What's the problem?" Meg held a dripping piece of beef up for her attention. It was charred on the outside. "See this?!"

"I do," Quill said mildly.

"Is it cold in the middle?"

Quill touched it. "Yes."

"Everything I learned from that jackass colonel about how fast this meat cooks compared to Angus?"

"Yes?"

"Bogus!" She threw the steak back on the grill. "And the timing for the dinner is ALL OFF!"

"That's okay, Meg. John and I will take care of it."

"The colonel's filled with baLONEY!" she roared the last syllables and flipped the steak with the wooden spatula. "I want to see him THIS MINUTE!!"

"Okay," Quill said.

"Right now!"

"Gotcha." Quill walked back to the dining room with a determinedly casual pace. She whispered briefly in the colonel's ear. He excused himself and followed Quill back to the kitchen.

"Can I be of assistance?"

Meg showed him the beef. "Cold," she said. "Not medium rare. You said it cooks faster. It's not cooking faster."

The colonel examined the beef with a grave air.

"I knew I should have gotten those articles from Laura," Meg said fretfully. "Damn it all."

"Perhaps," the colonel said carefully, after a long look at her extremely ill-tempered expression, "you might think about cooking it longer than you have, but not as long as you might."

Meg scowled. Turned up the flame on the broiler. Seared the steak, counting under her breath. She whipped it off the grill, cut a small piece, tasted it, then said cheerfully, "Now that works."

"Good," Quill said.

"I'm glad to hear it," the colonel said. "If you'll pardon me? I have decided to give my speech now." He gave Quill a long look, pregnant with meaning.

"She gets," Quill said, "um . . . excitable when she has to cook."

"I can see that."

"But things will be fine now."

"But the meal will be twenty minutes off schedule," Meg said, the thunderclouds returning.

"I have several extra slides I could present, if you require an additional twenty minutes. The time will fly by. I assure you."

"Do it," Meg said, indifferent to the additional boredom about to be inflicted on her guests.

"I shall be delighted."

"And it's not my fault."

"Absolutely not. Do you mind if I get back to the dining room now?"

"Go right ahead," Meg said generously.

He bowed, replaced his hat on his head, and left.

"I should get back, too, Meg."

"I know you're worried about somebody bonking the colonel over the head in the middle of the meal. Since I'm not going to do it, at least not right now, you go back and hover over him like the mother hen that you are."

"Thank you *so* much," Quill said sweetly.

She returned to the party. Maybe the colonel had so bored those in his vicinity that they'd all fallen asleep and hadn't noticed that he'd been murdered. He was alive and well and in full spate, despite the fact that poor Harvey was bravely struggling with his introduction speech. Quill reseated herself, replied reassuringly to Miriam's half amused question about Meg's equanimity, and drank a full third of her Vouvray without stopping.

"Well, I think it's wonderful," Miriam said with a trace of defensiveness.

Quill dragged her attention back to her dinner companions. The mayor wound down his speech to scattered applause, and the colonel rose from his seat and put on his hat.

"What's wonderful?"

"Marge and Harland." Esther adjusted the spit curl

over her left ear. "Would you look at them? Behaving like a couple of teenagers."

"Really?" Quill smiled. "It *is* wonderful. Harland's been so lonely since June died. Where are they?"

"Over by CarolAnn," Esther said. "Would you look at that, and in public, too."

The extent of Harland's rowdy behavior was that his right arm was draped casually over the back of Marge's chair. Miriam rolled her eyes. "I wouldn't call that anything but sweet, would you, Quill?" She tapped her on the knee. "Quill?"

The colonel began his speech. Quill scarcely heard him. CarolAnn Spinoza was staring at him, eyes narrowed, fingers turning her steak knife over and over again. John turned down the lights so that the slide show could begin. Quill could see nothing in the darkness but the flash of the silvery blade, turning over and over again in CarolAnn's restless hands.

"CarolAnn?" Meg said some hours later. "You're kidding, aren't you?" Her hair was sticking up in tufts all over her head. Her face was pink. The dinner had been an enormous success; at the conclusion, the crowd had refused to leave until Meg appeared. She had received a standing ovation.

Lally Preston, speaking importantly into the camera over the background of cheers and whistles, had said, "You're witnessing the important launch of what's sure to be an incredible successful, healthful product. Texas longhorn beef!"

"You should have seen her, Meg." They were in Quill's bedroom. Quill took off the white dress and pulled on a pair of jeans and a dark pullover. "As soon

as the colonel started to speak about the cattle, she looked
. . . well, vicious is the only word.''

"CarolAnn looks vicious in church."

"Then when the entrée came out—do you know the
colonel is *still* asking about that marinade recipe, Meg—
and everyone went bananas over it."

"They did?" Meg's face got even pinker. "I was so
worried about the timing."

"They did. They loved it, Meg. You heard them at the
end. It was a triumph," Quill said. "But I'm sure
CarolAnn's the murderer. She turned purple with rage
and stamped out."

"Out? She left."

"Huff doesn't even begin to describe it. The beef's a
success. There's no way even she can stop the permit
going through, even with all the underhanded tricks she
knows. She's stymied, thwarted. Boxed in. I know all
she's thinking about is that feedlot and the smell. And
she's crazy with rage."

"Boy, it seems like a thin motive for murdering three
people."

Quill held up one finger. "Means. She's a tough,
strong woman. And boning knives are a dime a
dozen . . ."

"Not good ones," Meg said seriously.

". . . and she's been everywhere the Q.U.A.C.K. group
has, every time, so she had opportunity."

"And motive?"

"Meg, this case has fanatic written all over it for motive."

"But how do we prove it?"

Quill sat down on the bed and began to pull on her
tennis shoes. Meg, who'd worn jeans and a T-shirt under

her toque, hadn't needed to change. "Proof," Quill said vaguely.

"Yeah, proof. You know, that little thing you can't get convicted without?"

"There isn't any proof, is there?"

Meg began to bounce on the bed. "We need a boning knife, with her prints and Candy's blood on it. We need the blunt instrument that scattered poor Laura's blood all over the clinic floor. We need the shoe that kicked poor Tye . . ." She stopped the manic rant. "Hey. That might do it. CarolAnn's shoes. With Tye's fur on the toe. CarolAnn would never think of that."

"I don't know that proof she kicked the dog would convict her of murder, Meg. Everyone knows she hates animals already. Are you ready to go?"

"You still want to go to the clinic? Why?"

"You bet I do. I told Brady we'd meet in an hour outside the Croh Bar. Think about it, Meg. What possible reasons could CarolAnn have for trashing the clinic?"

"I have no idea. To conceal something? To look for something?"

"Think it through, Meg. What did those cattle need so that Harland could put them on his feedlot? Health certificates. Proving that the cattle were free from bovine encephalitis. *That's* what she was looking for. That's why she trashed the office. Laura must have come in, caught her at it, and CarolAnn killed her so that Laura wouldn't turn her in."

"Well," Meg said dubiously, "it's a scenario which fits the facts. So, we go to the clinic to look for the health certificates, and if they aren't there . . ."

"We know that someone took them. Because Laura had the results, she told me so."

"And if they are there . . ."

"Maybe CarolAnn didn't find them. That," Quill said impatiently, "is not the point. The point is the proof, Meg."

Meg squeezed her eyes shut and muttered under her breath.

"Open up, Meggie. If CarolAnn caught us at the clinic tonight, what do you think she'd do?"

"If she's the murderer, bash our heads in with a tire iron."

"Brady will be with us. Concealed in another room. We get a confession out of her . . ."

"Wait, wait, wait. You're planning on letting her know we're going to the clinic? How? I mean, I'm all for dragging confessions out of the killer, which is the done thing in my favorite mystery stories, but I'm not about to walk into the proverbial basement. Gothic romances are NOT my thing."

"I told you. Brady will be there." Quill thumbed through the thin Nynex phone book for Hemlock Falls, found CarolAnn's number, and picked up the phone.

"Wait a minute, Quill. What if Brady did it?"

"Then we have CarolAnn to protect us," Quill said flippantly. "I'd match her against a crazed killer any day."

"You have a point," Meg said. "Okay, go ahead."

Quill tapped in the number. After three rings, CarolAnn's distinctively sweet tones said, "Hel-lo?"

Quill dropped her voice to a whisper. "I saw what you did. I know what you want. I'm going back there to get it. You didn't get them all."

"Hello? HELLO?!"

Quill hung up. Meg fell backwards in a fit of nervous giggles.

"What's going on?" John walked through the open

door. He, too, had changed out of his evening kit and into his standard chinos and polo shirt. "Quite a night, Meg. Congratulations."

"Thank you," she said demurely.

"Andy called. Sent his love. Said he was sorry he couldn't make it. Asked you to call him at the hospital as soon as you could."

"Got it. I'll be back in a bit, Quill."

She banged in to her room. After a moment, they heard her murmuring lovingly into the phone. John eased himself into the rocking chair. Quill, suddenly conscious that she was sitting on her bed in a half-dressed condition, tucked in her T-shirt and tied her sneakers.

"Quite a night." John put his hands behind his head. "I'd like to do a business proposal, Quill. Set up shares in a partnership to market this beef. I think there's a set of customers out there that are going to buy it at a premium price."

"A partnership?"

"Among you, Marge, Harland, and a few other wealthy investors. It should give us the capital to get started, set up a web site, contact distributors to get the beef where people can find it."

"But we don't have any money," Quill said.

"You have the Palate. As of tonight, this is the only retail establishment where it's available. That's worth money in the bank, Quill."

"That's great. Does this mean we can sell it and buy the Inn back?"

He smiled. "We'd be selling the recipes, Meg's marinade, the fact that right now this is the only place to get a Texas longhorn beef meal prepared by a gourmet. I doubt that the new owners would allow the Inn to serve the same meals. You'd be barred from serving longhorn beef for a period of time. A noncompetition clause increases the value of the Palate to a buyer. Do you understand?''

''Of course. And I don't mind not selling the beef. I don't like to think of eating those cows.'' She tucked her feet under her. ''John, you've been a godsend.''

He waved his hand dismissively. ''All in the day's work of a consultant.''

''Is it? Will you invest in this, too?''

''I'll be auditing the books. I can't.'' He grinned. ''But I would if I could.''

''So, you'll be going back to Long Island?''

His glance took in her tennis shoes, the dark T-shirt, the jeans. His smile broadened. ''You don't need me to solve this case. Not with Brady at hand. So, yes, I'll probably be traveling back to Long Island.''

Quill bit her lip. ''It's a great job. And I'll bet that nurse misses you.''

''I'm rethinking the job. And the nurse and I are good friends.''

''You're going to quit?''

''I'm a businessman, Quill. I've always wanted to be in business for myself. I've made enough contacts in the bank job to establish a private list of clients.''

''You mean you're going into the consulting business?''

''I'm giving it serious consideration.'' He got up, drew aside the drape, and looked out onto Main Street. ''As a consultant, I can live just about anywhere. There's a bit of traveling involved, of course, but with a fax machine, e-mail, and a phone, I can set up anywhere.''

''Well,'' Quill said. She took a breath. ''Well.''

''Hey!'' Meg came into the room. ''Andy says 'hi'

and where can he buy the beef? He says if Michael Debakey eats it, he wants to eat it, too.''

"I'll talk to Harland in the morning,'' John said. "And
I'm bushed. I'm going to bed.'' He looked at them
sternly. "You two be careful.''

"At what?'' Meg said innocently.

"Just be careful. And tell Brady—thanks for the tip.''
He left quietly, closing the door behind him.

"Who would have thought that Brady would be a
blabbermouth?'' Meg said with some indignation.

"It's a guy thing,'' Quill said with a wise air. "You
ready?''

"Ready, Watson.''

The who was Holmes and who was Watson argument
hadn't been settled by the time they picked Brady up at
the Croh Bar, and continued all the way down Route 15
to the clinic.

"Hush up,'' Meg said as they bounced down the
gravel road.

"Why?'' Quill asked reasonably. "There's no one
there at this time of night. And, Brady,'' she twisted
around so she could see him in the backseat, "you're
supposed to be there, anyway, right? To feed the animals.''

He didn't respond right away. "Right,'' he said finally.
Then, "I brought my pistol.''

"Oh, God,'' Meg muttered.

"We've told you we're pretty sure CarolAnn Spinoza's behind this,'' Quill said. "You aren't going to
shoot her?''

"Don't think I could shoot a woman,'' Brady admitted. "Even if she . . . well, I just can't believe she'd kill
Laura. That's all.''

Quill pulled the Olds to a stop in front of the clinic.

The outdoor halogen lights were on, flooding the gravel yard. The perimeter around the buildings was dark. There was a hint of rain in the midnight air, and the moon had a gauzy veil over it.

"Do you think we should hide the Olds?" Meg asked anxiously.

"No. We told her we'd be at the clinic. Or rather I told her I'd be at the clinic. Why would I hide the car?"

"Because if she sees the car, she'll think it's a trap," Meg said.

"That's reasonable enough."

"Pull it into the shed." Brady pointed with his thumb. "Where do you all want me to be?"

"There's an examining room just off her office," Quill said. "Why don't you hide in there, and Meg, too, while I go through the desk until she comes. Then we'll have two witnesses to her confession."

"We should have brought a tape recorder," Meg said. "Some detectives we are."

"Laura's got one so she can keep records," Brady said. "I'll take that into the closet with me." He shook his head. "I think you ought to let me take care of the rough stuff."

"She expects to see me there," Quill pointed out. "This will work, guys, trust me."

She pulled the Olds out of sight against the wall of the shed. Now that they were close to trapping CarolAnn, Meg's high spirits were gone. She looked pale in the light from the outdoor lamps.

Brady had a key to the office. They came in after him. He found Laura's tape recorder in the bottom drawer of her desk, and checked it to make sure the batteries were live and that a tape was in place. Quill found a flashlight under the tape recorder and took it out. Brady and Meg disappeared through the door to the examining room. Quill—out of some sense that it was more fitting to conduct a search at night in the dark, switched the office lights off, turned the flashlight on, and began to search methodically through Laura's files. Despite the chaos on her desk and couch, her files were in excellent order. She listed her patients by customer name, and Quill thumbed through the manila folders looking for Rossiter, then Longhorn Cattle, and finally, Calhoun.

No health certificates. The stack of data in the Rossiter file was thick, and the contents a dense collection of data related to genetic testing, back fat, and composition and disposition of fat throughout the Longhorn carcass. Quill came to a letter from the research lab from Cornell University, and, more out of a sense of relief that she could understand the language, read it quickly. Then she read it again. More slowly.

Laura Crest DVM
Paradise Veterinary Practice
Box 36, Route 15
Hemlock Falls, N.Y.

Dear Laura,

It is with a great deal of interest that I report the results of the DNA testing of the Rossiter Texas longhorn carcasses. This is not, as you surmised from your visual examination, one hundred percent pure Texas Longhorn, but a Longhorn-Angus cross. The attached lab results will verify that the cattle are crossbreds.

While final reports on the fat composition are yet to be collated, it is clear that the cholesterol and fat index of these cattle are closer to those of the Angus, rather than the leaner longhorn, which clearly invalidates any claims of health benefits in human consumption. Please call me at your earliest convenience. If beef from these carcasses is being marketed as one hundred percent Texas longhorn, it is clearly a case of consumer fraud and a matter for criminal investigation.

Very truly yours,

N.D. Phillipone, DVM
N.B. Glad to hear that Brady is back in your life.— Neville.

Quill read the letter a third time. She sat down in Laura's chair. So it wasn't the health certificates CarolAnn was looking for. It was this. Evidence that Rossiter and Calhoun were selling—could she call it adulterated beef? It seemed a pretty strong term for it, but the U.S. Attorney's office might not think so.

And what would have led CarolAnn to believe there was fraud, anyway? She'd never even looked at the beef up close, refusing to eat it at the menu tasting, demanding a vegetarian meal tonight. Quill frowned. Her lovely little case was collapsing around her. And CarolAnn was probably at home right now, calling the folks at the local rubber room to come and take her, Quill, away. Well. Since CarolAnn clearly wasn't coming—and the cops she'd probably called would—it didn't matter whether her search was in the dark or not. She reached up and flipped on the overhead lights.

Her breath stopped in her throat. "Colonel! You scared the dickens out of me."

"Hand me the letter," he said.

"This letter?"

"I've talked to Neville Phillipone. I know what's in it. I told him he received the wrong carcasses by mistake. He's going to redo his tests. Withdraw his allegations."

Quill handed it to him. His hat was off. He was breathing shallowly. His face was distorted with some emotion Quill couldn't name.

The rage in his voice was unmistakable. It was rage that transfigured his face. "Pollution," he said. "Pollution. My purebred line. My bull."

And the penny dropped.

"You killed Royal, didn't you?"

He blinked at her, bewildered. "Ma'am?"

"You killed Royal because he was out crossing the cattle with Angus. Because of the taste. He didn't think people would eat leaner meat. So he modified the cows, didn't he?"

"Royal was a man driven by money," he agreed. "Not by principle."

Quill hoped very much that the tape recorder was on, that Meg and Brady were getting all this. She darted an involuntary glance toward the examination room.

"Oh, I came through that way," the colonel said softly. "She isn't going to bother either one of us, now, Miss Quilliam."

Quill felt herself turn pale. "Meg!"

His arm shot out and grabbed her wrist. He was dismayingly strong. He held her with one hand. In the other was a knife. A boning knife. Quill looked away from the fresh red stain and wanted to scream. "She can't hear you."

"What about—" Quill stopped herself just in time. She took a light breath. She was aware that she was cold, aware that her hands were stiff, that she was almost inarticulate with hate and grief. But she said, "Tell me. Tell me about the cattle."

"Oh, you know. You know what Royal did. Did I kill him? No. But I would have."

"And Laura? Why Laura? She loved cattle. She wasn't in it for the money." Quill took an imperceptible step backwards. Then another. Calhoun followed her, his eyes hot on her face, the knife raised.

"She knew the samples were from Rossiter's herd. She and Neville Phillipone had done research at the lab together. He knew she wouldn't make a mistake. So I told him. I told him Rossiter had made the mistake. Or I would have had to kill him, too. Because she knew, of course. That my bull had been with Angus heifers. And I could never sell that bull once word got out. Lost half my net worth when Rossiter pulled that scam. And the shame of it. Couldn't hold my head up in the meetings again. So . . ." He raised the knife. Pushed her backwards.

Quill gasped. "Candy? What about Candy?"

"Candy!" His face twisted and he wailed, "Candy! I wouldn't touch Candy." Quill brought her knee up into his groin. He jackknifed forward, whooping. Quill jerked her head, but she was too late. The knife clipped her cheek. She twisted hard to the right, his heavy body pinning her so that she couldn't move. Then he jerked hard against her, in a strange orgasmlike way that froze her in terror.

He collapsed against her, facedown, head twisted to the side.

He coughed.

Blood spilled from his nose to the floor. She saw the knife in his back and looked up, terrified.

"Hey," Brady said. "A man's gotta do what a man's gotta do. Sorry, kid."

And he raised the pistol he'd brought to protect her.

# CHAPTER 12

Quill stared at the dying man at her feet. Brady bent forward and pulled the knife from his back with a grunt of effort. "Not right," he said, "to take him in the back. But I thought he had you."

"Meg," Quill choked the word out. A part of her registered the terror in the whisper. She fumbled at her cheek. Her hand came away slick with blood. She pushed herself away from the desk. She was aware of Brady's blue eyes, of Calhoun's sodden black coat in strobelike flashes of time. She ran to the back room, stumbling on legs drained of strength by fear. Her hand was wet; she fumbled with the door latch.

"Don't *push*!" came a cross, beloved voice. "I can't get *out*!"

Quill stepped back. The door opened. Meg fell into the room. Blood covered her T-shirt.

She screamed, "Oh, my God! Oh, my God! Oh, Quill. Quill!"

And the room went dark.

• • •

"Just lay still. I said, lay there."

"Lie," Quill corrected the voice. "Objects lay, people lie."

"What the *hell.*"

She opened her eyes. Trooper Harris loomed over her. Meg's face hovered over his right shoulder. She was in the office, on the couch. The room was filled with people. Ambulance lights flashed red/red/red/ outside the office window.

"Get out of the way, dammit." Meg shoved Harris to the side and knelt on the floor. "Hey, you."

Quill closed her eyes again. She felt sick.

"Are you going to barf? You look pretty green. Shall I get a wastebasket?"

Quill laughed, and regretted it. Her cheek hurt like the devil. "Remember horse camp?"

"Of course I remember horse camp. I was sick as a dog from the heat, and I thought I was going to die. You got the hut wastebasket. Worked a treat, as Doreen would say."

"I want to sit up." Meg put her arm around her. Quill could feel her trembling. She shoved Quill upright. Quill swung her feet off the couch and onto the floor. Her head swam.

"Maybe you'd better lie down again."

"No. No, I feel so . . . It's too scary. Where's Calhoun?"

"Dead as a doornail, the lying snake." Meg sat next to her, her arm less shaky, her voice steadier. "Your color's coming back."

Quill blinked. Her head cleared. John leaned against one wall, his face pale, his eyes on hers. Harris and his men walked in and out of the office. A tarp partially covered the body next to the desk. Blood seeped from underneath it. Quill made out the shape of an out flung hand, the fingers curled around the handle of the boning knife. "Wow." She looked at Meg. Her T-shirt was stiff with drying blood. Her eyes were clear, her smile a little uncertain. She was okay. Quill put her hand out and touched her cheek. "What happened?"

"Just call me Vincent." Meg tucked her hair back. "Calhoun got the bottom of my left ear. It bled like the dickens."

"I thought he . . ." Quill started to shake.

"Well, he didn't. When he came at me, I just fainted. Not for long. But I was so scared, Quillie."

Quill squeezed her hand. "Where was Brady all this time? Where's Brady now?"

"We need to talk about that." Meg lowered her voice. "Don't say a thing to Harris, okay? Not until we . . ."

"You ready to talk?" Harris crossed the room with his deliberate, heavy tread. "I want to know what the hell went on here."

Meg looked at John and lifted her chin slightly. He sprang forward as if released from a heavy chain. He came to Quill and took both her hands in his. "I'm getting both of them to the hospital, Harris. Your questions can wait."

"The med tech said nothing much was wrong with either one of them. And I'm going to talk to them now." His voice was ugly.

Meg tightened her hand on Quill's shoulder, then she screamed, "John! Quill's going to pass out again! Harris, get the medic!"

"I'm not either," Quill began indignantly. Meg shoved. "I . . . oooof!" She fell against the side of the couch. "I give up," she muttered, and closed her eyes.

She kept them closed while the medics put an oxygen cone over her nose, strapped her on a stretcher, carried her from the room and into the ambulance. She felt Meg's knees against her right arm, sensed John's presence on the left. She peered through her eyelashes; a med tech was at her feet, busily snapping the stretcher into place. She heard Harris's complaining voice outside, abruptly cut off as the doors slammed shut. The siren went on, and the van took off, moving slowly for all the noise.

Quill muttered behind the oxygen mask. Meg pulled it off her face.

"Hey," said the medic. The name stitched over his lab coat pocket read: Oliver. "You start messing with the patient, I'm leaving you on the side of the road."

"I'm fine," Quill said. "Honestly. Just a little lightheaded. I think it's the oxygen, actually, that's making me feel woozy."

"Huh." Oliver crouched forward. He took her pulse, looked into her eyes with a penlight, then slapped a blood pressure cuff on her arm. "Jeez," he said after a few moments. "You're in better shape than I am."

"Can you unstrap me, then?"

He shook his head. "Against regulations until we get you to the hospital."

"Can you call ahead?" Meg asked. "Make sure that Dr. Bishop's there at the E.R.?"

"Jeez, I . . ."

"Just let him know Meg and Quill are coming in. And that we're fine," Meg added hastily. "If you could let me talk to him."

The medic scratched his head. "Well, I . . ." He pulled his cell phone from his pocket and punched the automatic dial. He talked into it, then handed it to Meg.

"Before you say anything, I just want you to know we're fine." She listened and pulled a face. "I'll tell you when we get there. Just a little cut, Andrew. Honest. Quill's a little worse off, she has a nasty thing on her cheek."

Quill tried to smile. She did have a nasty thing on her cheek. John's hand curled comfortingly around hers.

"Just hang on, we'll be there . . ." The ambulance took a turn, then stopped. "Right now." She handed the phone back to Oliver.

Quill suffered the next hour and a half in impatient silence. Once she was in Andy's capable hands, Meg and John disappeared. She was checked into the hospital, her cheek was stitched by a tired-looking plastic surgeon who murmured reassuring things about scarring, and finally she was wheeled out of emergency surgery, exhausted, and increasingly annoyed. "We're going to get you right into that nice bed," the nurse pushing the wheelchair said. "You just hang on a minute." She was a large woman, about Quill's own age. Her bossy, repellently happy attitude reminded Quill of someone, she couldn't think who.

"Miss Francis," she said suddenly.

"Yes, dear."

"This perfectly horrible kindergarten teacher."

"Mmhm."

"We all hated her. Underneath that big fat smile, she was mean as a snake." Quill gave an exasperated sigh. "You haven't seen my sister?"

"Or your boyfriend, either," the nurse said cheerfully. "Heeere we are." She made a sharp right turn with the wheelchair, into a hospital room.

"He's not my boyfriend," Quill said crossly. "Where are they?"

The nurse's patience was apparently inexhaustible. So was her insufferably cheery tone. "You'll see them in the morning, I'm sure. Here, now you can walk, can't you?"

Quill quelled the urge to punch her. "I can walk."

"Then I'll just help you into this nice bed."

Quill glared at her. "Do you know how I got this cut?"

"No, dear, I don't."

"In a knife fight." Quill bent forward. "The other guy died."

The nurse's eyes widened.

"I can get," Quill said ominously, "into the bed myself." And she did. She refused a sleeping pill, asked the time, and when she learned it was well after four in the morning, gave it up and went to sleep.

She woke to sunshine streaming through the window. Someone was snoring. Doreen was asleep in the chair by her bed, head flung back, mouth open, gray hair as wild as kudzu. Quill got up and went into the bathroom. She looked in the mirror. What she could see of her face was a mess. A gauze bandage covered half her face from her cheekbone to her chin. Her hair was a bird's nest, and she saw, a lot redder than usual. She felt it. It was stiff with dried blood.

"You're supposed ta be in bed."

Quill jumped. "Doreen? Where is everyone?"

"Meg'll be here in a minute."

Quill poked at her hair. "I hope she brings some shampoo."

"You get back inta bed."

"I don't *need* to be in bed."

"The minute you step outta this door, Harris is goin' to give you the third degree."

"I've got to tell the police what happened," Quill said reasonably.

"You talk to Meg first."

Fortunately for her state of mind, Quill didn't have to wait very long. Meg and John came in minutes later, John holding a paper bag that gave off a delicious smell of yeast and cinnamon, Meg with a cardboard tray of cafe lattes.

"All right," Quill said, when they were settled with coffee and cinnamon croissants. "What's going on?"

Meg, curled at the foot of the bed, looked reflectively into her coffee cup. "Some of this is what Brady told me. Some is what I deduced."

"What you deduced? Ha! Both of us thought that CarolAnn Spinoza did it."

"I never thought CarolAnn Spinoza did it. You were the one who—"

"Meg," John said quietly, "we can't put Harris off too much longer. Howie said we'll be a lot better off if you two cooperate as soon as possible."

"Oh. Right. Anyhow, there were three bodies, Quill, and three murderers. It's why you couldn't get the timing right."

"Neither one of us . . . never mind. Go on."

"Rossiter killed Candy. Over Mrs. Rossiter. So you were right about that."

"You mean Rossiter discovered they were having an affair?"

"It's not that so much as the fact that Candy wasn't going to give up Shirley unless Rossiter paid him off. They got into a squabble, and Royal knifed him and left him for dead."

"But he wasn't dead."

"Not right away. Calhoun found him."

"Calhoun?"

"Rossiter told Shirley about the crossbreeding. She told Candy. When the colonel found him, he told the colonel."

"I don't understand. Why didn't Calhoun get Candy help?"

"I don't know," Meg said soberly. "Shirley said that Candy had known about the crossbreeding for at least a year. Calhoun must have left him for dead. Out of revenge."

"So Calhoun killed Royal Rossiter?"

Meg bit her lip. "No. Brady did."

"Brady did?! Why?!"

"Because he and Candy went way back. Because Candy saved his life more than once. Because Brady, too, found Candy in the park. By the time Brady got to him, Candy was gone. You remember how you saw him in the park that morning? And we thought that perhaps he had killed Candy until we discovered how long the poor guy had been lying there? Brady told me that Candy died in his arms, Quill. And Brady swore revenge."

"And Laura. The colonel killed her."

John nodded.

"And Brady. Brady saved my life."

"When you passed out on me, I was terrified. Brady called the medics, called the cops, and told me what I've just told you before they all got to the scene."

"And Meg told him to run," John said.

Doreen patted Quill awkwardly on the shoulder. "Any guy'd save your life like that, I woulda tolt him to run, too."

"So, here's the scoop." Meg took a deep breath. "I told Harris I killed Calhoun."

"You're kidding!?"

"I'm not kidding."

Quill lay back on the pillows. "Oh, my goodness."

"So we've got to get our stories straight."

"You mean, lie to the police?"

Meg nodded.

"But, Meg. Won't there be a trial?"

"Howie says unlikely. Justifiable homicide or whatever."

"Did you tell Howie about all this?"

"We didn't think it prudent," John said.

"No one knows but us." Doreen scrubbed her nose with her fist. "That son of a gun Calhoun would have kilt you, if he could. And Meg, too."

"Why wasn't Brady in the examining room with you, Meg?"

"Nobody thought CarolAnn Spinoza killed Laura Crest except you," Meg said blithely. "Brady left me there with the tape recorder and went around to the front so that he could follow Calhoun when he came in. Only problem is, Calhoun came in the back way, found me, and almost got you before Brady got him." Meg gave Quill her sunniest smile. "Got it?"

"I guess so."

"So we're agreed? On what you and I tell Harris?"

Quill lay back.

"You have some problems with this," Meg said. "I knew you would."

"Not with letting Brady go," Quill said. "I mean, he saved us both."

"No. It's not that. John, could you and Doreen leave us alone for a second?"

Doreen, put out, opened her mouth to protest. John put a gentle hand on her arm and led her from the room. Meg waited until the door closed, then said. "It's Myles."

"He wouldn't understand at all, Meg."

"It's up to you, kiddo. I have to say I agree with you. This will put a barrier between the two of you. Maybe a final one."

"No maybe about it," Quill said wryly.

"It's not too late to tell Harris the truth, you know. He doesn't think much of women anyway. He's one of the few men we know who'd be perfectly ready to believe we were too stricken with girlish fear to know what went on. And he sure didn't like Brady."

The door burst open. Harris walked into the room. Quill looked at him a long moment, lay back against the pillows, and said in a faint voice, "Oh, Meggie. He's here. He's not going to take you away, is he?" She struggled winsomely to sit up. "Sergeant, what my sister did, she did because she loves me."

"Oh, Quill," Meg said.

"Oh, Meg," Quill said.

"Now, girls." Harris sat down in the chair by the bed. "You just take your time and tell me all about it."


Quill sat on the back porch, rocking in the evening air. They'd closed the dining room for the evening, and the house was finally quiet. There'd been a stream of visitors that afternoon, after she'd left the hospital. Miriam and Esther, with a bouquet of flowers. The mayor and Adela, shocked and sympathetic. Howie, who looked closely at both Meg and Quill, then said, "I don't want to know a thing about it," and left as quickly as he'd come. Dookie Shuttleworth, who had been shocked into sympathetic speech and run on so long that Doreen had told him to git. There'd been media, as well. Lally Preston had thrown up her hands and gone back to New York, but the Syracuse television station had been hanging around the Palate all afternoon. John had given them a brief statement, and Quill was sure there was going to be a (very unflattering) shot on the evening news of both her and Meg driving away from the hospital in their battered Oldsmobile. She still hadn't had time to wash her hair.

She'd left word for Myles.

Doreen poked her head out the screen door. "You okay out there?"

"Yeah, but if I don't wash my hair soon, I'm going to faint all over again."

"You want a hand? You can't get that face wet."

As she scrubbed Quill's hair in the kitchen sink, Doreen said, "Sher'f comin' back?"

"At some point."

Doreen dug her fingers into Quill's scalp. "You know what I mean."

"I left word on his voice mail."

"Voice mail," Doreen muttered. "Best way to dodge a relationship ever invented." She rinsed Quill's hair in warm water, then wrapped her head in a towel. Quill heard the phone ring, then stop. She sat up. Water dripped down the back of her neck.

Meg came into the kitchen, her face pensive. "Myles is on the phone."

"I'll take it upstairs."

She went up slowly. Her face ached. She was tired. She sat in the rocking chair next to the window and picked up her extension. Below stairs, she heard Meg yell, "Got it?" and she shouted, "Yes." She waited a moment, then put the phone to her ear. "Hey."

"My God, Quill. What the hell's going on?"

"The usual. Murder and mayhem."

"You're all right, I take it."

"Fine. A scratch on my cheek. A couple stitches. No biggie."

"And Meg?"

"She's fine."

"I've talked to Harris."

"Before you talked to me?"

"I wanted to get the facts straight. I don't think there's going to be a problem. It's clearly a case of self-defense." No suspicions in his voice. Quill wanted, suddenly, to weep. "Do you need me?"

"No," Quill said. "No. We're just fine." She asked him about the job he was on, received assurances that things were going as well as could be expected. Promised to see him soon, and rang off.

"You didn't say, 'I love you,'" John said. Quill looked up in surprise. "Sorry. I didn't mean to startle you. Just wanted to let you know that Marge and Harland are downstairs. Are you too tired to see them?"

"No. What...?" She smiled at him. "You look pretty happy. Don't tell me, she's ready to sell."

"Almost better than that, I've got a buyer for the Palate. But we'll get to that in a bit." He held out his hand. "Come on, Quill. We've got an Inn to buy back."

"We're still one hundred thousand short," Quill said glumly. They were in the kitchen of the Palate. The meeting with Marge and Harland had been brief the night before, much longer this morning. They'd managed, somehow, to serve the lunch trade, while discussing ways to raise the five hundred thousand dollars Marge wanted to sell the Inn at Hemlock Falls back to them.

"We've got the four hundred," Meg said worriedly. She sent an absentminded smile toward Bjarne, who set a plate of fresh strawberries in front of them.

"Yes." John put his pencil down. "The Marriott wants to run the Palate as a signature restaurant for the longhorn beef."

"All the publicity about the crossbreeding isn't going to put customers off?" Quill asked.

"It shouldn't. The purebred beef is as advertised, Quill. And the Marriott name carries a lot of weight with the consumer."

"The bank'll give us the hundred k," Doreen said. "Whyn't we just go with that?"

John shook his head. "Not a good idea. They want a second mortgage, nine percent interest, and personal loan guarantees. No way."

"There's got to be some way to raise that money." Quill frowned.

"It's five-thirty," Meg said. "I'll make some coffee and we'll do some brainstorming."

"You cannot," Bjarne said. He put the filet knife carefully in its slot on the butcher block, folded his arms, and stared at them.

"What do you mean, we cannot?" Meg said crossly. "Make coffee in my own kitchen?"

"Talk business in *my* kitchen." His glare was icy, made even more intense because his eyes were such a pale gray. "Who has worked, worked in this kitchen while Herself has been off in New York interviewing for the TV cameras?" He flung his hand at Meg. "Who is the real talent behind the Palate? Who has been browbeaten into cooking for my sworn enemy, those (here he said what must have been a very bad Finnish word, since Quill didn't understand it. The enemy of my people?) And who has DONE it! I, Bjarne Bjornson."

"My goodness," Meg said.

"Oh, dear." Quill got up and went to him.

"No and no!" Bjarne folded his arms. "I will give you the four hundred thousand. In exchange for ownership."

"You've got four hundred thousand dollars, Bjarne?" Meg rolled her eyes. "I must be paying you too much."

"*I* do not have four hundred thousand American dollars," Bjarne admitted. "But my government has."

Quill blinked at him. "Your government has?"

John grinned, something Quill had rarely seen him do. "The Russians," he said. "Is that it?"

Bjarne made a spitting motion. "I have contacted my sponsor in Helsinki. If the Russians can invest in America, so can we."

"But . . ." Meg trailed off. She tugged at her hair with both hands. "The Finns?"

"Why not the Finns?" Bjarne said. "You have something against Finns?"

"It'll work," John said. He leaned forward and began to make rapid notes. "We provide an opportunity for you to bring Finnish citizens to work for the Inn . . . I'll want to talk to Howie Murchison, Bjarne, and your people. Will they spring for a trip to Helsinki?"

"Oh, yes," Bjarne said. "It is very beautiful in Helsinki in July."

# EPILOGUE

It was late summer in Hemlock Falls. The warm gold light of August wrapped the rose garden in drowsy quiet. The Queen Elizabeth roses were in splendid bloom, the bush loaded with more flowers than had ever been there before.

The dog sniffed at the base of the tallest bush with eager interest. A strong odor of cow, not that old. He raised his nose to the breeze, but the odor wasn't carried to him from anywhere else. Just here, in this garden, with the fish swimming in the stone pond.

He jumped over the low stone wall surrounding the garden and trotted to the lip of the Gorge. The waterfall filled the air with more intriguing scents. He stiffened. Rabbit. Definitely rabbit. He plunged down the side of the hill to the stream beneath.

"Max!"

One floppy ear bent back.

"Max! Dinner!"

Rabbit? Or a dish of dry food in the stone flagged kitchen at the Inn? He sat down, scratched heartily, and went back up the hill.

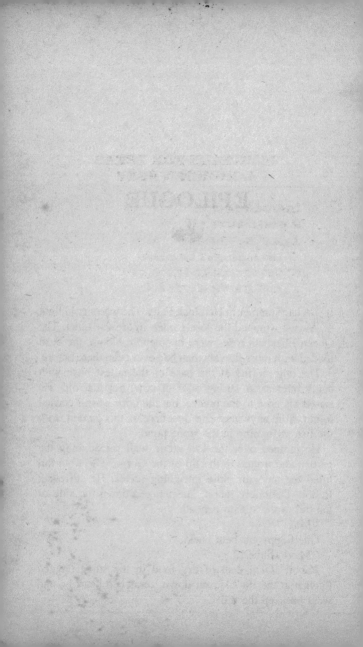

## MARINADE FOR TEXAS LONGHORN BEEF

**Ingredients:**
**2 parts olive oil**
**1 part soy sauce**
**ground ginger to taste**
**dry mustard to taste**
**1 part papaya extract**

Mix, pour over beef, and chill for several hours.

**CLAUDIA BISHOP** is the author of seven Hemlock Falls novels, and is at work on the eighth. You can learn more about Texas Longhorn beef on the Website http://www.silverhill.com

# Jane Waterhouse

"Waterhouse has written an unusual story with plenty of plot twists. Garner Quinn is a memorable creation and the book's psychological suspense is entirely successful."
—*Chicago Tribune*

## GRAVEN IMAGES

A murder victim is discovered, piece by piece, in the lifelike sculptures of a celebrated artist. True crime author Garner Quinn thinks she knows the killer. But the truth is stranger than fiction—when art imitates life...and death.

___0-425-15673-7/$5.99

A Choice of the Literary Guild®
A Choice of the Doubleday Book Club®
A Choice of the Mystery Guild®